Share

Larkspur Book One

Zoe Piper

Snare (Larkspur Book 1) by Zoe Piper

Published by Apollo8 Publishing

Cover design: Designs by Morningstar
Professional Beta Reader: Megan Dischinger, Blue Beta Reading
Editing: Penny Tsallos Editing & Proofreading
Proofreading: Corrinne Beehre

ISBN: 978-0-473-55371-5 (mobi)
ISBN: 978-0-473-55370-8 (epub)
ISBN: 978-0-473-55369-2 (print)

Snare – Blurb

Kellet James has few regrets in life, except maybe one. Jamie Larke. Walking away from their shared dreams of fame and fortune for responsibility and family was the hardest decision he'd ever had to make.

Seventeen years later, Jamie is back, offering Kellet the opportunity of a lifetime. Larkspur, the band they formed in high school, needs a new drummer for the last leg of their world tour.

With the help of a meddling teenager and his best friends' support, Kellet reluctantly agrees to Jamie's offer, and is immediately thrown into a whirlwind of rehearsals and sold-out shows across North America. Adding to the maelstrom is the connection he and Jamie still share. A connection Jamie wants to rekindle.

Can Kellet and Jamie have a second chance at love, or are they destined to be a one-hit wonder?

Acknowledgements

Thanks firstly, as always, to you the reader, for choosing to read my book. I couldn't do this without your support. Please consider leaving a review. Even just a few words can go a long way for an independent author like myself.

Thanks to the following people for making Snare what it is:

Megan Dischinger at Blue Beta Reading for strengthening up the story.

Elle Keaton for "translating" to American English for me. Greatly appreciated.

Penny Tsallos for editing and polishing.

Corrinne for proofreading. As always, any sneaky ninja typos that got through are my fault, not yours.

Morningstar Ashley for the gorgeous cover and creation of the Larkspur logo.

My fellow Kiwi Rainbow Authors - thanks for the support and encouragement.

Jackie C, this one is for you. Thanks for being my number one supporter and cheerleader.

Prologue

!MUSIC NEWS NOW!

**** BREAKING NEWS ****

Larkspur Tour in Jeopardy

It has been announced today that Larkspur's drummer, Mark Sullivan, is leaving the chart-topping group. In an official statement, band management has said that Sullivan is departing for personal reasons and that no further details will be released.

The Californian hitmakers are due to start the last leg of their world tour in early July, playing in twenty cities across North America. Larkspur first charted sixteen years ago with their single, 'When the Sun Rises'. Lead singer, Jamie Larke, has tweeted a message of support for his bandmate, wishing him well.

A source close to the band has told MNN that Sullivan has been unhappy for a while and was asked to stay until the end of the tour. His premature departure now leaves fans wondering if the tour will go ahead.

In a separate statement, promoters have advised they will issue updates on developments as they happen.

Chapter One

Jamie flicked his phone to silent and dropped it onto the table as he leaned back in his chair, taking in the expressions of the others in the room. His remaining bandmates had similar pained looks on their faces as they read the many social media notifications that flashed across their own devices.

"What are we going to do, Miles?" Jamie asked wearily. The events of the last few days had resulted in sleepless nights as he worried about the group's future.

Their manager, Miles Cartwright, smiled sympathetically back at him. "You have two options, Jamie. You can either cancel or find someone to fill in on drums for the rest of the tour."

"Ugh. How are we going to do that?" Seth asked. "Do we even have time to audition and get someone up-to-speed on the set list?"

"It would be tight, but we could make it work," Miles said, nodding at the lead guitarist. "There are some good session musicians out there we could look at."

"What about Joey Billings?" Liam suggested. "We used him when Mark was out with a strained wrist two years ago."

"He's working with that kid from the boy band that's just split up," Jamie replied. "Is there no way we can convince Mark to stay for the last three months of the tour?" he asked, already knowing the answer.

Miles shook his head. "No. I've tried everything. He's burned out Jamie, you know that. He's never coped well with the touring; as much as he loves creating the music, he hates being away from home, and his stage fright is getting worse. It's starting to affect his performance, and you know he's a perfectionist. He'd rather not play at all than play badly."

"I know, had to ask though." Jamie looked at Seth and Liam. "So, what do we want to do?"

"I want to tour, but if we don't get the right person, then the fans will be as unhappy as if we canceled," Liam said.

Seth nodded in agreement.

The room was silent as each person mulled over the problem. The late spring sun filtered through the windows, reflecting off the neighboring high-rise buildings of downtown Los Angeles, casting long shadows in the air-conditioned conference room.

"Where's the list of guys you have for us, Miles?" Seth asked, leaning his forearms on the table. "We may as well look at them now. Sitting on our thumbs will not make the problem go away or solve it any quicker."

Miles pressed a few keys on his laptop, and a list of names appeared on the wall screen.

"Unfortunately, there are less than a dozen available for the time frame we need. I've already weeded out those I know won't work with and the ones with other commitments."

"Well, you can take Finn Harris off the list," Jamie said, pointing to the top name.

"Why? He's the best of the bunch." Miles said, frowning.

"Oh god, tell me you haven't fucked him?" Liam groaned.

"Fuck off! No, I haven't fucked him," Jamie said, rolling his eyes. "He's got a little dependency on the white stuff."

"What? How'd you know that?" Seth exclaimed, eyes widening in shock.

"I haven't heard of any problems with him," Miles said. "Are you sure?"

"I… ah… um… may have slept with his ex who let it slip that was the reason they'd split up," Jamie admitted, slinking down into his seat to avoid looking at his friends.

"Fuckin' horn dog," Seth chortled. "Okay, so Finn's off the list. What about the rest?"

They spent the next hour debating the merits of each person Miles had listed, and Jamie soon realized that the problem was bigger than they'd thought.

Every person was good in their own right. Still, each of the guys had a reason they didn't want to work with a particular person. Jamie had always insisted that all four—now three—band members had to be in agreement when it came to decisions about the group and their business. Miles was their voice of reason, but even this time, he couldn't help sway them.

"It has to be someone we trust implicitly, who can fit in with our dynamic, and play our music, as well as Mark did," Jamie stated when they'd failed to come to an agreement.

"Y'know, this was so much fuckin' easier when

we were just a little no-name indie group playing in bars and lugging our gear round in the back of Liam's van," Seth said.

"What? You'd give up the last fifteen years and go back to that life?" Jamie asked. "You'd give up all the traveling we've done, your big fuck-off McMansion in the hills, your Maserati?"

Seth shook his head, grinning. "I never said that J. Y'know, I'd never give up my baby."

"I think you're the only person I know that has a picture of his car in his wallet rather than a picture of his family," Liam teased.

"Yeah, well, the car is a lot more reliable than my fuckin' family, that's for sure," Seth retorted, eliciting nods of agreement from the others in the room.

A cough from Miles had the three men pause in their banter. "There is one person we haven't considered."

"Who? I thought you'd gone through all the available session musicians?" Jamie frowned at their manager.

A strange look crossed the older man's face. Jamie sat up straighter in his chair.

"I know that look, Miles."

"What look?" Miles asked, trying for an air of innocence but failing. Jamie knew him too well. Miles had been with them every step of the way for the last seventeen years and was an integral part of their success. He was eight years older than Jamie but could easily pass for younger. He was as fit and toned as any of the guys in the band. With the flecks of gray at his temples and in his close-cut beard, he was heading nicely into silver fox territory.

"Come on, Milesy Boy, spill," Seth said, waggling his fingers in a gimme gesture.

"There is one person we could ask. He isn't actively working as a session musician, but I know he keeps his hand in, and he'd fit perfectly with you guys."

A tingle crept up Jamie's spine as Miles looked at him pointedly.

"No!"

"Come on, Jamie, you know he's the best option after Mark," Miles said. "Was the best option before Mark, to be honest, no disrespect to Mark."

Seth and Liam were frowning at the two of them.

"Who?" Liam asked.

"He won't want to," Jamie said, pushing himself out of his chair, unable to sit.

"You don't know that," Miles said as he tracked Jamie's pacing in front of the large windows.

"I fuckin' do!" Jamie all but yelled back. "He didn't want to seventeen years ago, so why would he want to now?"

"That was then. Circumstances change. Responsibilities change. You've got nothing to lose by asking him."

Jamie shook his head. He leaned against the window, looking down onto the busy street below. Miles was wrong. He did have something to lose. Seventeen years ago, his heart had been shattered into a million pieces. It had taken a long time for him to heal, and he knew it wouldn't take much for him to lose it again.

Fuck Mark! Why couldn't he have just hung on for a few more months? Jamie immediately felt contrite at the thought. Mark was a good man and friend. It wasn't his fault he suffered from anxiety, and the stress of performing live had gotten to be too much for him.

"I have his number; do you want me to call him?" Miles asked, dragging Jamie out of his thoughts.

"No," Jamie heaved a sigh. "I'll go and see him. Feel him out. See if he's as good as he was back then."

"He is. I caught him playing a month or so ago, and he's still the best drummer out there."

"Still confused over here," Liam said, waving a hand in the air. "Who are we thinking of asking?"

Seth cuffed Liam over the back of the head. "Idiot. Who do you think? The *only* person who could do this."

Liam frowned as he thought hard. Jamie chuckled softly as the moment he realized who they'd been talking about.

"Fuck, yes! He has to do it, J. Don't leave until he says yes."

Seth nodded in agreement. "Whatever it takes, man. He's the one for us."

With an internal groan, Jamie shoved his hands in his pockets and looked at Miles, who was trying to keep the smug smile off his face. "Looks like I'm taking a trip home. What's his address?"

"I'll email you his details," Miles said, already tapping away on his keyboard. "You've got a week to get this done, Jamie. We can't afford to let it go any longer than that."

Jamie nodded and picked his phone up off the table. "See you in a week then." With a nod to the guys, he left the room. This was going to be a fucking disaster.

Chapter Two

The clash of symbols had Kellet James wincing as he sat at his desk in the back office of the restaurant bar he co-owned. He twitched and tried to focus on the spreadsheet in front of him, resisting the urge to interfere.

Another crash and a yell had him rising out of his chair. He paused as a brief knock at the door sounded, and before he could utter a word, Andi pushed her way into the office, waving a tumbler of whisky at him.

"Thought you might need this," she declared with a wry grin.

Kellet sank back into his seat and eyed his co-owner. "It's a bit early for that, isn't it?"

"Think of it as medicinal," she told him, placing the glass on the desk.

"I think I need the entire bottle if I'm going to numb the pain of that racket," he answered, reaching for the glass. As he inhaled the smoky scent of the amber liquid, he recognized the signature tones of their best brand. He took a sip, closing his eyes in appreciation.

"I'm surprised you've lasted this long," Andi commented dryly. "I expected you to be out there ten minutes ago."

"It's been a struggle, but Wil was adamant that he didn't want my help. It's his band; he's got to learn how to audition people."

"Hmm, he gets his stubbornness from your side of the family," Andi said with a smirk.

Kellet coughed as the sip of whisky he'd just taken went down the wrong way. "Excuse me, your side has its fair share too. You can't blame me for all of it."

"True, but he's definitely your son," she retorted. "He's got your height, your hair, your musical talent, and your stubbornness."

"He got your eyes, though. And your brains."

Before Andi could retort, the office door opened with a bang, and the subject of their conversation stumbled into the room.

"Whoa, buddy. Where's the fire?" Kellet asked, placing his glass down on the desk, preparing to rush out to the main bar.

"Dad, Dad. There's a guy out there asking for you," Wil said excitedly, pointing in the direction of the bar before noticing his mother. "Oh, hey Mom," he said, leaning down to kiss Andi on the cheek. "I thought you were going to the movies with Ma?"

"Hi, love. We are, but your other mother had to call into Grammie's first, so she's meeting me here."

"Wil, who's here? Who wants to see me?" Kellet interrupted, curious as to why their son had come crashing into the room.

"Oh. Dunno. He looks kinda familiar, but when I asked who he was, he just said to tell you Jack Sparrow is here." A frown wrinkled Wil's brow. "He's not Johnny Depp though; I'd recognize if it was him."

Kellet froze in his seat, his gaze flying to meet Andi's as she gave a soft gasp.

"Why would he be here? Now? After all these years?" she asked.

"I… I don't know," he stammered out, his heart racing. He'd thought he'd never see the man again, not after he'd walked away from him all those years ago. It had been the worst day of his life, and it still pained him to think of it.

"So, Dad, shall I bring him through?" Wil asked. "You obviously know who it is?"

"Um. Yes please, Wil," Kellet told his son, distractedly running a hand through his hair. Wil eyed him curiously before nodding and leaving his stunned parents.

"Here, finish this," Andi said, pushing the whisky glass into his fist. "Do you want me to stay?"

"I don't know," he repeated, his mind racing.

The sound of footsteps echoing in the narrow hallway had Kellet standing up slowly, rubbing his damp palms down his denim-clad thighs.

"He's through here," Wil said, waving through the person following on his heels.

Kellet gripped the edge of the desk as a familiar tall, lean frame stepped through the doorway. A baseball cap pulled low and dark sunglasses disguised the well-known features. A small smile tugged at the corners of a wide, full-lipped mouth and Kellet's stomach hitched in recognition at the sight.

"Hey, Kel, Andi. Long time no see." The husky tone sent a shiver down Kellet's spine.

"Jamie," Kellet nodded. "You're a long way from home."

"Not really." Broad shoulders shrugged, causing the black t-shirt he wore to tighten across his chest. "It's only a short drive up the road."

"This hasn't been your home for seventeen years."

"It will always be home, Kel. Just because I don't live here, doesn't mean it's not home," Jamie replied, slipping his glasses off and tucking them into the neck of his shirt before removing his cap and running his fingers through his dark hair.

"Holy shit! I thought I recognized you," Wil exclaimed excitedly. "You're Jamie Larke. Wow! Wait. You know my Dad?" he asked, his gaze bouncing between their visitor and his father.

"And your mom," Jamie nodded with a smile.

"Mind your language, Wilson James!" Andi admonished.

Kellet couldn't help the quick grin that escaped as their son rolled his eyes.

"Mom, I'm eighteen! I think I'm allowed to say 'shit'," Wil waved a hand in the air. "How do you guys know each other, and how come I've never known this?"

"We were in high school together," his father replied, glossing over the relationship that went deeper than just friends.

Jamie raised an eyebrow at Kellet's statement but thankfully said nothing.

"How long are you in town for?" Andi asked, relieving Kellet of the duty.

"Um… I've got a week," Jamie responded, his eyes darting to Kellet, as though it all depended on him.

"Why are you here, Jamie?" Kellet asked. "Not that it isn't good to see you, but we haven't heard from you in a long time. What's brought you back now?"

The clatter of heels in the hallway and a call of *"hello"* made Jamie pause in answering.

A tall, African American woman strode into the room, halting when she saw the gathered crowd.

"Oh, sorry. I didn't mean to interrupt your meeting. Tomas told me you were back here, and I didn't think to ask if you were busy."

"Hey, Ma," Wil said, kissing her on the cheek. "It's okay. An old friend of Mom and Dad's showed up. Ma, this is Jamie Larke," he declared excitedly.

"Forgive our son, Jamie. He tends to forget his manners when he's excited," Andi said with a fond smile. Wil blushed at the gentle admonishment and mumbled an apology under his breath, causing his parents to chuckle.

"Jamie, this is my wife, Rochelle." Andi made the introductions, and Kellet saw surprise flicker on Jamie's face before he hid it behind a bright smile.

"Hi, please call me Ro."

"Pleasure to meet you," Jamie said, shaking Rochelle's hand before looking at Andi. "I… ah… didn't realize that you'd got married."

"We've been together fourteen years, married for five of them," she told him with a beam. She stepped next to Rochelle, kissing her on the cheek. "Everything okay at your mom's?" she asked.

Ro nodded. "Yeah, but Wil, can you call in on your way home, please? She wants something from the attic, and you know I don't like going up there."

"Sure, Ma, no problem."

"We'd better get moving if we're going to catch the start of the movie," Andi told her wife. "Jamie, it's good to see you. I hope we'll see you again before you head back to LA. I'd love to catch up properly with you."

Jamie leaned over and hugged Andi. "I'd love to," he replied. "I'll get your number from Kel?"

"Yes, of course." Andi's piercing gaze pinned Kellet in place. "I'll talk to you later."

"Have a good night, ladies," Kellet returned. "Wil, you'd better head off too if you have to call into your grandmother's on the way home."

"But… but… I wanted to stay and get to know Jamie," Wil said plaintively, sounding more like an eight-year-old than an eighteen-year-old.

"Not tonight. But if Jamie is going to meet with your mom, I'm sure you can tag along then."

Wil opened his mouth to protest, but a raised eyebrow from his father had him sighing instead. "Okay," he agreed. He held his hand out to Jamie. "Great to meet you."

"Good to see you too, kid."

With one last glance at his parent, Wil left the office. Kellet looked at Jamie, taking in the changes that happen when you haven't seen someone in the flesh for nearly two decades. He didn't look too different from the twenty-year-old man Kellet had last seen.

His face wasn't as smooth as it had been back then, with fine lines around his eyes. It didn't detract from his good looks though, just enhanced them. Dark hair was brushed back, shorter than it had been, but still long enough to brush his collar. He'd bulked up with age, losing the loose-limbed lankiness of his late teens, and Kellet had the urge to trace his fingers across the broad chest, learn the new shape of the body below the worn shirt and faded jeans.

His gaze met Jamie's, amusement, and something else shining in the chocolate brown eyes. Kellet cleared his throat. "You're looking well, Jamie. Rock star life obviously agrees with you."

"Thanks, Kel. You're not so bad yourself," Jamie replied. He gestured to the chair, "Mind if I sit?"

Dropping into his own seat, he waved at the vacant one. "Why are you here? I... I didn't think you'd ever want to see me again."

"I need your help, Kel."

Kellet sat up straighter. That was the last thing he'd expected Jamie to say, although it didn't escape him that the rest of his statement hadn't been answered.

"You want *my* help?" He frowned. "What could I possibly have that you need, Jamie?"

A knock at the door prevented Jamie from replying. Kellet called out, and the dark auburn head of his bar manager, Tomas, popped around the frame.

"Sorry, boss. I know you're busy, but I wanted to remind you to order extra of that fancy pink gin. We've got a couple of bachelorette parties booked for the weekend, and we're almost out."

"Yes, I ordered that and some more vodka too. Should all be here with the delivery tomorrow," Kellet told him with a smile.

"Great, thanks Kellet. I'll leave you to it." Tomas smiled, and Kellet noticed his poorly disguised glance of curiosity at the man sitting in the chair.

"Thanks, Tomas. I'm going to head out if you've got everything under control here?"

"Yep. Evening crew is arriving, and I can't see there being a mad rush on a Tuesday. Just the quiz night regulars. I know where to find you if I need you."

"Great. Have a good evening, and I'll see you tomorrow."

Tomas nodded his goodbye and quietly closed the door behind him. Kellet returned his attention to Jamie, finding an inscrutable look on the other man's face. Sighing, he pushed away from his desk.

"Come on," he said, standing. "We aren't going to be able to have a decent, uninterrupted conversation here, and if anyone realizes that Jamie Larke is on the premises, then all hell will break loose."

"Where are we going?" Jamie asked, pushing to his feet and slipping the worn cap on before unhooking the sunglasses from his shirt.

"Back to my place. Did you drive or get a lift here?" Kellet inquired as he shoved his wallet into his pocket and picked up his phone and keys.

"I drove up from LA. What's your address? I can meet you there."

Kellet couldn't help smirking. "2708 Creek Road." He watched as realization dawned on Jamie's face.

"Well, I won't have any trouble finding that, will I?" Jamie said with a smirk of his own. A bubble of emotion popped in Kellet's stomach. He'd always loved Jamie's smirk. But then again, he'd always loved Jamie.

Chapter Three

Jamie's hands were damp as he gripped the steering wheel of his Range Rover. Stomach churning, he followed Kellet's Mustang out of the busy harborside area towards the suburbs of their youth.

He'd known that coming back to Juniper would be difficult. That seeing Kellet again would be hard. He'd only kept the barest of tabs on what his former lover had been up to over the years; not because he'd not wanted to know every detail of what he was doing, but because he'd accepted that staying away was the only way he'd heal his broken heart.

His parents had retired to Palm Springs and still kept in touch with old friends. In turn, Jamie had heard snippets of news, but maybe in deference to Jamie's feelings, they'd never said much about Kellet, Andi, or their son.

God, Wil James was almost a carbon copy of his father. Walking into East Bank, the bar Kellet and Andi owned, he'd thought he'd slipped through a time warp when the tall, lanky teenager with unruly curls had greeted him. It had taken a few seconds for his subconscious to catch up with the subtle differences between father and son. The main one being the bright blue eyes of his mother. Kellet's eyes were a shade of moss green that Jamie had never seen replicated in anyone else, and he'd stared into them enough times to know every slight change in them.

He chuckled as he remembered the look on Wil's face when he'd given the name Jack Sparrow. It was an old nickname Kellet had given him in their teens, a play on Jamie Larke and the fact that Jamie had dressed up as the character one Halloween.

Familiar landmarks flashed by as he traveled the highway out of the main business area into the hills where Kellet lived. Jamie had moved to the town when he was fourteen, and his first friends at Juniper's Lincoln High had been Kellet and Andi. They'd taken him under their wing, and he'd easily settled into high school life. Finding a shared interest in music with Kellet had cemented their friendship, and they'd formed a garage band with more enthusiasm than skill.

Kellet was a natural musician and could play most instruments, but the drums had spoken to him, and he had honed his skills with hours of practice. Jamie could play guitar and was passable on the keyboards, and as was typical with high school bands, they'd cycled through members until Seth and Liam had joined them after their own band had split up. The four teens had gelled and had begun playing small, local gigs.

Seeing Kellet indicate to leave the highway at the next exit, he changed lanes and followed him. He knew exactly where Kellet lived as he'd spent enough time at Kellet's parents house at 2711 Creek Road, just four doors away from where Kellet lived now.

It had surprised him when Andi introduced her wife. He'd known she and Kellet hadn't stayed together but were both active in raising their son. He suddenly wondered if Kellet had a partner. He shifted in his seat, uncomfortable at the thought. He had no claim on Kellet; that had been taken away from him seventeen years ago by Kellet himself.

He slowed the car and pulled into the driveway of a neat and tidy ranch house. Taking a moment to gather himself, he turned off the ignition and watched Kellet exit his Mustang. He greedily ran his eyes over the man, taking in the broad shoulders and muscular legs encased in dark denim. He tried not to linger on the firm backside that filled out the jeans just so, and with a deep breath, he opened his door and stepped out.

"Nice place you've got here," he commented as he drew close to where Kellet waited for him.

"It's not a rock star mansion, but it works for Wil and me," Kellet said with a grin before leading him onto the porch and opening the front door.

Inside was as tidy and as well-kept as the outside. Kellet led the way down a short hallway into a brightly lit combination kitchen-diner-living area. There was a comfortable sectional couch facing a large-screen television, a gaming console was on a small unit under the TV. There was a bookshelf laden with tattered paperbacks and framed photographs against one wall, and the whole room was warm and inviting.

"Want a beer?" Kellet asked from the kitchen.

Nodding, he wandered over to where Kellet was. "Thanks," he said, taking the proffered bottle.

Kellet waved to the worn kitchen table, and Jamie pulled out a chair and sat down, studying the features of his oldest friend. The years had been kind to Kellet. His hair was still a dark chestnut brown, but the red highlights had faded slightly, and it was shorter than it used to be. Jamie had lost count of the number of times he had pushed the unruly curls off Kellet's face so he could stare into the deep green eyes before kissing his soft, pliable mouth.

He gulped a mouthful of beer. This was harder than he thought it would be. Kellet met his gaze and quirked his eyebrow in a familiar gesture that had Jamie's heart flipping.

"You look good, Kel," he couldn't help saying.

"Thanks, but I know you didn't drive six hours from LA, after years of not seeing or hearing from you, to tell me how good I look."

"This is going to sound so egotistical, but have you followed me, I mean, the band, over the last few years?"

Kellet's gaze dropped to his beer bottle, and he idly picked at the label. "Sort of," he said shrugging. He lifted his eyes to meet Jamie's, emotion swirling in them. "I know you've done good, Jamie. I know you've achieved everything you always wanted. But," he paused, "I don't know any of the finer details."

"We have done good, Kel. It's a dream come true. We're just about to start the last leg of our current world tour. It's been an amazing ride."

"So, why are you here? You mentioned earlier you needed my help. What could I possibly have that you need, Jamie?"

"Mark left the band," Jamie answered and watched as Kellet frowned and slowly lowered his beer bottle to the table.

"Mark quit? Why?"

"He suffers from anxiety, and the stress of performing live has got so bad he can barely get on stage."

"Wow. I can't imagine how that would feel. He's a talented drummer. What are you going to do?"

Jamie took a deep breath. It was now or never. "We want you to come and join the band and play out the tour with us. Maybe even longer if it all works out."

♫ ♫ ♫

"No!" The word exploded out of Kellet as he pushed out of his chair and stood over Jamie. To his credit, the other man didn't react and sat calmly. For some reason, that infuriated him more, and he began pacing the small kitchen.

"You've got to be kidding me, right?" he asked, and Jamie shook his head, still silent.

"You're unbelievable, you know that? You turn up, out of the blue, no contact for years, and want me to drop everything and join your band." He glared at the achingly familiar man. "Have I got that right?"

"Look, Kel, I know how this looks. Do you not think that we looked at every other possible drummer before I came here? I knew what your reaction was going to be. I knew you'd say no, but I had to try. You are the best option we have," Jamie declared, brown eyes pleading for him to understand.

Kellet pushed a hand through his hair. "So, I'm your last resort, am I?"

"Oh, for fuck's sake!" Jamie blew out an exasperated breath. "Yes, you are, but not for why you're thinking. I told Miles and the others that you'd say no. You said no seventeen years ago. I knew you'd have no reason to change your mind now."

"Seventeen years ago, I had a baby to provide for and look after. I couldn't just walk away from that responsibility on the off chance that the band was going to be a hit." Kellet drew in a shuddering breath, trying to draw oxygen into his lungs. "Goddamn you, Jamie. That was one of the hardest decisions I have ever had to make, and then to see you and the boys make it. To see you on TV, in magazines, hear your music on the radio. Music I should have been making with you. Do you know what that did to me?"

Kellet turned to look out the wide kitchen window, his broad shoulders hunched, knuckles pale as they gripped the counter.

"I know, Kel. But now's your chance. Come on tour with us for the summer. It's not too late. You're still the best drummer I know. We need you, Kel."

"I can't just drop everything, Jamie. I may not have a baby anymore, but I do have a business to run, other responsibilities."

"I know," Jamie repeated. "But please, just hear me out and think about it. It's only for three months, and you'll be paid well. You can put the money towards Wil's college fund."

Kellet ran a hand down his face before slumping back into his chair. "Kid's got a full-ride scholarship. Got his mother's brains, thank God."

Jamie huffed a laugh, and Kellet met his gaze. "You're serious, aren't you?"

"As a heart attack," Jamie nodded. "We need you, Kel. You're the only one that could pick up the set list and do it justice and fit in with all of us."

"What do Seth and Liam say?"

"My instructions were 'Do whatever it takes, don't come back without him.'"

"Ahh, fuck!" Kellet sighed. "I can't Jamie. I can't leave everything here for the summer to go traipsing around the country playing in a rock band."

"Can you think about it, please Kel? I know it's not a decision you can make straight away. I… just… please?" Jamie's voice trailed off.

A noise in the doorway had Kellet looking up into the shocked face of his son. "Wil, I didn't hear you come in."

"Dad, did I hear right? Did Jamie ask you to go on tour with him and Larkspur, and you said no? Are you crazy?"

Pulling out a chair, Wil joined them, his gaze going between his father and Jamie. "Well? Are you honestly saying no?"

"Son, it's not that simple. I can't just up and leave. I have you and the business and– "

"Did you really have the chance to be part of Larkspur all those years ago, and you didn't because of me?" Wil asked quietly, cutting him off.

"Yes, and I'd do it again in a heartbeat, Wil. Being here for you was more important than being part of the band. It still is."

"But Dad, I'm an adult now. You don't need to be here for me." Wil laid a hand on his father's. "I'm heading off to college in the fall. I can stand on my own two feet. You need to start living your life."

"It's not that simple, Wil. I can't just up and go. What about the bar? Do you expect me to go off and leave your mom to run things? She and Ro are finally taking that trip to Europe that they've always wanted to do. I won't stand in the way of that."

"I think I should go," Jamie's voice broke into the silent battle of wills between father and son. Kellet nodded.

"Good to see you, Jamie. I'm sorry I can't help you and the guys out."

"Wait. That's it? You're just going to say thanks for calling in, have a nice life," Wil said in amazement. "Dad, you can't just say no. Why don't you sleep on it and talk to Jamie again tomorrow?" he pleaded.

"Wil, son. You don't understand—"

"It's okay, Kel," Jamie interjected, a sad smile on his face. "Wil, thanks for the vote of confidence, but your dad has always been stubborn. Once he's made his mind up, he rarely changes it."

"Tell me about it," Wil said dryly, his voice full of understanding.

Jamie chuckled at the young man before offering his hand to Kellet. "Good to see you, man. I'm sorry it's taken me so long."

Warm fingers wrapped around Kellet's, and a long-forgotten feeling of warmth spread up his arm. Jamie's fingers tightened briefly, dark eyes shining with an emotion Kellet didn't want to acknowledge. Kellet gave a small nod, clearing his throat.

"Yeah. Good to see you too."

Kellet reluctantly let go of Jamie's hand. Jamie turned to Wil, who was simmering quietly, glowering at his father. Kellet glared back and was unsurprised when his son didn't back down. He sighed. It had been easier when the kid was shorter than him and thought his dad hung the moon. Nowadays, they stood eye-to-eye, and Andi's earlier words about Wil being his son played in his head.

"Hey, Wil. Give me your number, and I'll arrange for some tickets for our LA concert. You can come down and hang with the band, see the show." Jamie cast a sideways glance at Kellet. "Of course, if that's okay with your dad."

"Really? That would be awesome." Wil's excitement was palpable, and Kellet couldn't help but smile at his son's pleasure.

He watched as they swapped numbers and a fist bump; before Jamie gave Kellet a last nod. Kellet nodded back, swallowing back an invitation to stay for dinner. He was torn between wanting to reconnect with his oldest friend and letting him go, just like he had all those years ago.

He followed Jamie out to his car.

"It was good to see you again, Kel," Jamie told him as he unlocked the Range Rover.

"Yeah, you too, Jamie. You gonna drive back to LA tonight?" he asked.

"Nah, I've got reservations at a hotel in town. I'll head back in the morning."

"What are you going to tell the guys?" Kellet stuffed his hands in his jean pockets, resisting the urge to touch Jamie for one last time.

"The truth." Jamie shrugged. "We'll come up with a solution, don't worry about it Kel. I always knew it was a longshot, asking you to come back." Jamie tapped the door frame with his fist. "Take care, Kel."

Kellet nodded and watched as Jamie backed down the driveway and disappeared out of his life again. He absently ran a hand over the ache in his chest. Why did it hurt more this time?

Chapter Four

Kellet was roused from a fitful sleep by a loud knock on his bedroom door and his son yelling to him to wake up. With a groan, he rolled into the pillow. He'd hardly slept, memories of Jamie keeping him awake half the night, and when he'd finally dropped off to sleep, fragmented dreams had plagued him.

"Dad! Come on! Get up!" Wil's insistent voice accompanied another bang against his door.

"Go away, Wil. I'm on the afternoon shift today," he growled back before pulling the duvet cover over his head.

The sound of the door opening had him rolling over to glare at his son. "What's wrong? Is something the matter?"

"Yes, there is. I've called a family meeting. The Moms are going to be here in ten minutes, so unless you want everyone in here, you need to get up and meet us in the kitchen." Wil glared at his father, hands on his hips.

"What? Why have you called a family meeting?" Kellet sat up, wide awake now. He scanned his son from head to toe, checking for injury or signs of distress. Wil looked tired, faint shadows under his eyes, and Kellet was instantly concerned. "Son, what's the matter?"

"Get up and meet me in the kitchen. I'll make you a coffee," Wil told him before turning on his heel and leaving the room.

Kellet rushed out of bed and took a second to use the bathroom before going to find his son. Voices led him to the kitchen where he found Wil, Andi, and Ro sitting at the table drinking coffee. Pulling out a chair, he took a grateful sip from the mug Wil had prepared for him.

He shot an inquiring glance at Andi, who shrugged in reply. Great, so she didn't know what was upsetting their son either.

"Wil, honey, why have you called us here?" Andi asked softly.

Wil's gaze bounced to his parents and briefly to Ro.

"Son, whatever it is, you know we'll do our best to fix it," Kellet told him, giving what he hoped was an encouraging smile.

"How old were you guys when you met?" Wil asked. Kellet paused as he lifted his mug to his mouth. He wasn't sure what he'd been expecting Wil to say, but it wasn't that.

"Um... I think we've told you before," Kellet said. "We met in high school. We were fifteen or so."

Andi nodded in agreement. "Yeah, we had tenth grade English together and ended up being partnered for a project."

"And was that when you started dating?"

Kellet and Andi swapped a glance. "We never really dated. We just hung out a lot," Kellet said. "Your mom became my best friend."

"So, if you weren't dating and were just best friends, how did I happen?"

Kellet's stomach flipped at the question. While they'd always been as honest as they could be with their son, he and Andi had never gone into the details of his conception. Tension filled the air as Andi looked at him, a query in her eyes. Kellet pinched the bridge of his nose as he gathered his thoughts.

"Son, your mom and I may not have dated in the traditional sense, and she may be my best friend, but I want you to know that we do love each other and you have always been our number one priority."

"Honey, what's brought this on? Has someone said something to you?" Ro asked.

"No, Ma. I just... just started wondering why Mom and Dad didn't stay together." Wil looked up, an imploring look on his face. "Not that I don't love you too, Ma. I can't imagine life without you in it. This isn't... isn't about you."

"It's okay, Wil. We know you love all of us as much as we love you. Tell us what is wrong. Let us help you. We're all your parents. It's what we're here to do." Kellet laid a gentle hand on his son's arm.

"How did you get Mom pregnant?" Wil blurted out, blushing at the question.

"Ah, son. I thought we covered the birds and the bees and where babies come from a long time ago," Kellet teased, and Wil's blush deepened.

"Daad! That's not what I meant! Christ, I know where babies come from," Wil said, rolling his eyes.

"Language!" Andi admonished and then chuckled when Wil rolled his eyes again.

The tension eased slightly, but Kellet realized that Wil would not be happy with anything but the truth. With an encouraging smile from Andi, he looked their son in the eye.

"Like I said, your mom and I were best friends in high school. We hung out with each other, and it was presumed that we were a couple. We'd both figured out that maybe we weren't like the other kids in how we felt about the opposite sex, but things were different back then. There wasn't the support in schools that there is today for kids who are questioning their sexuality. We only really had each other." Kellet paused to take a mouthful of coffee and gather his thoughts.

"We went to prom together, and it was held at The Renoir Hotel. We reserved a room. All our friends did, and it was sort of expected that we would too." Kellet closed his eyes as memories flooded back. "We... we weren't planning on having sex, but someone on the football team had smuggled a bottle of vodka in, and we had a few shots each, and we... we—"

"What your father is trying to say is, we were tipsy, we were curious, and one thing led to another and we slept together," Andi finished off when Kellet didn't continue.

"Didn't you use protection? I mean, that's the one thing you've told me over and over again, always use protection," Wil looked at them both, disbelief in his eyes.

"Of course we used protection," Kellet replied. "However, as we've also told you, it's not always one hundred percent effective. We were both inexperienced, Wil. We didn't know that the condom had failed until your mom missed two periods and did a home test."

"And before you even think of asking, no, at no time did we ever think about not keeping you. We knew it wasn't going to be easy, but there was never, ever doubt in our minds that we weren't going to try and be a family," Andi said.

"But you didn't stay together. Why not?" Wil pushed.

Kellet sighed and glanced at the clock on the wall. Was it too early for alcohol?

"Wil, like I said, your mother and I love each other very much. But only as friends, probably more like siblings. We're not in love with each other. We never have been. We were only eighteen when you were born. Your grandparents on both sides were and still are amazing. They helped as much as they could, but your mom and I knew that staying together for the sake of appearances wasn't going to work long term.

"We were lucky that we lived so close to each other and we worked our schedules so we both had equal time with you while working and going to college too."

"And… and you both have always known you were gay?" Wil stammered.

The three parents glanced at each other. Was this what this was about? Kellet had never thought his son would be nervous about coming out to them. Really, how could he be with his mother and Ro having been together since he was in kindergarten? True, Kellet hadn't been in any long-term relationships, but Wil had seen him with guys in the past.

"Wil, honey, you know we have no expectations or concerns with whatever your sexuality may be. And to answer your question, the night of senior prom - when you were conceived - convinced your dad and I that, yes, we were both definitely gay." Andi flashed a grin. "As sexy as your father is, he doesn't do it for me like Ro does."

"Eww, gross, Mom! I really didn't need to hear that part," Wil said, a disgusted look on his face, reminding Kellet of when they'd tried feeding him broccoli as a toddler.

Kellet and Ro burst out laughing as Andi leaned over to give her son a gentle hug and a teasing smile. "Are you afraid to tell us you're straight, honey? Is that what's worrying you?"

"It's fine if you are," Kellet added, struggling to keep from laughing. He knew Andi was trying to relax Wil, and teasing him was the best way to do it.

"Oh my god! You guys are unbelievable!" Wil huffed out before laughing like his mother had intended. "And I think I'm bi just so you know," he threw out with a satisfied grin of his own.

"That's cool. As long as you're safe, that's all we ask."

"Yeah, yeah. I know," Wil said, rolling his eyes.

"Great, now that's all out, can I go back to bed please? I'm closing the bar tonight and would like another hour or so to sleep." Kellet pushed his chair backward, stretching his arms above his head.

"Actually, that's not why I called the family meeting, but good job on deflecting, Dad."

Kellet dropped his arms onto the table and gave his son his full attention. "It's not? Then what is the family meeting about?"

"Mom, did you know that Dad gave up a chance to be part of Larkspur when I was little?"

"Wil, if this is about yesterday, then I've already told you—"

"Shush, Kel," Andi waved a hand at him and then nodded at Wil. "Yes, of course I knew. Every major decision in our lives we have made over the last eighteen years has always been in consultation with the other. What's this all about, Wil? What happened yesterday?" Andi asked, looking to Kellet.

Kellet shook his head. He should have known his son wouldn't leave things alone. He pushed away from the table to get a refill for his coffee.

"Kel?"

"Fuck!" he ground out before turning back to the table to the surprised faces of Andi and Ro. He rarely cursed around them, but this situation warranted it. "Larkspur's drummer has quit, and Jamie asked me to join the band to help them finish out the tour," he told them, leaning against the kitchen counter.

A slow grin spread across Andi's face, but before she could say anything, Kellet pointed a finger at her. "No, Andi! I already said no. I can't go, so just take that look off your face."

"But, Kel. Why not? It's the opportunity of a lifetime."

"That's what I told him, Mom. But he's doing this whole self-sacrificing routine," Wil said, as he tapped something out on his phone.

"What self-sacrificing thing? I'm not sacrificing anything," he told them, frustration in his tone.

"Let me guess, you told Jamie that you couldn't go because of the bar?" Ro asked, making Kellet squirm under her laser-like gaze.

"Yep, he did. And he used your trip, and he used me, like he did when I was a baby," Wil told his moms.

"All valid reasons," Kel shot back. "And, Ro, stop giving me your courtroom stare. I know you're a damn good lawyer; you don't need to use your tactics on me."

"Kellet James, I have admired and loved you from the first time I met you, and you welcomed me into your family. Not many men would have readily accepted someone into their son's life as freely as you did," she told him, love shining in her eyes. "But you really are a stubborn, blind man."

"Well, it wasn't hard, Ro. I could see how happy you made Andi, how easily you accepted that Wil and I were part of the deal. After Wil, Andi has always been my main priority."

"Yes, that's the problem. Wil, Andi and the bar have always been your top priorities."

"Why is that a problem? I agree our lives would've been different if Wil hadn't come along, but Andi would still be my best friend, and she still would've met you, and I would've—"

"You would have stayed with Jamie. You would have been the drummer with Larkspur, not Mark Sullivan," Andi interjected. She closed her eyes as if in pain, and there was a hitch in her voice when she spoke again. "Kel, I love you so much. You have never once given Wil and me anything but your complete self. But it has been at the detriment of your own happiness."

Kellet strode over to the table and dropped heavily into his chair. He reached over and grasped Andi's hands. "Andi, honey. I love you too, but I'm not unhappy. Whatever gives you the idea that I am?"

"I didn't say you were unhappy, Kel. I think you're comfortable with your life, but you're not complete. You've never let yourself go, not really. You work hard–and that's not a bad thing–but you don't play at all. You give everything you've got to us," Andi said, indicating them all, "but you don't give yourself anything other than the most basic of care."

Kellet was speechless. Is that how they really saw him? As a workaholic? He frowned at the thought. In the beginning, when Andi had told him she was pregnant, he'd immediately withdrawn his college application and gone to see his boss at the restaurant where he waited tables to ask if he could get more hours. After Wil was born, he and Andi had gotten into a routine. He'd signed up at the local community college and earned his business degree by taking night classes and studying around his work schedule and Wil's needs.

Andi had done the same, and they'd made it work. He'd never resented the path he'd taken, even if it wasn't his first choice. They'd both worked hard, and with help from their parents, they'd bought the bar and restaurant where Kellet had worked since he was sixteen, and they were now one of the top eateries in Juniper. Everything he'd done was what any self-respecting father would do.

"What did Jamie offer?" Andi asked, drawing him from his thoughts.

Before he could answer, the doorbell sounded. Wil jumped from his seat as though electrocuted. "I'll get it!" he yelled.

"Wilson James, what have you done?" Kellet growled out, a sense of foreboding crawling down his spine.

"I... I... I just want you to do something for yourself, Dad," Wil answered guiltily, glancing down the hallway as the bell rang again.

"Wil..." Kellet's words fell on deaf ears as Wil disappeared.

A muffled snort from Ro had Kellet looking across the table at her. He raised an eyebrow in question.

"Well, it looks like we can ask Jamie directly what the deal is," she announced, with a bright grin.

Kellet wanted to curse as Wil shuffled into the kitchen, Jamie close behind him. The smile on Jamie's face fading as he met Kellet's stony glare.

Chapter Five

The air crackled with tension as Jamie followed Wil into the kitchen. His excitement that maybe Kellet had changed his mind evaporated as he took in the pinched look on Kellet's face. He glanced at Andi and her wife, surprised to see them holding barely suppressed amusement.

"Sorry, is this a bad time?" he asked Kellet. "Wil said you wanted me to come over to talk."

Wil coughed next to him and seemed to fold in on himself as his father stood and crossed his arms across his chest. Jamie watched as the younger man tried to shuffle out of the door, but he froze as he realized that he wasn't going to be able to escape, and with a visible gulp, he slowly moved back to the table.

"Um… here, Jamie, you can have my spot," he offered, pulling out the chair and indicating for Jamie to sit down. Jamie glanced at Kellet, who rolled his eyes and gave a sigh before waving him into the seat.

"You," Kellet's voice was stern, "over there, where I can see you," he said to Wil, pointing to the spot between the ladies.

Wil dropped into the chair and slid down, staring at the tabletop. Andi patted his hand, and Ro leaned over to whisper something in his ear, making the young man blush and nod.

"Okay, I take it that you don't want to talk to me?" Jamie asked, looking at Kellet. He could see he was less than happy by his arrival. Stormy green eyes were hooded, and a muscle ticked in his jaw. Jamie's fingers itched to run a thumb along the light covering of stubble, to ease the tension he was probably the cause of.

"Jamie, Wil says you offered Kel a place in Larkspur for your summer tour?" Ro asked. She was a beautiful woman with caramel skin and long braids gathered in a high ponytail. Warm eyes sparkled with intelligence, and he could see her mouth twitching with amusement. At what, he wasn't sure.

"Yes, that's right. Mark, our drummer, has left the band because of some personal health issues. We have two choices; either hire someone else for the remaining leg of the tour or cancel altogether."

"And you want Kel to be the replacement drummer? Is there no one else you can ask?" Ro asked, leaning on the table.

Jamie felt as if he was on a witness stand with the intensity of her stare and he shifted in his chair. Kellet gave a small cough, and glancing at him, he was surprised to see that Kellet's stance had relaxed a little and something was amusing him. Jamie turned back to Ro.

"Yes, I want Kel, and we've gone through the list of available musicians, but we have an all-for-one policy in the band, and we couldn't all agree on the same person."

"Except for Kel," Ro stated, and Jamie saw Kellet twitch at the statement.

"Except for Kel," Jamie agreed with a slow nod.

"He knows our dynamic; he knows our music and style. He really is the most obvious choice."

"He is sitting right here," Kellet interjected. "Jamie, I really appreciate that you think so highly of me, but you have to face facts. I haven't played regularly for years, so I certainly won't be up to stadium performance level. Secondly, I haven't hung out with you and the band for over sixteen years; you have no way of knowing if I'd still fit your dynamic. And thirdly, I haven't listened to your music properly in years. I can't pick up a set in a matter of weeks. It would take months of rehearsals and hours of practice."

Wil mumbled something, earning a dig in the ribs from his mother and a glare from his father.

"Care to share with the class, son?" Kellet bit out. "Seeing as you've done so much already, you may as well give us your thoughts on this."

Jamie squirmed internally. Who knew Kellet in dad-mode would be such a turn on? He'd always been so easygoing and laid back when they were teenagers. It was strange to see him so authoritative, and Jamie found he liked it. A lot.

"I said, you're just making excuses," Wil bit out, glaring at his father, twin spots of red high on his cheekbones.

"They are not excuses; those are the facts, son." Kellet sighed and brushed a hand through his hair. Jamie tracked the movement, remembering the softness of the curls, and he wondered if Kellet still liked to have them pulled when being kissed.

A cough from Andi had Jamie returning his attention and her knowing smirk and raised eyebrow had him clearing his own throat. Busted, dammit. She'd always been able to read him, and she could probably work out where his mind had gone. With a quick wink, she faced her son's father.

"Kel, love, Wil isn't entirely wrong," she stated, causing Kellet to bristle and sit back in his chair, defensive barriers rising as he crossed his arms.

"Don't look at me like that," she said. "What you said is all true, but it shows that you have thought about Jamie's offer. Let's break it down," she suggested, raising a finger in the air. "One, you may not have played like you used to as a teenager, but you do play a few times a week; either here on your kit in the spare room or with Wil's band."

Before Kellet could interject, she raised a second finger. "Two, the four of you were as tight as tight could be, and before you interrupt me and tell me you were kids then—" Jamie covered a smile as Kellet was shot down before he could even open his mouth. "—I bet it would take less than fifteen minutes before you're shit-talking and carrying on as if the last seventeen years hadn't happened."

This time Jamie did chuckle, earning himself a glare from Kellet and a grin from Andi as she raised a third finger. "Three, you can play virtually any song after only hearing it once. You are a musical freak, Kel, and add in your stubbornness, you'd be more than tour-ready in the time Jamie needs you to be."

"Have you finished?" Kellet growled out, sending a shiver down Jamie's spine.

"No. I haven't," Andi replied haughtily and held up her pinky finger. "And number four; you are going to say yes to Jamie. You can use every excuse you can think of, but I'm telling you now, you are going on tour with Larkspur." With a satisfied grin, she sat back in her chair.

"Damn, baby. I love it when you get all bossy," Ro told her as she leaned across Wil to kiss her wife on the cheek.

"Oh, gross, Moms. How many times have I told you not to do that kissy-faced stuff in front of me?" Wil grumbled, pushing his mothers apart.

"Yeah, Andi, not in front of the children," Kellet deadpanned.

"You're just jealous," Andi shot back with a side-eyed glance at Jamie. A light stain rose up Kellet's neck and a tiny ray of hope slithered through Jamie. He wasn't sure what he was supposed to do now. Kellet seemed adamant he wouldn't join them on tour and Andi was just as certain he would.

"Look, guys, I appreciate you taking the time and all, but if Kellet's not going to say yes, then I have to head back to LA. We've got to decide by early next week, and I need to talk to Miles and the guys."

"What are the finer details, Jamie?" Ro asked.

"Um… what do you mean?" he replied, confused.

"When would you need Kel in LA? How long would he be gone? What sort of remuneration are you looking to pay?"

Jamie must have looked as stunned as he felt by the questions as Kellet laughed. "Don't mind Ro, Jamie. She's my lawyer, and she tends to take over, whether I want her to or not."

"Ah, that explains why I feel like I'm on a witness stand," Jamie retorted, smiling at Ro.

"Hey, you know that I watch out for my family, Kel. This decision affects all of us. We need to know all the facts."

"It's okay, Ro. I'm glad that someone wants to make an informed decision, rather than just blindly saying no," Jamie couldn't resist getting a jab in at Kellet, who glared at him.

"That look doesn't work on me, Kel. You should know that," Jamie said, without thinking.

Andi giggled, and Kellet turned his glare to her. "Be careful, Kel. You keep glowering like that, and your face will set permanently," she teased.

"To answer your questions, Ro, we'd need Kel in LA by the end of next week at the latest. We have contracts and business shit to deal with, as well as rehearsals and getting Kel up to speed on our set list." Jamie glanced at Kellet. "The tour is nineteen shows over seven weeks, starting early July in New York City and finishing in mid-August in LA. I told Kel last night that he'd be well compensated. It would cover Wil's college fees easily."

"Hmm, we could work with that timeline. Get your lawyer to send me the contracts so I can go over them. I'm not as familiar with entertainment law, but one of my partners is, so I can run them past him." She reached into her bag and pulled out a slim card. "Here are my contact details. Give them to your team and get the ball rolling."

Jamie quickly scanned the card, noting that Ro was a senior partner in her firm. "Thanks, I'll pass them to Miles Cartwright, our manager. He'll talk to the legal team at the label and someone will be in touch."

"Don't bother. I've told you I'm not going, and my decision is final," Kellet huffed and stood up from the table. "Thanks for coming out again, Jamie, but I'm afraid it's a wasted trip."

"Dad!"

"Kel!"

"Your family doesn't seem to think so," Jamie countered. He was getting frustrated with Kellet's attitude. The man was as stubborn as a bag of rocks, something that hadn't changed over the years, but Jamie thought that maybe he may have mellowed as he got older. Obviously not.

"My family doesn't know what's good for them," Kellet growled back and then had the grace to look shamefaced at the gasps from the others.

"Look, you guys obviously need to discuss this without me here." Jamie stood up. "I'll go and have a drive around the neighborhood and if I haven't heard from you by two o'clock, I'll consider your decision as final Kel, and I'll head back to LA."

"That sounds like a good plan. I'm sure we'll have it sorted out in the next couple of hours and I'll give you a call. Wil obviously has your number?" Ro said, standing and shaking his hand.

"Yeah, Wil's got my number," Jamie said with a grin. "I'll see myself out."

With a last look at Kellet, who had his back to him, staring out the window, Jamie once again left the house thinking it would be the last time he'd see him. And his heart cracked a little bit more.

Chapter Six

"I can't believe you just... just—" Kellet was so mad he couldn't get his words out.

"We just what, Kellet? Shot down every argument with a counterargument? Made you see that your excuses–because yes, that's what they are—were flimsy at best," Andi retorted, hands on hips as she faced off against him.

It wasn't often they didn't see eye-to-eye, but today was one of those rare occasions.

"Dammit, Andi. Stop and think for a minute. You and Ro are booked to go on your trip in three weeks. If I go gallivanting off to LA, who's going to run East Bank and look after Wil?"

"Dad! I've told you, I'm an adult. I don't need looking after," Wil said. "I'm moving away in the fall. This could be a trial run."

"Tomas is more than capable of running the bar. He's our manager for a reason, Kel. Jonas is doing a great job as assistant manager and if anything major happens, then either of our parents can step in, and you'll only be a phone call away," Andi countered.

"Dad, Mimi and Pops are four doors away! You know that Mimi will be around every day checking on me," Wil added to the argument.

Kellet paced as much as he could in the small kitchen. He knew his excuses were just that. If he was honest with himself, everything Andi and Ro had said was true. He did give all of himself to his family and the bar. He didn't hang out with friends often, preferring to spend his downtime with Wil or hanging out around the house.

Some people, namely guys he'd had brief relationships with, hadn't understood his driving need to be the best he could be for Wil, and that Andi and Ro were a major part of his life. Many a relationship had dissolved before it could even start when Kellet had chosen family and work over any potential long-term partner.

"What are you really afraid of, Kel?" Andi asked softly.

He stopped his pacing and leaned against the kitchen counter, sighing heavily. He'd known it wouldn't take long for Andi to get to the heart of the matter. His chin dropped onto his chest as he tried to escape her knowing gaze. He shook his head and shoved his hands into the pockets of his jeans. She knew the answer. He didn't need to reply.

"Wil, honey. How about you and I go and pick up some of your dad's favorite donuts from the bakery?" Ro said. The scrape of chairs signaled the sound of Wil being ushered from the room.

Andi's warm palm slid down his forearm, and he pulled his hand from his pocket and twined their fingers together. He looked into her blue eyes, sympathy shining there.

"I can't do it, Andi. It will hurt too much," he told her.

"Kel," Andi sighed. She tugged him into the living room and sat on the large sectional couch, pulling Kellet down beside her. She wrapped her arms around him, and he let himself relax into the familiar hug. It had been a long time since anyone had held him so close.

"It's time to live your life, Kel. You're being given a second chance at a dream you gave up. You're being given a second chance to be with the man you love."

"But what if he doesn't want anything more than my drumming skills? He may be in a relationship and seeing him with someone else day in and day out will be worse than not saying yes and not seeing him ever again."

A snort of amusement came from above him, and he craned his head to see Andi smiling brightly at him.

"What?"

"Jamie Larke still only has eyes for you," she told him, brushing a curl away before placing a gentle kiss on his forehead.

"What do you mean? How can you know that?" Kel asked, sitting up from her embrace and facing her on the couch. A flicker of hope stirred in him.

"He barely took his eyes off you when he was here, and he looks at you now like he did when we were kids. He's as much yours as you are his."

Kellet scrubbed his face with his hands. "But we're not kids anymore, Andi. Could we make it work as adults? Being on tour with him, seeing him every day; it's not going to be the normal situation of dating and getting to know each other again."

"True," she nodded, "but think of it another way; being together in the intense pressure cooker of a major music tour, with one of the biggest bands in the country, well, it will either make or break you."

"That's what I'm afraid of," Kellet whispered. "It broke me seventeen years ago saying goodbye to him. I couldn't do it again."

"You're the strongest man I know, Kel. We'll all be here to support you if it does crash and burn," Andi nudged his shoulder with hers. "And we'll also be here to plan the wedding when it doesn't."

Kellet couldn't help the chuckle that broke out of his chest. "I don't know why I love you, but I do. You're just as terrible today as you were twenty-odd years ago when we met."

"So, you're going to say yes? You're going to live your dream of being a rock star and be with the love of your life?"

Was he? Excitement and dread warred equally in Kellet's head. Could he live up to the standard of an international band? He was sure he could. It would be hard work for the next few weeks, but he knew he could give it a damn good try.

The biggest question, though, was could he bear being around Jamie again? Could he risk his heart again? And would Jamie want to risk his?

He gave a slow nod, and Andi bounced on the seat next to him.

"Yes!" she exclaimed, giving a fist pump before slinging her arms around him and kissing him on the cheek. "I'm so proud of you, Kel." She jumped to her feet. "Where's your phone? You need to let Jamie know so he can get the ball rolling."

"That's not going to work, Andi," he told her, grinning as her face fell.

"Why not? You just said you're going to say yes."

"I don't have Jamie's number. I'll have to get it off Wil." As Andi rolled her eyes, Kellet gave in to the excitement bubbling inside him and let himself hope.

♫　♫　♫

Jamie leaned back in his chair as he looked across the river that ran through the heart of Juniper. The small town was only forty minutes north of San Francisco and was a mix of families and young urbanites who commuted daily to the bigger city. From his seat he could see the bustling ferry terminal and throngs of people out enjoying the late spring afternoon.

He sipped at his coffee before checking his phone for the umpteenth time since he'd left Kellet's house. He had to hand it to Wil; getting Jamie there for what was obviously a family meeting had been a stroke of genius. Kellet had been right when he'd said that his son got his brains from his mother. It was totally something Andi would have done at the same age. He snorted quietly. In fact, if Andi had known his number, he was sure she would have called to set up a meeting. She'd been as heartbroken as he had been when he'd left Juniper. He wished now he'd kept in touch with her, but at the time, it had hurt too much, knowing she had a part of Kellet that he could never have.

His phone buzzed, clattering against his coffee cup, and he grabbed at it. The caller ID showed an unknown number, and he was tempted not to answer. Not many people had his personal contact details, and those that did were loaded into his phone.

A gut feeling had him swiping at the screen before lifting the device to his ear.

"Hello?"

"Hi, Jamie?" a female voice answered him.

"Yes." Jamie thought he recognized the voice but couldn't place it.

"Hi, it's Rochelle Patton, Ro. Andi's wife?"

"Oh, yes. Of course. Hi Ro. Is everything okay?"

"Look, I hate to do this to you, but is there any chance you could come back to the house? Kel's place."

Jamie's stomach hitched. Could this mean…? "Yes, of course I can. I'm just downtown at the moment. I can be there in fifteen minutes."

"Excellent." Happiness shone in Ro's voice. "We'll see you shortly."

Jamie hung up the phone and stood from the table, doing a quick check to make sure he had left nothing behind before striding to his parked car. He tried to keep his excitement at bay, but it was hard not to.

Fifteen minutes later, he once again pulled into the now familiar driveway of Kellet's house. He took a calming breath and made his way up to the door. Before he could knock, the wooden door was flung open, and a visibly excited Wil greeted him.

"Hi Jamie! Thanks for coming back," the young man said, bouncing on his toes as he let Jamie in.

"Wil! Let the man in, for goodness sake." Andi's voice floated down the hallway and Jamie chuckled as Wil rolled his eyes and waved him towards the rear of the house.

Jamie entered the large open plan space to find Andi and Ro smiling at him from the couch, and Kellet perched nervously on the edge of the recliner. Jamie smiled at them all and took a seat on the loveseat opposite them.

"Thanks for coming back, Jamie," Ro said, leaning forward. "Kel has a couple of questions for you."

"Sure, no problem," Jamie replied before looking at Kellet. "What did you want to know?"

Kellet cleared his throat before responding. "Are you one hundred percent certain there is no one else you can ask and that all three of you want me in the band again?"

"Yes, on both counts. It was actually Miles that suggested you after we'd exhausted the list of possibilities. You're the only one that all three of us said yes to without having to think," Jamie replied, glossing over his initial reaction to having Kel back. "I know this is a big decision for you Kel, and I appreciate that you have a life and responsibilities here. I wouldn't have come if I didn't know you were the best option for us."

"Okay. I'm still not happy about leaving everything at short notice, but Andi and Ro have convinced me they'll be able to cope without me here," Kellet said, glancing at the women on the couch, who nodded enthusiastically.

"And I'll be fine, Dad. The Moms are only away for three weeks and the grandparents will feed and water me," Wil added, grinning at his father.

"I know. But apart from that, this is our last summer together before you head off into the big wide world. I was planning on us taking a guy's trip, one last father-son bonding memory."

"There'll be other summers, Dad. This is the chance of a lifetime. You've said no before because of me. I won't let you say no again." Wil's tone was so reminiscent of Kellet's when he was being stubborn about something that Jamie had to smother a laugh.

"Kellet," Andi growled and gave Kel a stare so loaded that Jamie didn't need a translator to understand her message.

"Actually, I have a suggestion," Jamie said, causing everyone to look at him. "Wil, do you have any major plans for this summer?"

"No, not really. Just hanging out with my friends before we all take off to college, and yeah, that's about all," the younger man replied with a shrug.

"Why don't you come with your dad then?"

Stunned silence greeted his suggestion. It was something Jamie had thought of earlier and wished he'd suggested that morning when Kellet was throwing up defenses quicker than a castle under siege.

"I... ah... yeah, I do," Wil was lost for words. "Do you mean it? For real? Go on tour with Larkspur?"

"Yes, I'm serious. It's a win-win for everyone. Your dad stops stressing about you. Your moms can go on holiday knowing you're safe, and you get a once in a lifetime experience before you head off to college," Jamie said. "And, also, your dad will need a PA, so you can be it."

"PA?" Kellet queried.

"Yeah. We have a band personal assistant, Jax, who is amazing, and she looks after us all and keeps us where we're supposed to be, but we each have equipment guys who set up our gear and mics. Wil can be yours."

"Yes! I'll do it!" Wil declared, jumping to his feet.

"Hang on, son," Kellet said, waving his son back to his seat. "I don't think a tour is the place for an eighteen-year-old."

"He'll be fine, Kel," Jamie assured him. "It's not all sex, drugs and drinking, you know? We're actually pretty tame in our old age."

"Daadd! I'm not going to be corrupted. This is a great life experience. Besides, you'll play better if I'm there," Wil said smugly.

"Oh, and how do you figure that?" Kellet asked, arching an eyebrow as he settled back in his seat.

"If you leave me here, you'll be worrying about what I'm up to. Ergo, it will affect the way you play because your mind won't be one hundred percent on the job."

"You've been spending too much time with Ro," Kellet muttered, causing everyone in the room to grin. Jamie saw the moment that Kellet gave up his last defense. His shoulders relaxed and he took a shuddering breath. Moss green eyes met Jamie's, and Jamie couldn't stop the grin that spread across his face.

"Okay. I'll do it, and Wil can come with me," Kellet finally said the words that Jamie wanted to hear. "But he'll need a contract, and the crew are to be reminded that he's only eighteen."

Jamie felt like doing a dance on the spot as relief coursed through him. He nodded his agreement and took out his phone. "I'll call Miles now and get legal onto everything."

"Use my office if you want," offered Kellet, pointing to a doorway just off the hallway. With a nod of thanks, he walked away and dialed his manager.

He closed the door on the small office, noting the tidy desk and crammed bookshelves. Pictures of a young Wil dominated, and Jamie smiled at the sight of father and son over the years.

Miles picked up straight away and Jamie filled him in on what had happened and what contracts he needed. Miles was ecstatic and promised to get everything moving as soon as they hung up. He approved Jamie's idea of having Wil along as a PA for Kellet and assured Jamie that they could cover the cost with no issue.

Jamie had hung up and was sending a message to the band chat group when a small knock sounded, and Andi popped her head around the door. Seeing he was off the phone, she stepped into the room and closed the door behind her.

"I presume I have you to thank for talking him round?" he asked, slipping his phone into his pocket.

"Yeah. Thanks for offering a position to Wil. It means a lot to all of us."

"He's a good kid, Andi. You and Kel have done a pretty incredible job raising him."

"Thanks. Ro has been there for a lot of it too," Andi replied, features softening as she mentioned her wife.

"You're an amazing team. Anyone can see that." Jamie paused. "I'll look after him, you know that, don't you?"

"I do. He's scared, Jamie. He may sound like he's got it all together, but he's never gotten over you," she said, picking up on the fact he wasn't talking about her son.

"I never got over him either, Andi. I'm scared too. Our lives have been so different, I don't know if we can be the same people we were back then."

"You can't be," Andi told him, stepping closer. "You have to relearn each other. Get to know the men you are now, with all that life experience behind you."

"Does he want that?"

"He does, but he'll be stubborn about it. You've got your work cut out for you," she said with a smirk.

Jamie gave her a grin back. He'd always liked a challenge.

Zoe Piper

Chapter Seven

Kellet flopped front first onto the king-sized bed with a groan. He was exhausted. He ached from head to toe, and his brain was zipping around at a mile a minute trying to process everything that had happened in the last ten days, let alone that afternoon.

"Dad check this out, it's so cool," Wil's excited voice floated from somewhere in the hotel suite.

Kellet didn't bother answering; it would have taken too much effort. All he wanted to do was shower, eat, and sleep for the next three days. Then he might feel human again.

"Dad? Dad?" The bed bounced as Wil dropped next to him, and he moaned as his son pushed at his shoulder. "Hey, old man, are you okay?"

"Go 'way," Kellet said, his voice muffled by the pillow.

"Jeez, if you're like this after a six-hour drive and an afternoon of appointments, you'll never survive a seven-week tour across the country." The bed moved again as Wil rolled off, and Kellet heard him shuffling about in the next room.

The scent of coffee had him lifting his head as Wil placed a steaming mug onto the cabinet next to the bed.

"Here, drink this and then go and shower while I order us dinner. Jax said to just put anything we want on the room and it will all be covered by the label." Wil sounded way too excited at the thought, and knowing how much an eighteen-year-old boy could eat had Kellet calling out to his retreating back.

"Hey, don't go abusing the band's hospitality."

"I won't," came the aggrieved reply and Kel knew his son was rolling his eyes at him. "I'm only going to order steak and all the trimmings."

"Sounds good. Thanks."

Kellet heaved himself off the bed and dug around in his suitcase for some old sweats and a worn t-shirt. He'd feel better after a shower and something to eat. The large marble bathroom took his breath away, and he gave a quiet chuckle as he realized he'd better get used to it. The last week and a half had been a crazy rollercoaster of tidying up his affairs in Juniper. Of course, Andi and Ro had been in their element, organizing both him and Wil.

East Bank was in the more than capable hands of Tomas and his assistant, Jonas. His parents had agreed to look after his house and keep an eye on things while Andi and Ro were on their European trip.

Then there had been the lawyer's meetings. Kellet thanked whichever deity had brought Ro into Andi's life all those years ago. She had gone through the contracts with a fine-tooth comb, enlisting the help of another partner in her firm to ensure that he and Wil were not being exploited. Not that he'd thought Jamie would do that to him. They may have gone their separate ways, but Jamie was still an honorable man.

Add in hours of practice behind his drum kit, listening to the whole of Larkspur's back catalog and familiarizing himself with the provisional set list Miles had sent him, and Kellet hadn't had much downtime.

The hot water streaming from the massaging shower head was doing wonders for his tight shoulders and aching neck. They'd had a quiet family dinner the night before, but despite his best efforts, he'd not been able to sleep as he worried if he was doing the right thing.

He and Wil had left before dawn for their trip to downtown LA, hoping to beat some of the traffic, which of course had been impossible. They'd made it to the hotel just in time to check-in before the band's PA, Jax Burton, had met them and whisked them off to a meeting with the label.

After the brief, but intense talk with Miles and the record label's senior members, they had taken him and Wil to a private clinic for a full health checkup. It had surprised him when Ro had told him that it was mandatory for all the band, and he didn't think he'd ever been so thoroughly checked out before. He understood why though. The label was investing a lot of money in him and the others, and they needed to be in peak condition.

A bang on the bathroom door and a yell from Wil that dinner had arrived had him quickly finishing up. He found Wil in the small lounge area, staring down at the mountain of food that had been wheeled into the suite.

"I thought I told you not to go mad," he said as Wil lifted one of the plates to sniff appreciatively at the thick steak lying on it.

"I didn't. God, this smells divine," Wil declared as he grabbed some silverware and took a place at the small dining table in the corner of the room. "Eat up, Dad, before it gets cold."

It didn't take long for them to clear their plates, and as they lounged back on the couch in front of the television, Kellet finally relaxed.

"Do you think we'll see Jamie and the rest of the guys tomorrow?" Wil asked.

"Hmm, I should imagine so. We've got a lot of ground to cover in the next few weeks. I probably won't be great company in the evenings."

"S'okay. Jax said I'm going to be pretty busy myself learning the ropes." Wil rolled his head on the couch back to look at his father. "She's scary, Dad. I thought Ma could be intimidating, but, wow, Jax is a whole 'nother level."

Kellet chuckled softly. "She'd have to be to keep Jamie, Seth, and Liam in line. They used to be real hell-raisers, and I doubt they've changed much."

"Dad?"

"Hmm?"

"Can I ask you a question?"

"You just did."

Wil groaned and nudged his father on the shoulder. "I know you are a dad, but really, telling dad jokes at thirty-seven should be against the law."

"Sorry. What did you want to ask?" Kellet glanced over at the sprawled teenager, noticing that there was a tenseness in his face. Recognizing the look, he sat up, turning to face Wil. "Are you having doubts? Do you want to go home? I know that it's not too late for you to pull out if you want to."

"No. Definitely not," Wil assured him. He stared

at the TV for a moment before facing his father. "What's the story with you and Jamie?"

Kellet sighed. He knew that Wil would need to know the full story one day, and if he was going to be hanging around not only Jamie, but Seth and Liam, he deserved to learn the truth from the source, rather than bits and pieces the guys might drop into conversation.

"Well, I think I told you we met at school?" At Wil's nod, Kellet continued. "He joined our school halfway through tenth grade. His dad's company got relocated to San Francisco, and rather than live in the city, they bought a place in Juniper. Just out on Lake Road," Kellet said, mentioning the street that was only a block away from their home.

"It was hard for him joining halfway through the year, but he and I were in a few classes together and we just sort of bonded. We had the same stupid sense of humor, and then we found we had the same taste in music, and we started hanging out more and more."

"Is that when you started your band?"

"Yeah." Kellet snorted at the memory. "God, we drove our parents crazy. Pops finally agreed to soundproof the shed at the back of his garden so we'd have somewhere to practice. It was small, but we spent so many hours in that shed, practicing until we were pretty decent."

"When did Liam and Seth join you?" Wil asked, enraptured in the story his father was telling.

"Um… I think it was the beginning of our senior year? Liam had an old van that he'd saved up to buy so we could start doing local gigs. We didn't have a lot of gear, but we made do with what we had." Kellet grinned at the memory of how'd they'd squeezed three guitars, the rudimentary sound gear, and his drum kit into the back of the old beater. They'd become experts at car Tetris.

"What happened then, Dad?"

Kellet sighed and pinched the bridge of his nose before turning to face the TV. This was the hard part of the story, and it still hurt all these years later.

"I'd already figured out that I was maybe, probably gay. I loved being with your mom and everything, but when I looked at Jamie, my stomach would flip and, well, let's just say that I imagined doing things with him that I didn't imagine doing with Andi." Kellet laughed as Wil made a retching noise.

"Did Jamie feel the same way?"

"I was too scared to ask him," he admitted. "I was too scared to let him see because I didn't want to lose his friendship and upset the band dynamic."

"Did Mom know?"

"Yeah, we were best friends and told each other everything."

Wil frowned at him. "So how did you end up with Jamie then?"

"Well, after your mom and I hooked up after prom, we were embarrassed and avoided each other, and Jamie was the only one that was brave enough to ask what was going on?" Kellet replied, his mind easily casting back to that day.

"Hey, Kel, what's up with you and Andi?" Jamie asked as he tuned his guitar before their practice. Seth and Liam were running late, and he was glad

that he had a bit of time alone with Jamie.

"Nothing, why?" he'd prevaricated.

"You guys have hardly spoken all week. Did something happen at prom?"

"Don't say anything to anyone, but, well, we… ah… um… slept together," Kellet stammered out. He knew he probably shouldn't be saying anything, but the urge to get it off his chest was too great. He hadn't been able to talk to Andi about it, obviously, and Jamie was his other best friend, so it made sense to tell him.

"Oh. Was it, y'know, your first time?" Jamie asked, and it surprised Kellet to see a blush color Jamie's fair skin.

"Yeah."

"Was it horrible? Is that why she's not speaking to you?"

Kellet fired a drumstick across the room at his bandmate. "No! It was fine, I guess."

"Fine? Wow. I wouldn't be talking to you either if you described having sex together as just 'fine'," Jamie teased.

"I didn't mean it like that," Kellet said, frustrated. "I… look, Andi is amazing, and I love her, but I'm not… she doesn't…"

"What, Kel? Come on, use your words."

"I'm gay, okay," Kellet blurted out, sick of Jamie's teasing. Silence greeted his statement and Kellet risked looking at Jamie. Chances are he'd just lost his second friend in a week. To his surprise, a look of wonder was on Jamie's face, and he slowly put down his guitar.

"You are? Are you sure?"

"Yeah, last weekend pretty much confirmed it for

both of us," Kellet said dryly and then realized he just outed Andi. "Shit! Please don't say anything about Andi."

Jamie waved a hand at him. "Y'know I wouldn't. Huh, that explains a lot," he muttered to himself.

"What do you mean?"

"Well, you and Andi are affectionate with each other, and you can see that you both love each other, but there was always something missing in the way you interacted."

"So, you're okay with it?" Kellet asked quietly, trying not to hold his breath as he waited for the reply.

"Oh, I'm more than okay with it," Jamie murmured, and Kellet looked up to find his friend standing in front of him. Brown eyes searched his face before Jamie lifted a hand and brushed a wayward curl off Kellet's forehead, before trailing his fingers along his brow and down his cheek before sliding his hand around to the nape of Kellet's neck. "I've wanted to kiss you for nearly three years."

Kellet's breath hitched as he realized what Jamie was saying. He leaned forward, pausing a hairsbreadth away from his lips. "Me too," he whispered before pressing his mouth to Jamie's.

As first kisses went, it was perfect. Although hesitant with each other, Kellet immediately felt the rightness in it all. Jamie's lips were soft under his but different to how Andi's had been. There was more strength, an underlying firmness in the way Jamie kissed him and the slight rasp of stubble against his skin had Kellet deepening the kiss.

They broke apart a few minutes later, breathless

and flushed. They'd looked at each other and then burst out laughing as a sense of freedom bubbled through Kellet.

"So, you and Jamie became a couple?" Wil asked, and Kellet was glad to see that his son wasn't upset at the idea.

"Sort of? We were out to Seth and Liam, and of course your mom, but we didn't flaunt it in public. I came out to your grandparents after Andi and I agreed that acting as a couple would be harder to do if I was in a relationship with Jamie, and we didn't want any misunderstanding why we weren't together anymore."

"We told friends we'd decided to split up as we were heading to different colleges in the fall and didn't want to do the long-distance relationship thing, and everyone believed us. Then, your mom found out she was pregnant with you."

"And what? Jamie dumped you because you were going to be a dad?" Wil asked, sounding angry at the thought.

"No. God, no. He was amazing. He was there for both your mom and me. I wouldn't have been able to get through it if he hadn't been there to support me, listen to me when I was scared shitless and worried about how we'd cope."

"But why then did you break up? What happened that you're not still together?"

"Miles Cartwright happened."

"Miles, Larkspur's manager? The old dude we met today?"

Kellet chuckled at Wil's question. "Miles's not old. He's only in his early forties, I think." He glared at Wil. "And have a little respect; he's a really great guy. Larkspur owes a lot to him."

"If you say so, but he broke you guys up," Wil said, obviously not convinced.

"No, he didn't. I was trying to earn as much money as I could. Aside from waiting tables at the restaurant, we were still playing gigs. Miles was there one night and liked what he saw." Kellet stood up, needing to move around. He wandered over to the window and looked out over downtown LA.

"At first, the guys said no, not believing that he would get us a record deal. But then he came back with contracts and everything, and it was too good an opportunity to miss."

"But you didn't sign," Wil said. "Why not? Surely it would have given you the money you needed, rather than a minimum wage waiting job?"

Kellet turned to look at his son. Love swelled through him as he took in the familiar features, so like his own at that age. "It would have, but there was one clause in the contract that I couldn't agree to." He dropped back onto the couch and laid a hand on Wil's knee. "I would have had to move to LA, and I wasn't leaving your mom and you. You were, and still are, my world."

"But what about Jamie? I thought you loved him?"

"I did. But I loved you more. From the first time I held you, you stole my heart. You became part of my soul. I couldn't leave you, regardless of how much money Miles offered."

"How did Jamie take it?"

"Your birth may have been the best day of my life, but telling Jamie it was over? That was the worst."

Kellet yawned as he made his way to the practice shed. He was so tired. Who knew that a baby could make that much noise? Especially at two in the morning. Thank God his mother had been there to help ease Wil back to sleep.

"Hey babe, you look shattered." The sound of Jamie's voice chased away some of Kellet's tiredness. The warm hug that enveloped him had him melting. He nestled his face in Jamie's neck and inhaled the familiar scent of wood and leather.

"Long night?" Jamie asked as he ran a hand up and down Kellet's back.

"Yeah, Wil got an upset stomach or something. Mom got him to sleep, but it took a while."

Jamie pulled away and gave him a gentle kiss before guiding him to the old couch that was squeezed into the corner. "It's good practice for when we're on the road," he said with a grin.

Dread flooded through Kellet. He'd hoped to avoid having this conversation, but Jamie and the other guys needed to know. He reached over and tenderly ran a thumb along Jamie's jaw, drinking in the features of the man he loved.

"I love you, JJ," he said, trying to stop his voice from trembling.

"Love you too, Drummer Boy," Jamie replied, a soft smile playing on his lips.

"I'm... I'm not signing the contract," he blurted out. Jamie stared at him in confusion before

understanding dawned and he pushed away and moved to the opposite side of the room.

"But—" Jamie began before Kellet interrupted him.

"I know what you're going to say. I've thought of every possible argument. I've looked at this from every angle and weighed up every pro and con, and it all boils down to one thing," Kellet looked at Jamie imploringly. "I can't leave Wil. He's my everything."

Hurt flashed across Jamie's face before he could hide it, and Kellet jumped up and strode over to him. "That didn't come out right. I love you so much it hurts, but he's my son, Jamie. Please, try to understand."

"I'm trying to, Kel, but you're my everything. How am I supposed to do this without you?" Jamie's voice cracked, and he turned away.

"This is your dream. You have to do it, and I'll always be here. When you're rich and famous, you can come back and keep me in the style I deserve," Kellet told him as he wrapped his arms around Jamie's slim waist and rested his head between his shoulder blades. A shudder ran through the lean body.

"I don't want to do it without you though," Jamie whispered.

"I know, but you have to. You, Seth, and Liam are amazing, and together as Larkspur, you'll be the biggest rock band in the world."

Jamie spun around and cradled Kellet's face in his hands. "Who are we going to find who is as talented as you? You're the backbone of this group. We need you. I need you."

76

"There are other drummers out there," Kellet replied. He winked, trying to break the tension. "Of course, none as good as me, but good enough to back you guys up."

"Please, Kel," Jamie whispered desperately.

"I can't, JJ. I'm sorry, but I can't."

A familiar ache spread through Kellet's chest as he spoke, and he absently rubbed at it. "It took a few days, but eventually Jamie accepted that I wasn't going to be part of Larkspur, and he and the guys moved to LA pretty much straight away. They auditioned and found Mark and he was a good fit for the band, and the rest, as they say, is history."

"Was last week the first time you've seen or spoken to him since?"

"No, he came back to Juniper when his parents moved. We had a beer and caught up, but our lives were so different. Larkspur had started to get a name for themselves and I was finishing up my degree."

"Do you regret it?" Wil asked.

"No, son. I don't regret a thing. Some days I wished I was out there with them, especially when you were being a little brat," he grinned, "but, no. I made my choice, and it was the right thing to do."

"What happens now? Are you and Jamie going to get back together?"

"I don't know," Kellet answered with a shrug. "The next few months are going to be hard work. I doubt we'll have time for anything other than doing our jobs. Besides, Jamie's moved on. He won't want to rekindle a teenage romance."

"But, if he did want to…" Wil said, a mischievous

gleam in his eye, very reminiscent of his mother's.

Kellet stood up and turned off the TV. "Go to bed, son. We've got another long day ahead of us tomorrow."

Wil grumbled good-naturedly as he made his way to his room on the opposite side of the suite. "I'm just saying, Dad. Don't pass up the opportunity. You deserve to be happy."

"Goodnight, Wilson."

Wil's laugh echoed as he closed the door.

Chapter Eight

Jamie's stomach fluttered with nerves as he followed Seth and Liam down the hotel corridor toward the conference room. He still couldn't believe Kellet had agreed to join them, and he was equally nervous and excited to see him again.

As they entered the large meeting area, Jamie immediately sought out Kellet, relaxing as he spotted him in the corner, talking on his cell phone, a soft smile on his face. Wil was perusing the coffee and pastries laid out on a table against the back wall.

"Fuck, Kel, you haven't aged a day. What's your secret?" Seth cried as he dragged Wil into a huge bear hug. Jamie laughed at the horrified look on the young man's blushing face.

"I... I'm n... n... not—" Wil stammered as Seth let him go.

"S'alright, kid. I'm just messin' with ya," he told him with a grin before turning to greet Kellet, who had hung up his phone and come to stand by his son. Seth looked him up and down before they were hugging and back slapping each other.

"Damn, Kel. It's good to see you," Seth said huskily.

"You too," Kellet replied as they broke apart. Kellet's gaze caught Jamie's briefly before Liam was there and more hugs were exchanged.

A sliver of envy pricked at Jamie at the ease the guys greeted each other. He and Kellet needed to have a proper talk, see if they were on the same page, and until then, Jamie couldn't risk being any more than a friend and bandmate. If he started touching, then he wouldn't be able to restrain himself from going further.

"Sorry about before, Wil," Seth apologized. "But you really do look like your dad. You couldn't see it as much when you were a baby, but yeah, you're definitely Kellet James's son."

"You... you saw me as a baby?" Wil asked, looking a little starstruck.

"Of course we did. We were at your dad's place more than our own. Your grandmother started keeping our favorite snacks in house. It gutted us when your dad said he wasn't joining us, but we totally understood why. You were a cute kid," Liam told him.

"You've grown out of that now though," Seth teased, causing chuckles around the room.

"Okay guys, there'll be plenty of time to reminisce and catch up later. We need to go over this schedule so Kellet can get up to speed, and we can make this tour the most successful we've ever had," Jax's no-nonsense tone broke into the happy reunion.

There was good-natured grumbling as they all got coffee and snacks and took seats around the table. Seth and Liam sat on one side, and Jamie slid into a seat on Kellet's left. Wil sat on his father's other side, pulling a legal pad and pencil towards him. Kellet gave him a warm smile, before turning to face Jax and Miles at the head of the table.

"Right, first thing today, Kellet, the audiologist will be here shortly to do the molds for your in-ear monitors," Jax said, glancing up the table before returning to her list. "Wil, you're getting a set too."

"Then we have Tam and Debbie coming over to go through wardrobe and styling, and you are all booked for the photo shoot tomorrow morning at ten. A car will collect you and take you to the studio."

"Who are Tam and Debbie, and what photo shoot is she talking about?" Kellet leaned back in his chair and half whispered to Jamie.

Jamie gave a grin, leaning in a little closer than was perhaps necessary, but he couldn't resist. "Debs is the band stylist, and she looks after our wardrobe and Tam, well, he's our chief hairstylist and make-up guru."

"What do I need a make-up guru for? I'm a drummer, not a model," Kellet side-eyed him, "or a diva lead singer."

"I dunno, Dad. You'd probably look good with some mascara," Wil said with a snicker, causing Jamie to lean across Kellet to high-five the teen.

"Don't worry, Kellet," Jax reassured him. "It's only for the photo shoot and will only involve a little foundation and powder."

As Jamie leaned back in his seat, he muttered so only Kellet could hear, "My guyliner used to turn you on, Drummer Boy."

Kellet stiffened in the chair next to him but didn't respond. Jamie was just beginning to think he'd maybe pushed a little too far, too fast, when a large foot gently pressed down on his own for a few seconds. Jamie gave an internal grin.

Jax continued to run through the list in front of her, making notes as she went. "A press release is going out in two days' time, announcing you as Mark's replacement. We need to get your social media presence up-to-date, and I'm going to leave that in your hands, Wil."

Wil beamed at the news and jotted a few lines onto the pad, nodding as he did. Jamie noticed that Kellet was softly tapping his fingers on the table-top, and he recognized the nervous gesture for what it was. His own fingers twitched to reach out and cover the broad hand and reassure him that everything was going to be okay.

He'd always loved Kellet's hands. Wide, with long tapering fingers that could coax any instrument to sing for him. Jamie remembered the way the calluses on Kellet's palms and fingers had felt against his own skin. He shifted in his seat as warmth flooded through him at the memory.

His attention was brought back to the meeting as Jax said his name. "Jamie, you're in charge of getting Kellet and Wil moved out to your place." Kellet stiffened beside him and angled in his chair to look directly at him.

"Why are we moving to your place?" he asked, suspicion radiating off him.

"It's easier for us all to be closer together rather than you and Wil battle this god-awful traffic every day trying to get to rehearsals," Jamie explained. "We take it in turns to host the practice sessions. We've all got home studios set up, and it's just easier. A couple of weeks before the tour starts, we'll do rehearsals on the actual stage set up, and the lighting and sound techs will tweak everything before we head out."

The wary look on Kellet's face eased as he nodded his understanding. "Okay. That makes sense."

"There's plenty of room at my place, so you don't need to worry that we'll be on top of one another," Jamie murmured. Kellet raised an eyebrow and smirked, and Jamie realized what he'd said. He smirked back and winked causing Kellet to shift in his seat before they both returned their attention to Jax. Hmm, maybe Kellet was on the same page as he was?

"Kellet, do you have any questions?" Jax asked. At the negative shake of his head, she beamed at them. "Excellent. You know how to get hold of me if you do. Wil, there are a few things I need to go over with you. Kel, once we've finished here you need to look over the drum set up Mark had. Any changes you want to make, let me know and I'll get them organized."

As Jax spoke, Jamie took the time to study the man beside him. Kellet had always been good looking as a teenager, and the years had been kind to him. His shoulders were broad, back tapering to a narrow waist. Corded muscles in his forearms flexed and tensed as Kellet fidgeted, fingers still tapping out an unheard beat. His dark curls weren't as long as they'd been when they were growing up, but there was still enough length in them for Jamie to want to run his fingers through.

Sitting this close, he could see a few strands of gray at his temples. Fine lines fanned from the corner of his eyes, crinkling when he grinned at something Seth said. Kellet may have been good looking as a teen, but he was drop-dead gorgeous as a grown man.

"Right, I think that just about does it for today," Jax's voice broke into Jamie's musings. There was a brief knock at the door before it opened, and an unfamiliar face appeared.

"Oh… um… hi," the blond man stuttered, his face turning a fiery red as he took in the occupants. "Sorry to interrupt, Jax, but the audi… audiologist is here for Mr. James."

Jax waved him into the room. "Perfect timing. Come in, Cal, let me introduce you to everyone." If it was possible, the stranger turned an even brighter red as he cautiously stepped inside, pushing his dark-rimmed glasses up his nose.

"Guys, I'd like to introduce you to Cal. He's assisting me over the next few months, so you'll be seeing a lot of him." She glared at them pointedly. "If he asks you to do anything, it is a request from me, so I expect you to do it as though you had heard it directly from me."

"Hi, Cal," Jamie said with a warm smile, hoping to put him at ease. "Welcome to the craziness that is Larkspur."

"Yeah, we promise to be gentle with you," Seth said, dropping a flirty wink, making Cal pale and then blush furiously again. Jamie was starting to worry that Cal may have a blood pressure problem with the constant blushing.

"Seth!" Jax growled, causing him to grin at her. Sighing in defeat, she introduced the rest of them. "Cal is Sarge's cousin," she said with a pointed glare, and Jamie bit back a laugh when Seth paled at the news. The threat of their lead bodyguard and

Jax's husband was enough to make anyone pale.

As the meeting wrapped up, Jamie snagged Kellet's arm. Not that Kellet was going anywhere, but Jamie had to touch him, just once.

"As soon as you're done here, we can head out to my place."

"You don't need to stay around and wait for us," Kellet told him. "Give me your address and I'll put it in the GPS, and we can let you know when we're on our way."

"Nah, that's fine. We've got to see Tam and Debs anyway, and I caught a ride in with Liam. We thought maybe we'd all hang at my place tonight, y'know, have pizza, a few beers. Catch up."

"Cool! Sounds great," Wil enthused, and Jamie grinned at his excitement. "Come on, Dad. The quicker we get this done, the quicker we can get out of here."

Kellet frowned at his son. "Why does that sound familiar? I'm sure I've heard that phrase before. Oh right, I remember now. I've said it to you a million times over the last eighteen years!"

Wil rolled his eyes at his father. "Whatever."

Jamie snorted and then laughed out loud when Kellet glared at him. "What? He's not wrong. Go and get your ears gooped."

"My what?"

"They make a mold of your ear canal, so the monitors fit comfortably. To do that, they squirt a blue goop into them," Jamie told him, and then chuckled at Kellet's shudder. "It's not so bad, only takes a few minutes." He nodded to the corner of the room where Wil was sitting and chatting with a woman who had a huge syringe in her hand.

Kellet sighed and ran a hand down his face. "Come and join our band, they said. It will be fun, they said," he muttered. "There was no mention of goop, and stylists, and… and make-up gurus when I agreed to all this," he told Jamie resignedly.

Jamie patted him on the shoulder. "It's okay, Kel. We'll get to the fun stuff, don't worry."

♫ ♫ ♫

Kellet squirmed under the piercing gazes of Tam and Debs. They had made him stand in the middle of the room and were slowly circling him. Scanning him from top to toe, occasionally pausing to comment to each other in voices too low for him to hear. He felt like a bug under a microscope and really didn't appreciate the calculating look Tam was giving him.

"Kellet, darling, what have you brought with you in the way of clothes?" Debs asked, tapping a finger against her chin as she contemplated god only knew what.

"Um, jeans, shirts, a couple of pairs of khakis, casual at home clothes," he replied with a shrug. "Was I supposed to bring a tux or something?"

"No, no. That's good. Where possible, we like to shoot you in your own gear, with the occasional new piece. I really need to see what you've brought, so I know what to bring in with me tomorrow," Debs told him as she held out a tape measure. "Let me get your measurements and then I can check what I've got on hand."

"Dad, why doesn't Debs come up to the room with me and I can show her your stuff as I pack up while you stay here with Tam. Kills two birds with one stone."

Kellet glared at his son.

"What?" Wil cried. "Dad, I'm your assistant for the next three months. You have to let me, y'know, actually assist."

"He's right," Liam piped up from where he was slouched in the corner, tapping away on his phone. Kellet wasn't sure why his bandmate was still here and not gone off with Seth and Jamie.

"Okay, fine," he huffed and Debs gave him a grin as she quickly finished what she was doing before picking up her bag and following Wil out of the room.

Tam beckoned him to sit, and Kellet thought the worst was over. But no, Tam lifted his chin and stared intently at his face, humming under his breath as he smoothed a thumb along Kellet's cheekbone and across his forehead. He tried to relax, but it was hard when the other man was only a few inches away from him.

"Your skin isn't actually too bad. What's your routine?"

"My routine? I get up, I go to work, I come home."

Tam gave him an exasperated look as Liam snorted. "He means your skin care routine, Kel. By the end of tomorrow, you'll have washes and creams and lotions galore."

"And I will expect you to use them every day as instructed," Tam told him, straightening up and putting his hands on his hips. With his blue hair and ice-blue eyes, he looked like a Smurf, but wisely, Kellet kept that thought to himself.

"But why? I've managed for thirty-seven years without a routine. Why do I need all this shit now?"

"Kellet, my love, for the next few months, you are not going to live life normally. You will have long days, less sleep than you're used to; you're going to be under glaring hot lights for shows where you're going to get a physical workout that you haven't endured before. And then, you're going to meet fans, PR reps, do interviews–on TV and radio–and everyone, and I mean, everyone, is going to notice every blemish and flaw on your stupidly handsome face."

"I'm not handsome," Kel retorted.

Tam threw his hands up. "Really? That's what you took out of all that?" Leaning forward, he got into Kellet's personal space again. "Believe me when I say, I have worked with some of the biggest names in the entertainment business, from supermodels to A-list actors. If there's one thing I know, it's faces. And yours is a good one. With a bit of love and attention, it will be devastating. There'll be people lined up at the back-stage door begging to have your babies."

"Been there, done that. Got the teenager to prove it," Kel retorted with a smirk.

"Yeah, and like Jamie is going to let anyone near you?" Liam muttered and blushed when Kellet and Tam turned to stare at him. "Oops! Did I say that out loud?"

Tam's glance whipped between the two of them and then stopped to look speculatively at Kellet. "You and Jamie?" He nodded slowly. "Hmm, makes sense now."

"What? What makes sense now? And there is no 'me and Jamie'," Kellet said, squirming in his seat. What had Liam meant? He was the second person after Andi to say that Jamie still carried a torch for him. Was it true? Could they possibly rekindle what they'd had all those years ago?

"Don't worry about it, honey," Tam announced, waving a hand in the air. Picking up his bag, he smiled happily at them. "I'll see you gorgeous men tomorrow. Kellet, shampoo your hair tonight, rather than in the morning. It'll make it easier for me to work with."

With a jaunty wave, the exuberant man left the room.

"Come on, Kel. Let's go and find the others and then head home. I think we could all do with a beer."

Kellet followed Liam, still pondering his words from earlier. He wasn't going to ask the bass guitarist for information on Jamie. He needed to talk to Jamie directly.

Zoe Piper

Chapter Nine

Kellet drummed his fingers against the steering wheel of his Mustang as he crawled along the highway, battling LA's notorious traffic. He was hyper-aware of the man sitting next to him. Jamie was half leaning against the passenger door, his body angled towards Kellet. This was the first time they'd been alone since Jamie had shown up at East Bank nearly two weeks ago. Wil had bailed on his father the second he'd seen Seth's Maserati Grand Turismo, and the lead guitarist had told him to hop in for the ride to Jamie's place.

The inane chatter of the DJ on the radio broke the awkward silence.

"... and we hear from sources close to the band that Larkspur may have found their new drummer..."

"Shit!" said Kellet. "I thought Jax said that they weren't announcing anything for a couple of days?"

"She did," Jamie replied, pulling his phone out of his pocket and tapping at the screen before lifting it to his ear.

Kellet returned his attention to the road in front of him while trying to follow Jamie's half of the conversation.

"Yeah, Jax. Have you leaked the news about Kel early?"

From the corner of his eye, he saw Jamie nod.

"Uh, huh. Nah, just some DJ on the radio made a comment." Jamie shifted in his seat, stretching his long legs. "Okay then. No, that's fine. Yep. See you tomorrow." He gave an aggrieved sigh. "We won't. Yes, I'll make sure Seth behaves. Bye Jax!"

Kellet quickly glanced at Jamie and got a grin in return.

"What did she say?"

"She definitely hasn't announced anything yet, but it could have been someone from the hotel. It's no secret we've been looking, and one of the staff may have made a call about our meeting. She said not to worry, if it breaks early, she'll deal with it."

Kellet felt slightly better. "I suppose I'd better get used to all this," he said, gesturing at the radio. "My life's not going to be my own for the next few months, is it?"

"There will be some initial buzz, and everyone will want to know everything about you, but the label will do their best to manage it all. They'll have a rep travel up to Juniper to help with any reporters who go digging into your family and your life up there. It will die down once the first concerts are out of the way."

"I don't want Wil dragged into this. Or Andi and Ro," Kellet told him, his stomach clenching at the thought of his family's privacy being invaded.

"They're already part of it, Kel. Andi and Ro are fully aware that there will be questions about all of you. How your life works; their relationship, not only with you and Wil, but with each other." Jamie gave a soft sigh. "I'm sorry, Kel. I know this is why you were so adamant against saying yes. You've always protected those you love, and this is going to be hard for you not to jump in now."

Kellet felt humbled by Jamie's words. He was right, and there wasn't much that Kellet could do except trust that the record label would honor their word and look out for his family. At least having Wil with him would mean he could control things a little easier where he was concerned.

"You're right," Kellet conceded and glanced across when Jamie snorted. The sight of the huge grin on his face warmed Kellet.

"I usually am," Jamie snarked back and laughed harder when Kellet flipped him the bird.

Tension broken, they spent the rest of the journey chatting about mundane, everyday things until they exited the highway and began the drive into Laurel Canyon where Jamie's home was.

Kellet slowed when Jamie pointed to a driveway just ahead of them, and as they drew closer, Jamie pressed a fob on his keyring to open the large wrought-iron gates that protected the property.

"Just pull up by the garage," Jamie instructed him as they drove in. He looked up the short driveway to the sprawling house in front of them. He was surprised to see an adobe style home, painted in light terracotta tones and surrounded by lush gardens. He stopped in front of a large three-car garage and turned off the Mustang.

"This is gorgeous, Jamie," he said as he got out of the car and took in the property. "How long have you lived here?"

"Thanks. I was lucky enough to get it about eight years ago. It needed some work done to it because the previous owners had only used it occasionally. It had all but been abandoned for about four or five years before it came on the market."

Kellet could tell how much Jamie loved his house, his voice resonating with passion, and his features animated as he described the state the house had been in when he bought it.

"Come on, let's get inside and I can give you the proper tour," Jamie told him, nodding towards the front door.

Popping the trunk, he pulled his and Wil's suitcases out. There were some other bags and boxes, but Wil could bring those in later and sort them out. He followed Jamie up the short pathway and paused as the other man unlocked the house and disabled the alarm.

"I'll give you and Wil keys and the alarm codes once he gets here," Jamie said over his shoulder as headed down a short hallway.

Kellet followed, taking in the décor of cream walls and warm terracotta tiles. He came to a halt beside Jamie, who was opening the door into a large, light and airy bedroom.

"This is one room," he said, before nodding to another door on the opposite side of the hallway a few feet down. "And that's the other. Both have their own bathrooms, so you can pick whichever one you want, and Wil can take the other."

Kellet stuck his head around the door and glanced at the room. It was sparsely decorated, with the usual bed, dresser and small bookshelf in the corner. He dropped Wil's case on the bed.

"Wil can have this one, and I'll have the other," he said as he followed Jamie down the hallway. He pushed into the other room and found it like the previous one, only this had a sliding door that opened onto a glittering pool.

"Great. If you want to freshen up, go ahead. The others will be here soon. Come on through when you're ready," Jamie said to him with a big smile. Kellet's stomach flipped. He could see how happy Jamie was to have him, and it made him feel good that he had put that smile on his old friend's face.

"Thanks, Jamie," he said, his voice a little husky with emotion. "You didn't have to open your home up to us. I know this... this will be strange, but I'm grateful."

"You're welcome, Kel. There's nowhere else I'd like you to be. Make yourself at home while you're here."

Jamie gave him a nod and then left him alone. Kellet dropped his bag onto the bed and unzipped it. He needed a few minutes to gather himself, so would start on his unpacking.

♫ ♫ ♫

Jamie leaned against the kitchen counter, staring across his yard, not seeing the pool or the lush gardens surrounding it. All he could see was Kellet-*fucking*-James in his house. In his spare bedroom.

He'd lied when he said that there was nowhere else he'd like Kel to be. Oh, he wanted him in his home, but he didn't want him in his spare room. No, Kel belonged in his bedroom, in his bed, in his life.

The buzz of the gate intercom had him shaking thoughts of how to get Kel from the spare room and upstairs. The front door opened, and he could hear Wil's excited voice calling out for his father. Kel's deeper voice rumbled an admonishment to his son.

Seth sauntered in; a grin plastered across his handsome features.

"I take it Wil enjoyed the ride home?" Jamie asked as they fist bumped.

"Yeah, took the long way around. Kid's cool. Kel's done a great job with him."

"Does one of you fuckers wanna give me a hand here?" Liam's voice echoed from the front door.

Jamie and Seth looked at one another before yelling back together, "Nah!"

"I'll help," Wil called and a few moments later he and Liam came in laden with pizza boxes and beer.

Kellet was just behind them, looking a little lost.

"Kel, come and grab a beer and some food," Jamie told him.

"My God, how many people are coming tonight?" Kellet asked as he saw the five pizzas spread out on the table.

"This is the best pizza you'll ever eat, Kel, trust me. We've been known to demolish more than this, especially when we're writing and recording."

"It looks great, but I doubt it's better than Dad's," Wil said as he grabbed a slice.

"You cook, Kel?" Liam asked, popping the top on his beer.

Jamie was surprised to see a dull flush stain Kellet's face.

"Um, yeah. Nothing flashy or gourmet, but good enough that we don't starve or live on takeout."

"Feel free to use the kitchen here whenever you like," Jamie told him. "If there are any special ingredients you need, just put them on the board next to the fridge and my housekeeper will get them in for you."

A hum of appreciation sounded from Wil. "Actually, Dad, this is pretty good."

"What do you want to drink, Wil?" Jamie asked, suddenly remembering they had an eighteen-year-old amongst them. "I've got bottled water or soda?"

Wil turned pleading eyes on his father, and Jamie smothered a grin at Kellet's put-upon sigh.

"One! You can have one beer and that's it," Kellet ground out and then chuckled as Wil did a little jig where he was standing.

"Thanks, Dad!"

"I got some non-alcoholic beer, Kel," Liam told him.

"Thanks Lee, appreciate it." Kellet turned and pointed to his son. "One normal beer and only a couple of the non-alcoholic ones, okay?"

"Yes, Daaadd!" Wil sing-songed back as he took the bottle Seth was holding out to him. "Thanks."

"Come on, let's sit outside," Jamie suggested, herding them towards the sliding doors that opened out onto the pool.

They gathered up their food and beers and soon settled in the comfortable loungers he had dotted at the pool edge.

"Ahh, this is the life!" Seth said, stretching out his long body. He lifted his beer bottle in a toast. "Welcome back, Kel. I know I speak for everyone when I say how happy we are you agreed to join us. We're gonna rock the fuck out of this tour."

A chorus of agreement rang out, and Jamie was

relieved Seth and Liam were just as happy to have Kellet back in their lives as he was.

"Thanks, Seth. I hope I can do the job justice."

"You'll be fine. We'll start rehearsals tomorrow, so tonight, kick back and relax. Bring us up to speed on your life for the last few years," Liam said.

Jamie sat and listened as Kellet told them about getting his business degree and how he and Andi, along with their parents, bought East Bank ten years ago. How they'd taken a worn-down bar and restaurant and turned it around to be one of Juniper's most popular eateries and hangouts.

A sense of pride went through him as he watched Kellet animatedly tell a story about a particularly raucous bachelor party that had taken place. Kellet may have ended up on a different path to what he originally dreamed of, but he'd made a success of what he'd done.

"What's that building over there, Jamie?" Wil asked, pulling Jamie's attention from the main conversation.

Jamie looked to where Wil was pointing. "That's the guest house there," he said, gesturing to a small cream building set back into the gardens before pointing to a slightly larger building, "and over there is the studio."

"Cool," Wil enthused. "I bet it's great having all that space to practice in."

"It is," Jamie agreed.

"How come we're not staying in the guest house?" Kel asked, catching Jamie off guard.

"Because you're not guests," Jamie replied, before draining the rest of his beer.

"What are we then?" Wil asked, gaze switching between his father and their host.

"You're family."

Wil gave a small nod, as though it was what he expected to hear. Kel's face gave nothing away, and Jamie decided he needed a few minutes to himself. Standing up, he gestured with his empty bottle. "Anyone want a refill?"

Everyone nodded their heads, and Jamie headed towards the house.

He wasn't surprised when he heard someone enter soon after him and he braced himself to face Kel, but it was the younger James who had followed him.

"Everything okay, Wil?"

"Yeah. Just came to help you carry the beers back," Wil answered cheerfully.

"I could've managed, but thanks," Jamie told him with a smile. He popped the lids on four regular beers and gestured to the young man. "Soda or…?"

"I'll have a fake beer, please," Wil said, causing Jamie to laugh at his description.

"So, hey… um… Jamie?"

Jamie passed Wil his drink along with another one. "What's up?"

"Look, I realize this will sound really weird, but… ah…. I just wanted you to know…"

"Know what, Wil?" Jamie watched in fascination as Wil's face turned a faint shade of red as he shuffled on the spot.

"Dad filled me in on your past… y'know, you and him when you were my age, and I just… just wanted you to know that I think it's cool and all, and like, if you and him were to… y'know… then

I… I'd be cool with that."

Jamie suppressed a grin. Kel would cringe if he knew his son had given his seal of approval on their relationship; not that they had an actual relationship as such.

"Thanks, Wil. I appreciate you telling me. If anything happens between your dad and me, then it's good to know that you're okay with it all."

Tension eased out of Wil's frame and a big grin spread across his face. He was about to reply when he tensed up again, worry replacing the grin, and he reached out a hand to Jamie.

"Don't say anything to Dad though, okay? He'd kill me if he knew what I'd just said."

"It's all good, Wil," Jamie reassured him, grinning. "Come on, before they send a search party for their beers."

Chapter Ten

Kellet tried not to fidget as Tam buzzed around him. He'd closed his eyes, so he didn't have to see what the cheery stylist was doing to him. Strong fingers ran through his hair several times; Tam humming under his breath as he worked. The pop of a cap being removed, and the brisk rubbing of hands was all the warning he got before Tam was massaging his scalp as his short curls were tamed into some semblance of order.

Kellet wasn't a vain man and not one to worry too much about his appearance in general. He had a regular haircut every six weeks and kept clean shaven, only allowing his stubble to grow through on weekends and on the occasional holiday he took. He rubbed a hand against his jaw, only to have it slapped away, Tam tsking under his breath. Wil had given him a delayed message the night before not to shave, and his skin was prickly with his morning growth.

In the background, he could hear the other guys teasing and chatting with the studio crew. It sounded like they were relaxed and unfazed by all the activity, which Kellet supposed they were. They'd been doing things like this for years, and he'd be lying if he didn't admit to himself, he was completely out of his comfort zone.

He jumped and his eyes popped open as a warm grip settled on his arm and he met Jamie's grinning gaze in the mirror in front of him.

"You okay there, Kel?"

"Yeah, just fine," he replied. Jamie's eyebrow quirked disbelievingly, and Kellet grinned ruefully in return.

"Okay, so I'm a little nervous about all of this," he admitted, waving a hand in the air.

"Oh, honey, you'll be fine," Tam told him as he reached for a large make-up sponge and a bottle of foundation. "Just relax and take your cues from the other guys. Now, close those gorgeous green eyes for me."

Kellet did as he was ordered and felt the gentle dab of the sponge against his skin. There was a scrape of a chair being pulled across the wooden floor, and he could sense that Jamie had sat down next to him.

"We'll only be here a few hours, and then we'll head home and we'll play around in the studio."

"Sounds good," Kellet replied. He was eager to get behind a kit and lose himself in the music. He was also excited to be playing with the guys again, and he hoped that he wouldn't let them down.

"Okay, Kellet, open up and look towards the ceiling for me," Tam instructed. Kellet leaned back as Tam loomed over him with a sharp-looking pencil in his hand.

"Relax, I'm just going to put a bit of eyeliner on you. I was considering some mascara, but you have obscenely long lashes that many a top supermodel would kill for."

Kellet tried not to flinch as Tam gently ran the pencil along his lower lid and let out a sigh of relief when Tam stepped back to admire his handy work.

"Annd, my job here is done," Tam said, obviously satisfied.

Kellet blinked at the reflection in the mirror. He looked the same, but also… different? His hair was artfully tousled, as though he'd just run his fingers through it, and his eyes seemed bigger and darker. He leaned forward and he could see the eyeliner, but it was so subtle it was almost like it wasn't there.

"You were expecting to look like Alice Cooper, weren't you?" Jamie said with a chuckle.

Kellet's gaze flicked to Jamie, and then to Tam, and then back to Jamie. "Umm…"

"It's okay, Kellet. I knew you were worried and really, it's all about highlighting your natural features without making you look like a circus clown." Tam patted him on the shoulder, and Kellet gave him a grateful smile.

"Thanks, Tam. I appreciate it."

"You're welcome. Now, go and see what Debs has brought for you while I sort out Mr. Larke here."

Standing up, he stretched out his back before heading to the corner where there were racks of clothes laid out. As he got nearer, he saw four stations, one for each band member. There was a selection of shirts, t-shirts, jackets, jeans, and footwear ranging from sneakers to motorcycle boots.

"Excellent timing," Debs said with a welcoming grin. "I've just sorted out Seth, so you are next up. She ran an appraising eye over him. "Tam has worked his magic again, I see. Right then, let's leave on the jeans you're wearing and put this on with it," she ordered him, thrusting a plain black t-shirt towards him.

He grabbed at the hem of his t-shirt, but a grip on his wrist had him pausing.

"Ease that over your head so you don't undo any of Tam's work. You'll never hear the end of it!" Debs told him with a grin.

Kellet nodded his understanding. He didn't want to get on the wrong side of the fiery man before he'd even been in the job a day. Once he had on the black t-shirt, he stood as Debs tugged and smoothed it into place. It felt tight, and he rolled his shoulders.

"How's that feel?" Debs asked.

"Hmm, a little snug," he admitted.

"No, it's fine. You're just not used to it," she reassured him. "You've got to remember, Kellet, you're not just a bar owner and dad now; you're the drummer in one of the biggest bands in the world. Your image has got to reflect that."

"You've got to get your sexy on, Kel," Seth told him with a grin as he appeared from across the room.

Kellet looked the lead guitarist up and down. The undercut on his faux hawk had been trimmed with the longer hair on top teased up, causing Seth's sharp features to stand out. Light glinted off his brow piercing and his dark brown eyes had also been lined in kohl. He wore ripped jeans and heavy biker boots and a black muscle shirt that showed off his biceps and the inked sleeves that ran up both arms.

Kellet knew that both sexes clamored after Seth, and the man certainly had never hidden his light under a bushel. Even as a teen, Seth had a certain swagger and innate sexiness that drew individuals to him. Kellet had no doubt that he was rarely without company when he wanted it.

"Okay, people! Let's get this show on the road!"

The strident voice of the photographer's assistant rang out across the studio and Kellet took a deep breath before following Seth over to the set where they were joined by Jamie and Liam and stood waiting for instruction.

"We're going to start with some basic shots against the white background of all four of you together, then we'll work some individual pictures, okay?"

The photographer stood back behind his camera and stared at them intently for a few moments. His assistant leaned into him and together they had a quiet conversation before the assistant nodded and walked towards them.

"Liam, you stand here," he said, directing the bass guitarist to the right of the set. "Then you Jamie, yep, that'll work. Then you Kellet, and Seth, you on Kellet's right."

Seth dropped an arm over Kellet's shoulder. "Breathe, Kel. It's a camera, not a firing squad."

He rolled his shoulders and tried not to squint at the bright lights. The photographer took a few test shots and stepped back to the computer attached to his camera. Kellet could see Jax and Miles pointing at the screen, and Wil caught his eye from his position just behind them and gave his father a thumbs up.

Satisfied with what he saw, he started shooting in earnest. Kellet was moved left, right, forward, back. As time went on, he relaxed, and a running commentary from Seth had him laughing, and soon he was teasing and throwing insults with the guys as though he'd never been away.

"We're nearly there, gentlemen," Jax told them as they took a quick break and wardrobe change. Kellet was about to shrug on the leather biker jacket that Debs had given him when the photographer called out.

"No, hold the jacket. In fact, lose the shirt as well."

Kellet froze as Jamie stripped off his shirt and tossed it onto a nearby chair.

"Come on, Kel. No need to be shy. It's just your shirt."

Mouth dry, Kellet took off his t-shirt and passed it to Debs, who gave him a smile. "You're doing great," she whispered.

Tam bounced over to them, make-up sponge in hand and began dabbing at Kellet's shoulders and chest.

"What are you doing?" Kellet asked, trying to push the man away.

"Oh, stand still!" Tam admonished. "I just need to take the shine off your shoulders. Heavens to Betsy, I'm not going to hurt you."

Kellet stood and bit his tongue. He really didn't want to say something to offend Tam, but he was feeling rather vulnerable. He risked a glance over towards Jamie, who was watching with hooded eyes, arms crossed as he leaned against the table.

Heat crawled along Kellet's skin, and he closed his eyes and mentally went through the opening beats to Larkspur's biggest hit to distract himself.

A swat on his shoulder had him opening his eyes, and Tam wordlessly shooed him towards the set before turning to Jamie.

Kellet tried not to watch as Tam dabbed and blotted Jamie's smooth chest. He pushed down the urge to go over and haul the make-up artist away. He dropped his gaze when Tam stepped closer to Jamie, his hand resting on the curve of Jamie's shoulder, and said something to him that had Jamie grin and wink.

"They've never slept together," Liam's low voice startled Kellet, and he swung to look at the man next to him.

"What?"

"Jamie and Tam. They've never slept together. In fact, Jamie has a policy of not sleeping with the crew."

Kellet wasn't sure why Liam was telling him this and was just about to ask when Jamie joined them.

"Everything okay?"

Kellet nodded, not trusting himself to speak. He tried not to let Jamie being half-naked next to him affect him, but it wasn't easy. Long-buried memories surfaced, and Kellet shoved his hands in his pockets to stop himself from reaching out and tracing the line of musical notes that wrapped around Jamie's rib cage on his left side.

"Where's Seth?" Jax called out.

"I think he went to the bathroom," Liam said. "I'll go and find him." The bassist headed out of the room in search of his erstwhile bandmate, muttering under his breath as he left.

"We may as well do some shots with you two while we wait," the photographer said, and Kellet wished he could have a drink to calm himself.

"Jamie, you stand there, and I want you to look straight at me. Yes, perfect. Now, Kellet, stand to his right, but back a little. There's good, but angle yourself so you're slightly facing him. No, too much. Yes. There. Okay, hold that." The photographer jumped behind his camera, and the flash of lights and whirr of the shutter sounded.

"Jamie, tilt your head back a bit. Yep. Good. I want a bit more arrogance."

Jamie crossed his arms and glared moodily at the camera.

"Perfect. Now, Kellet, I want you to lean an elbow on Jamie's shoulder. Yes. No." The photographer canted his head to one side, squinting slightly. "No. You're looking too relaxed against Jamie's glare."

Kellet wasn't sure what was wanted of him, and he stiffened his shoulders up. He caught sight of Wil smirking at him, and he bit his lip to stop himself grinning back.

"No. Still not working for me, Kellet."

Wil shook with laughter as he tried to suppress his amusement, and Kellet shot him a glare. Wil turned aside, laughing even harder when Anton cried out, "Yes! Perfect. Keep that look."

Kellet hid his own grin behind his hand, and Anton snapped away excitedly. A few minutes later, Liam dragged a smirking Seth into the room, and they took some more shots of the four of them.

Kellet and Jamie were relieved of their duty, and Kellet gratefully wiped the make-up off while Liam and Seth had their pictures done.

"That was great guys. We got some excellent ones, and we'll use a couple tomorrow when the announcement goes out about Kellet," Jax told them, a smile on her face.

They thanked Tam, Debs and the photography crew before heading out. Seeing Wil wasn't with them, Kellet paused to find where he was.

He spied him in the corner with Cal, the other assistant, their heads close together. "Wil, we're leaving. Are you coming with us or not?" he called out.

Wil looked up and nodded to his father. He turned back to Cal and patted him on the shoulder. Cal shook his head, and when he saw them looking, his fair skin flushed bright red and he hurried away.

"Is everything okay?" Kellet asked as the teenager joined them.

"Yeah. He's just a little shy and nervous," Wil replied casually and Kellet wouldn't have thought anything of it except for the look his son threw at Seth who was ahead of them with Liam.

"Wil, you'd tell me if there was something going on, wouldn't you?"

"Of course I would, Dad. It's cool. Cal's good. It's nice to have someone closer to my age to hang with."

"I didn't realize he was that young," Jamie commented from the other side of Wil.

"Oh, he's not. I mean, he's twenty-six, but that's still younger than you lot," Wil said cheekily, dancing out of the way of the gentle cuff his father aimed at him.

Chapter Eleven

Jamie paused a few feet away from the door to his studio as the sound of the drums rolled through the air. He recognized Kellet's warm-up scales and wasn't surprised that he hadn't changed it over the years. Mark's had been as distinctive and personal as Kellet's was to him, and it was strange to hear a different tempo after all this time.

The ride home from the photography studio had been relaxed, the constant stream of chatter from Wil breaking any possible awkward silences. Once they'd arrived home, they'd eaten a quick lunch of sandwiches before agreeing to meet later to get the practice underway. Jamie knew that Kellet was nervous and had deliberately stayed inside when he'd seen the other man make his way around the pool to the music room.

He'd been hyperaware of Kellet all morning, especially when they'd stripped down to just their jeans and Kel had rested his elbow on his shoulder. Jamie had channeled all the willpower he could not to turn and take Kellet in his arms and feel his skin against his own.

Recognizing the tempo change as Kellet slowed down, Jamie took the few remaining steps and opened the door. From the outside, the studio didn't look much, just a narrow-bricked building. Once inside though, it stretched out, leaving lots of room for all their gear and to one side, a small but functional mixing desk. There was a bathroom and in the back corner was a kitchenette area. Several large bean bags were dotted about, and there was a sectional couch tucked in the back.

It worked well for them to practice and when they were writing and working on new material. Each band member had a similar set up, and they rotated around each other's places regularly.

Jamie nodded at Kellet as he entered and placed his guitar in its stand before heading to the equipment cupboard to pull out the amps they'd need. Kellet finished his last scale, and the sudden silence was deafening.

"There's some water in the fridge," Jamie said, nodding to the corner, trying not to stare at Kellet's flushed face. He was dressed in a loose muscle shirt and his arms bulged from the exertion.

"Thanks," Kellet replied as he wiped his hands on a small towel before picking up a bottle from down by his feet. "I brought one over from the house. I wasn't sure what you had out here."

"There's usually a supply of water and snacks out here. Help yourself to anything you want." Jamie dropped the amp he was carrying into place and began to set it up.

"I know I've already said it, and I'll probably say it again, but thanks, Jamie. You didn't have to take us in like this. I know you've got... friends that you'd have around, and I hope Wil and I aren't going to be in the way."

Jamie stopped what he was doing to look at Kellet, noticing the slight hesitation. There was a tenseness to his features that, despite not seeing him for years, Jamie was still able to interpret. He smiled, trying not to let his amusement show too much.

"I don't actually... entertain that often," Jamie replied with a similar pause. "I only normally have the guys around, Miles and sometimes Jax and Sarge. It's usually pretty low key and casual."

"Ah, okay then. That's good. I'd hate to put you in an uncomfortable position."

"Kel, you can put me in any position you want, and I assure you, none of them would be uncomfortable."

Green eyes flared at Jamie's statement, followed by a look of heat and desire. "So, you're saying..." Kellet's voice broke off as Jamie ran his tongue over his bottom lip and took a step towards him.

"Yes, Kel, I'm saying that we need to sit down and have a really good talk," Jamie cocked his head as voices carried across the air. "But sadly, we don't have time for that, or anything else, right now."

Kellet looked disappointed at Jamie's response but nodded in agreement. "Yeah, okay then. Raincheck?"

Jamie grinned as fireworks of excitement burst inside him. "Raincheck," he acknowledged before the door flung open, and Liam tumbled into the room with Seth laughing behind him.

"Ahh, this is just like old times," Seth exclaimed as he unlatched his guitar case. "Let's see if you've still got it, Kel."

"Guys, I appreciate your faith in me, but I want to state for the record that I'm nowhere near Mark's level. If you feel that this isn't going to work, then let me know so you can find someone else."

"Kel, stop worrying! And stop selling yourself short. Miles heard you play a few weeks ago and if he thinks you can do it, then so do we. We know it's going to be different, but you've got this," Jamie rushed to reassure him as he adjusted the strap of his guitar over his shoulder.

"Yeah, Dad! You're not normally so pessimistic," Wil piped up from the doorway.

"What are you doing here?"

"D'uh! I'm here to document your first practice and offer moral support. Y'know, do my job as your assistant," Wil said, holding up a small video camera.

Jamie chuckled at the glare Kellet threw at his son. "C'mon guys, let's get this show on the road. I thought we'd start with Blue Moon."

Liam and Seth nodded their agreement, and Jamie sent an encouraging smile in Kellet's direction. The other man took a deep breath before tapping out a 1-2-3 beat with his sticks and launched into the steady tempo of the opening bars to their last hit.

Seth picked up his cue, and as the familiar guitar riff sounded, Jamie began to sing. Although they were only in his small practice studio and not on a stage in front of thousands of fans, the same thrill went through Jamie. He loved his job and today, it was a hundred times better for having Kellet James on drums.

Jamie respected and liked Mark, both as a musician and as a person. Loved him like a brother, but the connection he felt with Kellet snapped back into place, as though they hadn't spent too many years apart. He grinned at Seth and Liam and got answering ones in return. They felt it too. Getting

Kellet back had been the right decision. This last leg of their tour was going to be their best.

♫ ♫ ♫

Kellet rolled his shoulders, trying to ease the tension. They'd played solidly for nearly two hours and he'd forgotten how hard that could be. He knew it would be worse once they were on tour and he'd be under the glare of hot lights.

Warm hands settled on his shoulders, and he tensed before realizing it was Wil.

"You did great, Dad," he said as he dug his thumbs into the base of Kellet's neck. "I've never seen you play like that before. It sounded really good. It's going to be amazing live in a huge stadium."

Kellet shook his head in denial. Although he appreciated the vote of confidence, his son was biased, and he didn't hesitate to tell him.

"No, the kid's right," Seth told him. "Yeah, there are some spots we need to work on, but considering it's been how many years since we all played together, it was good."

Kellet stood and stretched out his back before leaning over his kit to fist bump Seth. "Thanks, Seth."

"No thanks needed," Seth replied as he picked up his guitar case. "Laters. I'll see you all tomorrow."

"Where are you going?" Jamie called out.

Seth flashed a grin and a wink.

"Oh, for fuck's sake! Don't be late or hungover in the morning or else I'm setting Jax on you," Jamie warned.

"Relax, J. I'm just goin' to have a drink or two, and I promise to be in bed before the witching hour."

"That's what worries me," Jamie shouted to his retreating back.

"Is it something we should be worried about?" Kellet asked. Seth had always been a bit of loose cannon, rebelling against his parents from early in his teens.

Jamie sighed and shook his head. "No, not really. He's slowed down a little over the last couple of years, and he's always professional when we're out on tour, but he's still a bit of a manwhore. When he says he'll be in bed before the witching hour, he doesn't necessarily mean his bed, and he certainly won't be sleeping."

"None of you have got partners, have you?" Wil asked.

Kellet saw something flash across both Jamie's and Liam's faces before they both shook their heads. "Wil! That's a bit of a personal question," he admonished his son.

"Oh, yeah. Sorry guys. I didn't mean to pry."

"It's okay, Wil," Jamie reassured him. "Mark has a long-term girlfriend, and that's part of the reason he left. Being away from her for several months while on tour made it harder for him to control his anxiety."

"And we've all been too busy," Liam said. "I'm heading out too. I'll see you in the morning."

"Thought you were staying for dinner?" Jamie called out to him.

"Nah. I just wanna head home and chill," Liam replied, and Kellet couldn't help but feel that his friend wasn't telling the whole truth. Jamie didn't call him on it though, so Kellet gave him a hug and said goodnight.

"I'll go and get dinner started if you like," Wil offered.

"You don't have to do that," Jamie said. "You're guests."

"Ah, no. Last night, you said we were family, and in our family, we take turns cooking," Wil reminded him, eyes sparkling with mischief. "Don't worry, Jamie. I'm not as good as Dad, but I can put up something edible."

Wil loped off towards the house and Kellet finished wiping down the drum kit before picking up his trash. He turned to find Jamie watching him with an inscrutable look.

"You did great today, Kel. I've really missed your playing," Jamie told him softly.

"I'd forgotten how much fun it could be playing with you guys," Kellet admitted. "It doesn't feel real. I feel like I'm dreaming."

"You're not. It's very real. Wait until you walk out onto that stage with thousands of screaming fans. It's almost as good as sex."

"I'll take your word for it," Kellet said with a rueful grin.

"There's been no one special over the last few years?" Jamie asked curiously.

Kellet sighed and shook his head. "There were a couple of guys, but they didn't want to be saddled with a kid in their early twenties, and I guess I just gave up looking."

"Well, they're idiots," Jamie huffed. "Wil's a great kid."

"Yeah, he's not so bad, but we've had our moments. I can understand where they were coming from. When you're twenty-five you want to be out partying and socializing, not attending little league and parent-teacher conferences."

"I would have wanted to," Jamie said quietly.

Kellet saw the truth in his words, and some of the wall around his heart crumbled. "I know you would have, but our lives were on different paths. You were born to live this life, Jamie. Maybe in the future you'll have the dirty diapers and school recitals, but you took the path you were meant to take."

"Kel, I…"

"It's okay, Jamie. We both did what we had to do. What we had was amazing, but we're older now. Your life has been the polar opposite of mine, and I understand that there have been… people that have shared parts of it."

"There haven't been that many guys, Kel. Liam and Seth may live up to the typical rock star stereotype, but I've never been that guy."

Jealousy ripped through Kellet at Jamie's words, and he did his best to quash it. He knew it would be ridiculous for him to think Jamie wouldn't have been with anyone else. He hadn't exactly been a monk either, though he could literally count on one hand the number of guys he'd been with in the last few years. And wasn't that a depressing thought?

Kellet shook himself mentally. After he and Jamie broke up, he'd been too focused on raising Wil and working hard to provide for them both. It had helped to bury the pain he felt over Jamie leaving, and by the time he was ready to date again, the lingering memory of Jamie had meant that he'd found it hard to commit to anyone.

"Kel, I know things are a bit awkward now. We've not teenagers anymore, and as much as I'd like us to be more, the thing I've missed most is your friendship. Can we, I dunno, maybe start out by rebuilding that and see where it takes us?"

"I'd like that, Jamie. I've missed your friendship too. The next few months are going to be hard enough as it is, but knowing you and I are friends will go a long way to make things a little easier."

Jamie took a step towards him and then stopped. "Can we mark this friendship renewal with a hug?"

Kellet smiled and opened his arms wide. Familiar scents of leather and wood assailed him as strong arms wrapped around him. Home, a voice in his head said. He felt safe, and some of the tension he hadn't realized he was carrying, eased. He resisted the urge to nuzzle the soft bit of skin just below Jamie's ear. It was one of his favorite places on Jamie's body and he longed to touch his mouth to it. Before he could embarrass them both though, Jamie's arms tightened in one last squeeze and he reluctantly let go.

They stared at each other and Jamie's eyes flicked to Kellet's mouth before he gave a rueful grin. "Come on, we'd better make sure your son isn't burning down my kitchen."

"Yeah," Kellet agreed, his voice a little husky as he tamped down the emotions flowing through him. "I'd hate to ask Seth or Liam if we could move in with them."

Jamie's laugh buoyed Kellet's spirits further as he followed the other man toward the house. Maybe this wasn't going to be as hard as he thought.

Chapter Twelve

The tap of Jax's bright red fingernails against the side of her coffee mug had Kellet on edge. Her displeasure was obvious, and even though he knew he wasn't the cause of it, he still wanted to do or say something that would ease the frown off her face.

Cal, shifted uncomfortably beside her, his eyes glued to the tablet in front of him as he tapped and swiped the screen.

"Do you want me to call him?" Jamie asked, breaking the silence.

"No, thank you, Jamie. He's just messaged that he's a few minutes away," Jax replied with a tight smile.

Seth snorted quietly from the recliner he'd commandeered in Jamie's lounge. "Makes a change for Lee to be the late one."

The sound of the gate buzzer had them all looking towards the front of the house. A few moments later, Liam appeared from the hallway and stopped when he saw everyone was staring at him.

Kellet was surprised to see the normally put together bass guitarist looking a little pale and rumpled, as though he'd thrown on whatever clothes he'd found lying on his bedroom floor. His hair looked like he'd run a wet hand through it, and dark stubble lined his jaw. Dark glasses hid his eyes, and although he smiled, it wasn't the usual sunny grin he usually gave.

"Damn, Lee. Who rode you hard and put you away soaked?" Seth asked. "And more importantly, why didn't you call me to join you?"

"Ah, sorry guys. I… um… overslept," Liam said as he made his way to the remaining chair. "I didn't go out. I had a couple of whiskeys and fell asleep on the couch. I must have been more tired than I thought."

Seth threw a skeptical look at his bandmate but didn't make any further comment as Jax cleared her throat.

"Right, the press release goes out in about an hour's time and we've got several interviews lined up." She smiled at Kellet. "Today, we're going to run through some questions that will get asked and the answers you need to give Kellet."

"Okay. I think?" Kellet had been dreading this. He knew it was part of the job, but he was a private person, and the thought of being asked invasive queries about his personal life had him breaking out in a cold sweat.

"It's okay. Questions are usually submitted ahead by the media organizations, so we know what is going to be asked, or we give them a list of topics they're allowed to talk about." Jax nodded at the young man next to her. "Cal will ask some questions, and I want you to answer them as best as you can. I'll stop you if you need some guidance."

Cal looked up from his tablet and a faint blush stained his cheeks as he faced Kellet.

"Kellet, what's it like to be the new drummer for Larkspur?"

"Um… ah… it's great?"

Seth made a buzzer sound and leaned forward in his seat. "Nope. That's not gonna work. You need to be confident and not answer like you're unsure or asking a question."

Kellet's gaze flicked to Jax, who looked amused and nodded that he should try again.

"It… It's great. A real honor."

"You were one of the founders of Larkspur, weren't you? Why didn't you stay with the band?"

"Yeah, Jamie and I were at high school together and we formed Larkspur then. I… I had other commitments and couldn't stay with them when they were offered their contract."

Jax nodded, her blond ponytail bobbing. "That's better. Relax your shoulders a bit. You're looking defensive and it will make the interviewer want to dig and push a little more."

"Yeah, bloody vultures," Seth muttered.

"Unfortunately, they are a part of the business, Seth," Jax told him before nodding to Cal to continue.

"I understand your teenage son is with you on tour. What does he think about this?" Cal's eyes flicked to where Wil was slouched on a beanbag. Wil grinned at Cal, who grinned back, and Kellet blinked at how different the young man looked. Seth gave a small cough and then jumped up from his seat.

"Gonna grab some water; anyone want one?" he asked before disappearing towards the kitchen without waiting for replies.

Kellet glanced at Jamie, who was at the opposite end of the couch to where he was sitting. Jamie shrugged. Kellet focused back on Cal. He had enough to deal with without his bandmates acting weirdly.

"Ah, Wil, my son, is loving this. He's working as an assistant and learning lots," Kellet replied to Cal's question and Wil nodded enthusiastically.

Seth returned and handed out bottles of water. Kellet noticed that Cal blushed when he took his, and he groaned internally. He really hoped that Seth was as professional as Jamie had claimed because it looked like there was a serious crush forming there.

"There will be questions to you three about Kellet replacing Mark and also about Mark leaving," Jax said, looking at Jamie, Liam, and Seth, who all nodded. "Keep your answers short and to the point. Mark's reasons for leaving are his to tell. You will not elaborate on anything other than what has already been announced."

"Is someone looking after Mark?" Jamie asked.

"Yes, he's been directed to send all communications to the office, and it will be handled by one of our representatives."

"That's good. Having the media hit him up won't help his recovery," Jamie said, and his concern touched Kellet. He knew that Jamie would be watching out for his friend and former bandmate, despite the situation Mark had left them in.

Cal cleared his throat, and an uncomfortable expression crossed his face. He leaned towards Jax, pointing to something on the screen of his tablet. She nodded and Cal glanced up at Kellet with an apologetic look.

I'm not going to like this. Kellet braced himself for the next question.

"Um... y... you and Jamie were once in a relationship. What is it like to be back in each other's lives?"

And there it was. The one question he knew would be asked, and the one he wasn't sure how to answer. Did he go with option A?—Great! Option B?—Hell on earth. All I want to do is drag him into a corner and make him mine again. Or option C— A little bit of A and a little bit of B.

Realizing the room was waiting for a response, Kellet flicked a quick glance at Jamie before smiling at Cal. "It's early days yet, but it's great reconnecting with all the guys and I only hope I can do them proud."

"Good answer, Kellet," Jax nodded her approval. "I know it's not a nice question, but it will get asked in one form or another."

The gate buzzer sounded. "That will be Miles," Jax told them. Sure enough, their manager strode into the room, glancing at them all. Kellet noticed how Liam seemed to shrink further into the cushions, as if trying to hide from the piercing gaze.

"How's it going, everyone?"

Murmured greetings followed, and Miles stood in front of the large screen television that graced the wall. He was an imposing figure, a few inches taller than Kellet's six foot. His dark hair and close-cropped beard had flecks of gray. He wore suit pants and a business shirt, but no tie and his sleeves were rolled up his tanned arms. Strong looking arms. The man obviously worked out. He certainly didn't look like your stereotypical industry executive. If Kellet wasn't so hung up on

Jamie, he'd take a second look at their manager.

Kellet had had little to do with him other than a few short phone calls and meetings. Miles left most day-to-day things in Jax's more than capable hands, but Kellet knew there wasn't much that got past him. With his fists shoved in his pockets, he looked relaxed and happy, but Kellet was sure that the man's mind was taking in every nuance and reaction from each person in the room. This was reinforced when Miles's gaze stopped on Liam. A dark eyebrow raised in an unspoken question, and Liam sat up slightly and nodded briefly back.

The silver-gray eyes turned their attention to Kellet. "How are you settling in, Kel?"

"Yeah, good thanks." Kellet nodded. "I think rehearsal went okay yesterday, at least, the guys are still talking to me, so that's got to be a good sign, yeah?"

"A very good sign," Miles agreed with a twitch of his lips. "I just called in to let you know the press release has gone out and all inquiries are to be directed back to the office," he told the room. "Jax will have emailed you all a copy, so you know what we have said. The label has arranged interviews with you all over the next few days, and they're wanting a spot on one of the late-night talk shows and want to know if you're up for a live performance?"

Kellet's stomach plunged. He wasn't ready. He couldn't play on live television yet. He'd thought he'd have a few weeks before he had to perform publicly. He jumped when a warm hand settled on his shoulder.

"Breathe, Kel." Jamie's voice grounded him, and he took comfort in the gentle kneading of his shoulder.

"I don't think that's a good idea, Miles," Seth said. "Kel's not ready for that pressure. We need all the time we can get to practice and get the set for the tour rehearsed. It's not fair on him or our fans to push him out into the spotlight this early."

"Thanks, Seth," Kellet said, sending a grateful smile towards the lead guitarist.

"Hey, man. I'm just telling the truth. If you play like shit—" at Kellet's glare, Seth waved a hand to calm him down, "—not saying you will, but you won't play to the best of your ability right now, and if we don't give a great performance, the fans will be up in arms and it could potentially harm the tour."

"Fuck, Seth. When did you grow up and be the voice of reason?" Kellet asked, grinning to soften the words.

Seth flipped him the bird, grinning back. "Fuck off. I can adult when I have to."

"As much as this pains me to say it," Miles said with a sigh, "you're right, Seth. I'll stay and watch you do a couple of tracks, but I have already told management that you won't be ready yet."

Kellet breathed a sigh of relief and felt a little bereft when Jamie removed his hand and returned to his spot on the couch.

"Well then, if there's no other business, let's get rehearsal started so I can return to the office and report in."

♫ ♫ ♫

!MUSIC NEWS NOW!

**** BREAKING NEWS ****

Larkspur Replace Drummer

Today, a press release from the management of chart-topping Larkspur has announced Kellet James as the replacement for drummer Mark Sullivan, who left three weeks ago citing personal health reasons.

James is an original member of the band from their early days before they struck the big time with their hit 'When the Sun Rises'. It is understood that James is in intensive rehearsals with the band and that all signs point to the final leg of their world tour starting as planned on the Fourth of July at Madison Square Garden.

Sullivan will be a hard act to follow and here's hoping Kellet James can do the role justice.

Chapter Thirteen

Jamie leaned back in the lounger and stared up at the stars. It was a clear night, and he tracked an incoming plane as it glided across the inky blackness. He sipped from the beer in his hand and let his mind wander, and his body relax.

It had been an intense couple of weeks as they had rehearsed and practiced for hours on end. The results were worth it though; their sound was as sharp as it had ever been, and Kellet had slotted into the band like he'd never left.

A splash broke the semi-silence and Jamie sat up and peered over the edge of the balcony that led off his second-story bedroom. He was rewarded by the sight of Kellet's long body gliding through the water as he did a leisurely lap of the pool. Jamie smiled to himself, right on time. Kellet had taken to swimming late in the evening after they had gone their separate ways after eating together, and Jamie wasn't going to admit it had become his favorite pastime spying on his house guest from his hidden perch.

They had stopped walking on eggshells around each other and were more relaxed in each other's company, but there was still an awareness that had them not going any further than the occasional palm-slap or fist bump. Certainly no more hugs since that first one and he was getting more and more frustrated.

He'd known that Kellet wouldn't jump straight back into his bed, but dammit if Jamie hadn't fantasized about dragging the man up the stairs to his room and doing all sorts of wicked things to him.

Below, Kellet finished his laps and rested against the side of the pool, his arms spread against the tile as he let his body float as he looked to the heavens. Jamie greedily eyed the long, tanned torso. His fingers itched to run across the smooth flesh that glittered with water droplets, reflecting the light from the subtle garden lights dotted around the pool. From his vantage point, he could see that Kellet's arms and chest looked more defined than they had three weeks ago; the hours of drumming were no match for an intensive gym workout.

Jamie wanted to run his tongue down the faint treasure trail running from Kellet's belly button to under the dark blue board shorts that bunched around lean hips and rucked up thick thighs. He dropped a hand to the swelling in his own loose-fitting shorts and squeezed, trying to stave off the erection that was growing by the second. It didn't help, of course, and he resisted the urge to slip his fingers beneath his waistband and take himself in hand.

Kellet floated for a few more minutes before slipping under the water and swimming to the opposite end of the pool, where he climbed the sunken steps. Water ran down his body in rivulets, and Jamie bit back a moan. What he wouldn't give to strip Kel of his board shorts and take the ass that was showcased by the sopping wet material clinging lovingly to every dip and curve. Kel had always had an impressive ass, but Jamie was sure it had gotten better over the years.

Jamie's view was cut off as Kellet finished rubbing his hair with a towel and wrapping the cloth around his waist. Jamie was disappointed; he'd hoped he'd get a front view, but he was out of luck tonight.

With a sigh, he headed into his bedroom. It took up most of the house's top story and easily fitted a huge California King bed that looked out over the valley below. There was a small sitting area to the side, and a family-sized ensuite bathroom. It was decorated in warm earthy tones and was one of Jamie's favorite places.

He dropped his empty beer bottle in the recycling and closed the door to the balcony. Picking up his battered notebook from the side table, he slumped onto the bed, plumping and prodding the pillows into place. He opened to the last page he'd been working on and re-read the lyrics he'd written the previous night. It wasn't his best work, but he'd found if he scribbled and jotted down odd lines, he could mold them later into something workable.

They wouldn't start on a new album until the new year which was still a good six months away. They always took a break after touring to recharge. Come January, they would get back together and all pitch in with lyrics and melodies that they had worked on during their downtime.

It was a process that Jamie liked, and it worked well for them, but tonight he couldn't get his mind off Kellet and he closed the journal with a frustrated sigh. His dick had subsided, but there was still the heat of desire thrumming through his veins. He wondered if he should have a cooling swim himself or just throw himself into a cold shower and see if that would do the trick.

With a groan, he rolled off the bed. He needed to do something to tire his brain out, and a few laps of the pool may just do it. Slipping into some board shorts, he grabbed a towel from the bathroom before making his way down the dimly lit stairs. He could hear muffled laughter from Wil's room, and he suspected the teen was playing on his gaming console with online friends.

He padded into the kitchen and paused to grab a bottle of water. As he closed the fridge door and turned to leave, he was startled by the shadow of Kellet standing in the entranceway.

"Jeez, Kel! Give a guy a heart attack."

"Sorry, I thought you'd heard me," Kellet said with a smirk. His gaze raked down Jamie's body, and he willed himself not to get hard under the stare. "Heading out for a swim?"

"Yeah. Can't get the brain to switch off," Jamie replied, no thanks to you. "Thought a few laps may help tire me out."

"Hmm, yeah. Good idea. Works for me. Although I'm pretty tired at the end of the day. I find a swim helps me relax."

"I've considered getting a hot tub, but I'm not a huge fan of them," Jamie said with a shrug.

"I don't mind them," Kellet told him before nodding toward the fridge. "I'm just going to grab a water, then head off to bed. I'll let you get to your swim."

Jamie shuffled to his right to let Kellet pass, gripping the bottle in his hand tightly as the warm heat from Kellet's body brushed his. Kellet was only wearing a pair of black sleep pants that hung low on his hips, causing Jamie to smother a groan as he was assailed with the scent of a freshly showered Kellet.

The soft close of the fridge door and the quiet crack of the water bottle lid being turned seemed to echo through the kitchen. He thought he heard Kellet's breath hitch, but waved it away.

He felt, rather than heard, Kellet step up behind him. "You okay, J?"

"Yeah, yeah. Just fine. I'm gonna go–" he flapped a hand vaguely in the pool's direction.

"Sure. Enjoy. Hope it works," Kellet said casually, his chest brushing against Jamie's shoulder as he eased past him. Jamie tensed and then slowly let out a breath. Dammit, Kel was not playing fair!

"Oh, and J?"

"Yeah?"

"If it helps, I won't be spying on you when you swim."

Jamie gaped at Kellet, who was smirking at him from the doorway. "Wha… what do you mean?" he asked.

Kellet put down his water bottle on the counter and stepped closer, amusement glittering in his eyes.

"You're not as subtle as you think you are."

"Oh?" Jamie said, quirking an eyebrow.

"I saw you last night, watching me swim from your balcony. Saw you again tonight." Kellet's eyes flicked down Jamie's body and back up to meet his gaze.

"Just relaxing. I can't help it if you're out there swimming at the same time."

"True," Kellet agreed, his eyes darkening as Jamie swiped his tongue against his bottom lip, his mouth suddenly dry at the close proximity.

"Kel?"

"Yeah?"

"I really want to kiss you right now." He was sick of pussyfooting around. He needed to taste this man, and he needed to do it now.

"Just kiss me?" Kellet asked, moving closer.

"No. I want to do more than kiss you, Drummer Boy, but I don't want to scare you off." He ran his thumb along Kellet's full bottom lip.

Kellet's lips parted and Jamie gave in to the desire raging through him. Their mouths met in a tender brush before a swipe of Jamie's tongue had Kellet opening for him. The long-forgotten taste of Kellet overlaid the faint hint of mint of his toothpaste. He slid his fingers into the hair curling at Kellet's nape and tugged, which elicited a moan from Kellet.

Warm hands landed on his hips, and he was pushed back against the kitchen counter with Kellet's body pressed against his. He blindly reached out to his left, trying to find the countertop to put down the bottle of water he still had clutched in his hand. He released it, only to have it clatter to the floor.

Jamie didn't care, he had both hands free now, and he wrapped his arms around Kellet, pulling him as close as he could. He missed this. It wasn't just desire and sexual attraction. It was the way they fit together, like two pieces of a puzzle. Over the years, no one else had come close to making Jamie feel like he did when he was with this man.

A muffled yell from the direction of Wil's room had them breaking apart, breathing heavily. For a moment, they just stared at each other, before Kellet pressed a brief, chaste kiss to Jamie's lips and stepped away. Jamie couldn't help but notice how the front of his sleep pants tented and Kellet didn't even try to hide it. There was no point, especially as Jamie's board shorts had a similar tent.

"G'night, JJ," Kellet said huskily. He picked up his water and left the room, leaving Jamie more frustrated than when he'd come down the stairs. He took a few calming breaths before reaching to the floor to pick up his own bottle along with his towel.

He quickly made his way out to the pool and dived into the cool, clear water. As he surfaced, he couldn't help the grin that spread across his face. He may have a case of blue balls, but he'd kissed Kel, and it gave him hope that they were a little closer to being more than friends.

Chapter Fourteen

Kellet's phone chimed on the bedside table, indicating a message from the band group chat.

Seth: Pushing back rehearsal to 1pm. Enjoy your morning off. You're welcome.

With a sigh, he dropped the phone onto the covers next to him and continued his inspection of the ceiling. Not that it needed any further investigation; he'd gotten a really good look at it last night as he'd replayed the kiss with Jamie over and over. He gave a chuckle as he recalled the expression on Jamie's face as he'd tried to appear innocent at being called out over his spying. Kellet had realized a few nights ago that he was being watched and he may or may not have deliberately gone swimming every night, even when he didn't want to, to see if Jamie would be there.

Seeing Jamie half naked in the kitchen had goaded him into teasing the other man. He hadn't expected the kiss though, and like when they'd hugged, it had felt like coming home. Maybe it was time to explore just how much further Jamie wanted to take their friendship. He wasn't sure if he could cope with a friends-with-benefits-while-we-tour situation. It was going to be hard enough to go back to his old routine and life as it was.

He hadn't dated in a long while, but maybe he and Jamie could do that. They'd never really dated as teens. Their relationship was a few weeks old when Andi found out she was pregnant, and it had seemed wrong to go out with Jamie on a romantic date when his best friend was carrying his child, and all their peers knew.

So, first plan of action, talk to Jamie and see how the land lay. He picked up his phone and glanced at the time. It wasn't too early, but he wondered if Jamie wanted to go out for breakfast. This was a conversation they needed to have without Wil wandering in on them.

He tapped out a quick message to Jamie, hesitating briefly before pressing send.

Kellet: Hey, where's a good place for breakfast around here?

He watched the screen and saw the message being delivered and a few seconds later showing as read. Nothing happened for a minute or two, and then the little gray dots started bouncing.

JJ: You sick of my cooking already, Drummer Boy?

As always, his stomach hitched at the nickname Jamie had started calling him when they'd first formed Larkspur.

Kellet: No. Just felt like a change. Want to grab a bite somewhere?

JJ: Sure. There's a diner near here that only the locals really know about.

Kellet: Great. Thirty minutes work for you?

JJ: Sounds good. Bring a ball cap and your shades.

Kellet: ??

JJ: It's standard uniform around here. You'll stick out if you're not wearing them ;)

Kellet huffed a laugh. He doubted anyone would recognize him, but he'd humor Jamie. With renewed energy belying his almost sleepless night, he jumped out of bed and headed for the shower.

Just over half an hour later, Kellet pushed open Wil's door to let him know he and Jamie were heading out. He silently chuckled at the mound of bedclothes; the only sign of there being anyone in the bed was a long foot peeking out from under the covers.

Heat from Jamie's body warmed him as the other man peered over his shoulder.

"Oh my god, he even sleeps like you used to," Jamie said in a hushed whisper. "If I ever needed any further proof that he's your son, that would be it."

Kellet smirked. "I still sleep like that."

Jamie's eyes darkened, and a shiver went through Kellet.

"Come on. Let him sleep. You can message him, so he knows where we are," Jamie said, stepping away from the door.

With a nod, he closed the door before pulling his phone out of his pocket and sending a quick message for Wil to see when he finally surfaced.

He followed Jamie outside and nodded when Jamie pointed at the Range Rover. There was no point in Kellet driving because he didn't know where they were going.

Ten minutes later they were pulling into the parking lot of a small adobe-style diner. It looked like any standard diner with red brick and large windows overlooking the parking lot. There were a few cars parked, most of them high-end, expensive models, giving away the nature of the clientele.

Before they got out of the car, Jamie tugged on a worn ball cap and slipped his sunglasses on and then looked at Kellet expectantly.

"Really?"

"Yes, Drummer Boy, really," Jamie nodded in amusement. "Your name and face are out there now, and although not many people will probably recognize you, it makes a difference."

"I don't see how," Kellet grumbled as he pulled on his Golden State Warriors cap. "I mean, doesn't it make it obvious that you're trying to hide who you are when you're wearing a cap and shades?"

"Like I said, it's kind of a uniform here, so it's basically ignored because everyone is doing it," Jamie shrugged as they got out of the car.

Kellet wasn't sure, but fell into step next to him, their strides automatically matching. Once inside, they were quickly seated in a small booth, and he was surprised to see that the windows were glazed with one-way glass, meaning they could see out, but no-one could see in. He discretely glanced around the room and spotted who he thought was an A-lister action movie star in the opposite corner.

A nudge on his shin had his attention returning to Jamie, who was sitting across from him grinning, and all thoughts about celebrities and whoever else may be in the diner fled.

Kellet removed his shades and picked up the menu. "What do you recommend?"

"Hmm, most things are good. I'm going to have double-stack pancakes with bacon," Jamie said, pushing his own menu to one side and leaning back in his seat.

Their server appeared and gave them both a sunny smile. "Good morning. What can I get you guys today?"

Jamie repeated his order and Kellet decided on the full English breakfast of eggs, sausage, bacon, with a side of hash browns, bypassing some of the healthier options listed. Once she'd left after promising to bring their coffee straight out, an awkward silence descended.

Kellet fiddled with the silverware, thoughts racing as he tried to come up with the best way to mention last night's kiss.

"So, about last night," Jamie said, and Kellet's eyes flew upwards to be met with a knowing smile and a flirty wink.

"Dammit, Jamie, you always could read me like an open book," Kellet groused playfully.

"I used to be able to, these days, maybe not so much," Jamie agreed. "But, I remember enough about you that sometimes you need a push to get your momentum."

Kellet huffed in agreement. He wasn't wrong. He waited until their server had poured their coffees, and after nodding his thanks, he returned his attention to Jamie.

"I never thought I'd be here with you," he said as he doctored his coffee with sugar.

"What, here in this diner?"

"Ass. Here in LA, with you."

"You once told me to come back when I was rich and famous and keep you in the style you deserved," Jamie said quietly, and Kellet found himself transported back to that horrible day when they'd broken up.

"I didn't think you'd take seventeen years to do it though," Kellet admitted, and Jamie's eyes widened at the words.

"You could have joined me any time you wanted to, Kel. All you had to do was pick up the phone. Don't put all this on me." Jamie's tone was frustrated and hurt, and Kellet reached across the table and laid his hand over Jamie's.

"I know. I didn't mean it like that. I... I'm just so confused and—"

Jamie turned his hand over and twined their fingers together. "I know, Kel. I am too. I don't have words for the way I feel having you back in the band; back in my life."

"I don't know how to do this, JJ," he whispered. Jamie's fingers squeezed his before pulling away, as the waitress was approached with their meal.

"Eat first, then we'll talk," Jamie suggested, pointing his fork at Kellet's plate. Glancing down at his food, he nodded before doing as suggested.

♫ ♫ ♫

They ate in companionable silence and once they had almost cleared their plates, Jamie picked up the conversation again.

"What do you want, Kel?"

Kellet swallowed down the last mouthful of food before taking a sip of his coffee. He wiped his face with the napkin, and Jamie recognized the stalling techniques for what they were. He met the mossy green gaze and quirked an eyebrow, encouraging him to talk.

"Has there been anyone special in your life, Jamie?"

"No, not really," Jamie admitted, running his finger around the rim of his coffee mug. He glanced up at Kellet. "There have been a couple of guys I dated for about six months. We've been so busy with touring and recording, there hasn't been time to consider anything long term. Besides, I saw what it did to Mark being away from Selena."

"Do you see yourself settling down?"

"Maybe sometime in the future, sure. It depends, of course, on the timing and circumstances."

Kellet frowned at him. "Timing and circumstances?"

"Yeah. I mean, once this tour is over, we'll take a break and then head back into the studio to do another album. We're contracted to one more with the label and then there'll likely be another tour on the back of that."

When Kellet didn't say anything else, Jamie gently kicked his shin. "You didn't answer my question, Kel. What do you want?"

"I want you, I know that much," Kellet said, and heat and desire shot through him at the hooded look.

"I want you too."

"But…"

"Yes, there'll be butts involved," Jamie said, trying to diffuse some of the sexual tension, and Kellet glared at him.

"But," Kellet repeated with emphasis, "I think we need to take it slow. God knows there's enough on my plate right now without adding the complication of us."

"I like the sound of there being an us, even if it is complicated," Jamie told him, leaning across the table to trace a pattern on the back of Kellet's hand.

"It is complicated. I mean, I don't think... no, I know, I can't just do a friends-with-benefits thing. Not with you. And then, if we do start something, what happens at the end of the tour? Do we go our separate ways? Do we try a long-distance thing? I just... I just don't know, JJ."

Jamie leaned back in his seat and eyed the downcast head of curls. He knew what Kellet was trying to say and totally understood his fears. He had them too. He leaned forward again.

"Kel. Drummer Boy. Look at me."

Kellet raised his head, and Jamie's heart hitched at the expression of longing and confusion.

"We don't have to make all the decisions now. You're right. There's so much going on that we need to focus on, but I want to be more than bandmates or friends, Kel."

"So, what do we do?"

"We could carry on as we are, but I think we both know that's not going to be easy. Kissing you last night was..."

"Yeah, it was," Kellet agreed, the corner of his mouth twitching, and it was all Jamie could do not to lean over and pick up where they'd left off the night before.

"Dammit it, Drummer Boy. Don't look at me like that!"

Kellet laughed, and the sound warmed Jamie through and he grinned back.

"I did have an idea, but, fuck, it sounds so silly," Kellet said, rubbing a hand over his face.

"I'm open to all suggestions."

"How about we date? Y'know, things like this, just get to know each other again and let things take their natural course?" A dull stain flushed Kellet's skin.

Jamie nodded slowly. It wasn't a bad idea, but knowing Kellet as he did, Jamie knew it would be a slow process until they were in the same bed together, but it was better than the alternative of not having Kellet at all.

"We can do that," he agreed, and a smile spread across Kellet's face. "In fact, we'll call this our first date, and seeing as you asked me, you can pay." He laughed when Kellet's smile turned to a scowl.

"Fine!" Kellet mock pouted and lifted his hips to reach for his wallet out of his back pocket. Jamie's body tightened at the sight and he shuffled in his seat.

"Come on, let's head home. We need to get Wil up before we go over to Seth's for practice."

Chapter Fifteen

The screech of a guitar's feedback through speakers echoed harshly around the cavernous warehouse greeted the band as they entered the building.

"Who the fuck is playing with my guitar?" Seth yelled, causing a pause in the hubbub of activity.

"Ah, the 'talent' is here," a voice shouted back, and Kellet could hear the air quotes around the word talent.

"Talent? I've got more talent in my dick than these guys have got collectively," someone else catcalled, provoking laughter from those that had stopped to watch them walk in.

"That's not what your wife told me last night, Larry," Seth retorted as he headed towards the stage.

Kellet joined in the laughter and felt a little of the tension ease from his shoulders, even though his stomach was doing a great impression of a washing machine on a full load. They were ten days away from their first show and today was their initial full rehearsal on the stage set up. The last few days of practice had been long and busy as they'd worked hard to get the sound perfect. It hadn't left a lot of time for him and Jamie to do much more than eat dinner and watch movies. Kellet suspected that their idea of dating would get even harder now that they were so close to the start of the tour.

He'd been surprised when the car that had collected them that morning had pulled into a famous studio lot. The guys had told him it was one of the best places to get the whole stage set up and give them a feel of how things looked and sounded in a large arena type situation.

They reached the end of the stage and were greeted by the man Seth had called Larry, a dark-haired man who looked to be in his late forties. He only came up to Seth's chin, but there was a wiry strength about his frame, and despite their back and forth, Kellet could see that Seth had a lot of respect for him.

"Larry, I'd like to introduce you to Kellet, our drummer," Jamie said after performing a complicated handshake with the guy. "Kel, this is Larry Finley."

"Good to meet you, Kellet. I've heard good things about you. It will be nice to have someone in the band who is somewhat of an adult."

"Thanks, Larry, although I'm sure what you've been told has been exaggerated," Kellet replied, warming to the man.

"Larry here is our tour manager. He makes sure everything, and everyone is where they are supposed to be at the right time. So if you've got any issues or need anything, Larry is your guy," Jamie explained.

"Yup, he's right. Sam is the drum tech, so he'll be here shortly to go over how you like your kit set up and he'll be available during every practice and performance should anything go wrong," Larry told him with a nod. "Not that anything will go wrong, of course."

"That's great to hear," Kellet told him with a smile. He nodded towards his son. "Larry, this is my son, Wil. He's tagging along and assisting as my PA. He knows as much about my kit set up as I do, so if I'm not around, he's the next best person to ask."

Larry stuck a hand out to Wil. "Good to meet you, kid. You have any problems with any of the crew, you come and see me, okay?"

"Hi, Mr. Finley," Wil replied cheerfully.

"Don't call me Mr. Finley, just Larry is fine," the older man said.

"Yeah, don't give him ideas above his station," Liam quipped with a grin.

"And so it begins," Larry responded with a put-upon sigh before clapping his hands together and taking on a serious tone. "Right then, let's get things moving. Kellet, I'll take you round and introduce you to the key guys you need to know right now. The rest of the crew you can meet and get to know later."

"You three," Larry said, pointing to the others, "go and say hi to everyone and meet me back here in thirty minutes. We'll have the set ready to go by then."

Kellet was amused to see that his bandmates all nodded their agreement before splitting off in separate directions. He'd never seen them so compliant.

"Come on, Kellet, first stop is the mixing desk. The guys will set up your in-ears and then go over what you need."

Kellet followed the wiry man across to the sound area that was set up about forty feet from the stage and was positioned so it sat directly opposite center stage. After introductions, Kellet was taken through how his in-ear monitors worked and given an overview of how the sound engineers kept everyone sounding the best they could. Kellet nodded but didn't really understand a lot of what they were saying. He was sure there was less equipment involved at NASA for the last rocket launch than there was on the desk in front of him and trusted that these guys knew what they were doing.

The dull thump of the bass drum had him turning back towards the stage, and he couldn't help but grin at the sight of Wil behind the kit, talking animatedly to a guy who looked a few years older than him. Kellet saw him nod and then launch into a rapid solo covering the whole kit.

"Huh, kid can play too?" Larry asked.

"Yeah, he prefers guitar and being up front, but he knows his way around the drums," Kellet said proudly. It gave him a thrill to see Wil up there and the reality that in a few short days, it would be him up there raced through him, causing his stomach to swoop and his vision to blur for a nanosecond.

"You alright there, Kellet?" Larry asked. "You look a little pale."

Kellet nodded and wiped a hand down his face, trying to compose himself.

"It just hit home, didn't it?" Larry said knowingly. He slapped Kellet on the shoulder. "Don't worry, once you're up there, you'll be fine. Come on, it looks like Sam and your boy have things ready to go."

With a brief thanks to the sound guys, Kellet followed Larry back to the stage and slowly climbed the steps onto the platform. The stage seemed huge from here. The main stage was about twenty feet across and sixteen feet deep with a walkway jutting out into the audience area for about ten feet. His drum kit was raised on its own podium, three feet above.

"Dad, this is sooo cool," Wil called out to him. You're gonna have the best seat in the house. "You can see for miles from up here."

The red-headed man next to him laughed. "He won't actually see much, Wil. Once the stage lights go on, you can't see two or three feet from the edge." Wil's face fell in disappointment.

"I think the best seat in the house is at the engineering booth, Wil. They can see everything from there," Kellet told him before holding out a hand to the stranger. "Hi, Kellet James."

"Good to meet you, Mr. James. I'm Sam Barnes and I'm the main drum tech."

"Please, call me Kellet or Kel. I can't see there being much formality around here."

Sam laughed. "You've got that right. The only time everyone is on their best behavior is when the label bigwigs show up, which is rare, thank goodness." He paused and then added with a grin, "And of course when Jax is around. No one messes around when she's here."

Wil gave a mock shudder. "She's scary, and believe me, if you knew my Ma, you'd know I wasn't exaggerating. Ma can make a grown man cry from fifty paces with her glare, but Jax has her beat."

"Wil, I'm not sure your other mother would like that comparison," Kellet gently admonished.

"I think Ma would take it as a compliment, Dad, and just for the record, I think it's great that her and Mom are away to Europe and will miss the start of the tour. Can you imagine Ma and Jax together in the same room?" Wil's eyes widened dramatically.

Kellet cuffed his shoulder. "Fair enough. Now, are you going to let me, y'know, do my job and move from behind the kit or are you planning to be the new drummer for Larkspur?"

"All yours, Dad," Wil said, handing over the drumsticks as he clambered out.

Kellet eased down onto the stool, his feet finding the kick pedals for the bass drum and hi-hat stand. He stretched out his back before twisting in his seat to get comfortable. He ran a practiced eye over the setup and nudged himself forward.

He went through his scales once and made a minor change to the position of the snare drum before nodding in satisfaction.

"This is perfect, thanks Sam."

"You're welcome. It's the same setup as Mark used, of course, but you're a bit taller than he is, so I just needed to make sure everything was positioned correctly."

"It's all good; thanks again."

"Just doing my job," Sam said with a smile, but Kellet could see he was touched by the compliment.

Kellet's attention was drawn away by Jamie coming onto the stage, microphone in one hand while he fiddled with his in-ear monitor pack. The sight of him in torn faded jeans, worn band tee, and his battered leather jacket looking so at home had Kellet catching his breath. God, he's beautiful.

As though he felt Kellet's eyes on him, Jamie turned and sought him out, a huge grin appearing when they locked eyes. A look of understanding passing between them. Yes, this is where we're supposed to be, Kellet thought as he winked at Jamie before settling into his seat.

Cory, the monitor engineer, appeared next to Kellet, and together, they got his in-ears set up and adjusted. Kellet ran through his scales a few times. It wasn't the proper warmup he usually did, but it was enough to settle his nerves and loosen up the tight muscles in his back.

"Right guys, we're going to run through the first three numbers just as if you were doing a live show," Larry's voice sounded from somewhere out by the mixing desk. "Once you've done that, we'll review before moving onto the next three, okay? Kellet, on your count please."

Kellet nodded, unsure of if Larry could see him. He glanced to each of his bandmates, who all responded and grinned their readiness. Locking eyes with Jamie, he took a deep breath and counted out a four-beat with his drumsticks before launching into the first song.

♫ ♫ ♫

Jamie strutted to the end of the walkway, his voice holding the last note before fading away, and the crash of drums and wail of guitar finished in a crescendo. The sudden silence was deafening before a quiet cheer echoed from the far reaches of the sound stage, and he grinned at Wil and Cal, who were waving their arms in the air.

"That was great, Jamie," Larry called out. "I want to run through Hard Up for Love one more time. The timing was off, Kel."

Jamie looked up to the drum stand and saw Kellet grimace as he replied.

"Yeah, I could feel it, but I'm not sure why."

"Let's take five and then we'll try it again. I know it's been a long day, so we'll do Hard Up one more time before we go over some admin shit Jax has sent through, then you can all go home."

Jamie turned his mic off and laid it on the pedestal next to the bass drum. He grabbed the small towel that was there and wiped his face before finishing his bottle of water. As much as he loved performing and being on stage, it always took a few days for his body to remember what a workout it was, singing and moving around the stage.

"You sound really good out there," Kellet said to him as he dropped next to him. A sliver of skin appeared, and Kellet's sweat-stained shirt lifted as he ran a towel over his head. Jamie wanted nothing more than to drag him backstage and lick him all over.

He met Kellet's heated gaze and knew that what he was thinking was probably as clear as day on his face.

"Don't look at me like that, JJ," Kellet growled.

"Why not? It's what we both want," Jamie countered and took a step closer.

"I know, but not here. I don't need the crew and their mothers to know that we're..." Kellet flailed a hand in the air.

"Kel, they're going to know eventually. Nothing is sacred on a tour like this. Believe me, everyone will know what color your boxers are before you've even decided which ones to wear in the morning."

Kellet smirked and leaned forward, his voice dropping so only Jamie could hear him. "And if I decide to go commando?"

"Fuck you, Drummer Boy," Jamie said, almost whimpering at the image.

"Raincheck, JJ," Kellet countered with an eyebrow waggle, and all rational thought flew from Jamie's mind, as all he could picture was Kellet James spread out on a bed just for him in all his naked glory.

Jamie half turned towards the back of the stage so he could discreetly adjust himself, ignoring Kellet's quiet chuckle.

"If you two have finished with your foreplay, can we get this thing done? I have places to be and people to see," Seth said as he sauntered past with a knowing grin.

"Dinner tonight, Drummer Boy. Just you and me. Date night," Jamie said under his breath and was glad to see Kellet nod his agreement.

They resumed their places and as Jamie listened for his cue as the opening chords to Hard Up for Love sounded, he hoped they got it right this time because he wanted to be alone with Kel as soon as he could be.

Chapter Sixteen

Checking his reflection in the bathroom mirror, Kellet ran a hand through his hair before adjusting the collar on his button-down shirt. He wasn't sure where Jamie was taking him for their date night, but he hoped the pale green shirt and black dress pants were appropriate. With a glance at his watch, he decided that he still had time if he needed to change.

He left his room just as Wil left his. A low whistle escaped from his son. "Wow, looking good there, old man."

Kellet ran a self-conscious hand down the front of his shirt before Wil smacked it away. "Don't do that; you'll wrinkle it," he said, his tone exasperated. "Chill out, Dad. It's only Jamie. It's not like you haven't had dinner with him every night over the last three weeks."

"I know," Kellet replied. The sound of feet coming down the stairs stopped him from saying more, and his breath caught as Jamie appeared at the end of the hallway. He was similarly dressed in a pale gray shirt and dark gray pants that clung lovingly to his hips and thighs. Kellet's body warmed at the sight. He'd seen Jamie in everything from ripped jeans and band shirts to comfy worn sweats around the house. Not forgetting of course, in his boardshorts, all wet and clingy from the pool. This version, though, of him in understated smart casual was a version that appealed to Kellet.

He was pulled from his perusal by the sound of Wil's phone chiming. Wil shrugged on the leather jacket he was holding. "My ride's here. I'll see you guys later."

"Remember, no drinking," Kellet cautioned as he held the door open for his son.

"Yeesss, Dad!" Wil gave the obligatory eye-roll. "It's only pizza and video games at Sam's place. He and Cal got your lecture this afternoon."

"Alright then. Call if you need anything."

"I will," Wil called airily as he trotted down the stairs to the path. "Oh, and Dad?"

"What?"

"Don't do anything I wouldn't do and remember to use a condom!"

Jamie chuckled as Kellet groaned, embarrassment sending a heated flush to his face. He gently banged his head against the door. Maybe he should have left Wil at home in Juniper.

He felt, rather than heard, Jamie step in behind him before a hand slid around his waist to rest against his stomach. Warm breath ghosted against his ear as Jamie leaned into him.

"Ready to go, Drummer Boy, or do you need a moment?"

"Yeah," Kellet said with a nod, answering both questions at once. A shiver coursed through him as Jamie pressed a soft kiss below his ear before moving away, and Kellet wanted to pull him back into his arms.

"Come on then." Jamie pulled his keys from his pocket and led them out to the Range Rover.

Once they were settled and on their way, Kellet asked where they were going.

"The Pump House. It's a steak house near here. It's an old converted fire station. Fraser, the owner and head chef, opened it about four years ago. I think you'll like it."

As promised, the drive didn't take long, and soon, they were pulling into a small parking lot of a beautiful brick building that Kellet could see had been lovingly transformed. Original features from the original station had been modernized and upgraded, but were sympathetic to when they had been first installed over fifty years prior.

They were greeted by a hostess who led them to their table. Kellet was impressed to see that most of the tables and booths were discretely shielded by tall plants and decorative screens. It could have given the area a cluttered feel, but the space was light and airy with the vaulted ceiling and large windows. The glow of shaded down lights added a warmth to the room, and Kellet instantly felt at ease. The professional restaurateur and bar owner in him appreciated the subtle details used to create an inviting and homey atmosphere.

The hostess left them at their table with menus, and Kellet eyed the array of choices. He wasn't sure what he was in the mood for, and there was plenty to choose from.

"See anything you like?"

Jamie's question had him glancing across the table, and his breath caught at the sight of Jamie in the subdued lighting. His cheekbones were thrown into stark relief above the thin cover of stubble. Amusement and heat danced in his brown eyes that were subtly lined.

"On the menu, Drummer Boy," Jamie said with a chuckle, nodding towards the folder.

Kellet smirked before glancing back down. "All of it looks great. Any recommendations?"

"Jamie! I thought you were on tour?" A voice broke through the gentle hum of conversation and Kellet looked up to discover a tall blond man in chef whites approaching their table with a huge grin on his face. He watched as Jamie stood and returned the hug and back slaps the blond was giving him.

"Fraser! Great to see you." Jamie turned and nodded towards Kellet. "Fraser Austin, this is Kellet James. He's an old friend and our new drummer. Kel, this is the genius behind this place."

"Hi, Fraser. Good to meet you," Kellet said warmly, shaking Fraser's hand. "I love what you've done here. Can't wait to try the food."

Jamie sat down as Fraser pulled a chair from an empty neighboring table. "Thanks. It's taken a lot of hard work to get it to where it is, but it's all paying off now."

"Kel has a restaurant and bar up in Juniper, just outside of San Francisco."

"Really? How long have you been there?" Fraser asked, his interest genuine.

"I started out as a busboy and kitchen hand at sixteen. Then about ten years ago, the owner retired, and we worked out a deal, and my business partners and I bought it. We've had to bring it kicking and screaming into the twenty-first century, but we're running pretty good now."

"That's amazing. And you've left it all behind to become a drummer in a band?" Kellet could hear the curiosity in Fraser's voice.

"Hey! Not just any band. He's drumming for Larkspur," Jamie said indignantly, aiming a soft swipe at Fraser's shoulder. Fraser laughed and dodged out of the way.

"Yeah, yeah, alright mate." Fraser hooked a thumb towards Jamie. "Do you know what you're getting yourself into, teaming up with this guy, not to mention the other two idiots?"

Kellet smiled lazily, his gaze tracking over Jamie's face. "Oh yeah, I know exactly what I'm getting myself into with this guy."

Fraser glanced between the two of them, a frown marring his handsome features, which cleared as understanding bloomed.

"Ah, like that, is it?" Fraser asked.

"Kel and I formed Larkspur when we were teenagers," Jamie explained softly, his eyes not leaving Kellet's. "He wasn't able to be part of the band when Miles signed us, but we're making up for that now."

"I shall leave you to it then," Fraser said, standing and returning the chair he'd been sitting on. "If you haven't ordered yet, I recommend tonight's special of slow-braised lamb. It's pretty amazing if I say so myself."

"Sounds good," Jamie said, holding out his hand. "Make sure you keep August 21st free. I'll get Jax to send you and Carlos tickets to our last show and the after-party."

"Thanks, mate. Have a great tour," Fraser shook Jamie's hand before offering it to Kellet. "Good to meet you, Kellet."

"Thanks, Fraser. You'll have to come up to East Bank when this is all over."

"I'd like that," Fraser said with a grin. "Have a good night, gents." With a final nod, he left them alone.

"Nice guy," Kellet commented as he picked up his glass of wine.

"Yeah, he is. We met just after I bought the house. He was working for a catering company at a party I went to. He did these little roast beef things that melted on your tongue. I got his name, and we became friends after I tried to convince him to be the tour chef."

"Just friends?" The words came out unbidden, and Kellet could have kicked himself. It was no business of his who Jamie had slept with. "Sorry, ignore that. None of my business."

"It's okay. You're allowed to be curious," Jamie said with a shrug. "And to answer your question, yes, just friends. He and his husband Carlos have been together for years."

"Ah, okay then. Good." Kellet took a gulp of wine. Jesus, could he be any more embarrassing? "Did I hear an accent? He doesn't sound like he comes from around here."

Jamie nodded. "Yeah, he's from New Zealand. He and Carlos met while working in Australia, and they've since worked together all over the world. They moved here when Carlos's father became ill and then they found this place and the rest is history."

Kellet was saved from embarrassing himself further by the arrival of their server. After both ordering the lamb, they fell into easy conversation about various restaurants and meals they'd experienced. Of course, Jamie was well traveled, and he had Kellet laughing at some of the tales of different foods the band had eaten in the many countries they'd visited.

Kellet had just finished his meal, which had been as good as Fraser had promised, when his phone buzzed. Fishing it from his pocket, he saw a message from Wil telling him he was staying the night at Sam's and that he'd meet them at the sound stage for the last rehearsal in the morning.

Emotions warred in Kellet. On the one hand he was happy his son had made some friends and was comfortable to stay over, but on the other hand, nervous anticipation was making the lamb he'd just eaten bounce around his stomach. With Wil not coming home, it would mean he and Jamie would be alone, and he wasn't sure if he was ready for that.

"Problem?" Jamie asked.

Kellet glanced up to see Jamie looking at him with concern. Shaking his head, he tapped a reply out to Wil before putting his phone down.

"No, Wil's staying the night at Sam's."

"Sam's a good guy; you don't have to worry that he's going to lead Wil astray," Jamie reassured him.

"Oh, I know. And Cal's there. He seems like a nice guy too. He's quiet, but he looks like he's got his head screwed on properly." Kellet paused, not sure how to continue. "I know I seem like I worry a lot about Wil, and well, I do, it's part of being a parent. We've been lucky that he was pretty level-headed through his early teenage years, but when he was young, he went through a patch of not wanting to be apart from either Andi or myself."

"How do you mean?"

"He must have been about five or six? Andi and I traded weeks with the custody. She and Ro had been together for a while, and Ro had recently moved in. One night I got a call from Andi, Wil was upset, asking for me, and she couldn't get him to settle."

Of course, I raced over, and we finally calmed him down enough to get out of him what was wrong." Kellet chuckled at the memory. "He'd suddenly realized that I was home alone while he was at his mother's, and he was upset at the thought of daddy being scared and lonely."

"The poor kid," Jamie sympathized. "What did you do?"

"We reassured him, of course, that Daddy was a big boy and was okay at being at home on his own." Kellet smirked. "Only Daddy hadn't been home alone. I'd been on a date for the first time in years and, well, yeah, you can imagine how that ended."

Jamie burst out laughing. "Oh, no! What did your date do?"

"He was very understanding, but we never had a second one."

"Looks like I'm one ahead of him then, doesn't it?"

Kellet frowned at him in confusion. Jamie waved a hand between them. "This is our second date. Breakfast was our first, remember."

"Very true. That also means that since this time you asked me, it's your turn to pay," Kellet informed him with a wink.

Jamie leaned across the table and traced his fingers along Kellet's wrist, causing goosebumps to skitter up Kellet's arm. "What I really need to know though, Drummer Boy, is do you put out on the second date?"

"It's been a while since I put out for anyone, Jamie," he admitted softly and saw a flare of emotion in Jamie's eyes at his words.

"That's okay, Kel. We won't do anything you don't want to. Maybe, I dunno, make out a little, see if I can get to second base?" Jamie waggled his eyebrows, causing Kellet to laugh and ease the tension between them.

"JJ, it's not that I don't want to do things with you. I just don't want to rush this." He twined their fingers together. "And yeah, I'm sure you'll make it to second base."

Heat flared in Jamie's eyes and he glanced across the restaurant. Catching their server's eye, he signaled for the check before reaching into his pocket for his wallet.

It felt like seconds later that Kellet found himself in the Range Rover and Jamie was driving them home. Anticipation thrummed through his veins. He wasn't sure if this was going too fast or not, but he needed to be with Jamie.

Chapter Seventeen

Jamie kept under the speed limit–just. As soon as Kellet had told him that Wil wasn't coming home, desire had shot through him, going from the simmering level it had been at since seeing Kellet all dressed up for their date, to boiling at the thought of them being alone for the night.

It had surprised him when Kellet had said that he hadn't been with anyone for a while, and he wondered how long it had actually been. Surely, he had more than enough opportunities with working and owning his own bar. Curiosity got the better of him, and he glanced across the dimly lit car to find Kellet watching him.

"How long's a while?" he asked.

"I was wondering how long it was going to take you to ask," Kellet replied with a chuckle. "The last time I went out on a date was about a year ago."

"A year? You mean you haven't been with anyone in a year?" Jamie's shocked voice echoed through the car.

"Yeah, I mean, it's not the longest dry spell I've had, but it's been a while."

"What do you mean, it's not the longest dry spell you've had?" Jamie was having trouble concentrating on driving with the revelations Kellet was spilling. He was grateful when the gates to his property appeared in the headlights. Jabbing a finger on the gate opener, he waited impatiently for them to draw back. He maneuvered the Range Rover into the garage and shut off the engine. Unclipping his seat belt, he turned in his seat to face the other man.

"Come on, let's head inside and continue this conversation there," Kellet said, releasing his own seat belt and opening the passenger door. He glanced back over his shoulder, "Though I don't understand why you want to talk about my sex life when you mentioned something about making out earlier." With a smirk and a wink, he slipped out of the car and headed towards the entry into the house.

Jamie scrambled to follow him and snagged Kellet's hand before he got too far. "Hold up, Drummer Boy."

Kellet laughed and tugged him closer to brush his mouth against Jamie's. Before he could react, Kellet was leading them into the kitchen. Tossing his keys carelessly onto the counter, Jamie reached for the grinning man standing in front of him.

"I don't remember you ever being a tease, Drummer Boy," he murmured as he stepped as close as he could, absorbing the warmth of Kellet's body. The faint tang of spicy cologne surrounded him, embedding the moment into his memory.

Kellet's hands rested on Jamie's hips, his grip firm as his fingers flexed, sending a bolt of desire through Jamie. Unconsciously, he pressed forward and groaned when his erection met with a matching hardness.

"Kiss me, JJ," Kellet whispered, lowering his head. Jamie's mouth met his, slotting together like a magnet finding its mate. Jamie's fingers slipped around Kellet's neck, holding him in place. His thumb rested on Kellet's fluttering pulse and it sped up as Jamie deepened the kiss. Kellet opened for him and their tongues slid and tangled in a long-forgotten dance.

Jamie wasn't sure how long they stood there. All he knew was that he could do this forever. A deep moan from Kellet as their lower bodies pressed together had him pulling his mouth away and resting his forehead against Kellet.

"Let's take this upstairs," he rasped out. Kellet nodded and let Jamie lead him to the stairs.

♫ ♫ ♫

Kellet's mind was a jumbled mess. He was equally heady with desire and the thought of being with Jamie again and nervous of somehow disappointing him. They'd been fumbling teenagers the last time they'd been together like this.

As if sensing his inner turmoil, Jamie squeezed the hand he was holding and paused before what Kellet presumed was his bedroom door.

"Relax Kel, I just wanna be with you any way you want to give yourself to me. We don't have to do more than kiss and cuddle, but it will be a hell of a lot more comfortable up here than in the kitchen."

Kellet nodded. "Yeah, I know."

Jamie brushed his lips against Kellet's before pushing open the door and tugging Kellet after him. Kellet nudged the door closed behind him as he took in the large room that was illuminated by the bright moon shining through the glass wall that led out to the balcony. Jamie left him as he flicked on the small bedroom lamp, adding a warm glow.

Jamie kicked his shoes off, aiming them towards a corner of the room. Kellet smirked, at least one thing hadn't changed. Jamie was not the tidiest person, with small piles of discarded clothes and shoes on the floor near what appeared to be a walk-in closet.

He watched as Jamie stalked towards him until Kellet's back was against the door. Jamie reached for the top button of his shirt, pausing as he wordlessly sought Kellet's permission. Kellet nodded, and nimble fingers made quick work of buttons before spreading the pieces of fabric aside to reveal Kellet's chest.

Eyes locked, Jamie traced along Kellet's collarbones before resting both hands on his pecs. Callused thumbs circled Kellet's nipples, causing them to pucker and a bolt of heat to shoot straight to his dick. His head dropped back against the door, and his hips punched forward, seeking friction.

Warm breath ghosted against his skin as Jamie leaned in and pressed small kisses against his throat, before nibbling along his jaw to the sensitive skin under his ear while continuing to tease and stroke his chest.

"JJ, please," he pleaded, his voice barely above a whisper.

Jamie slowly slid his palms down Kellet's rib cage, trailing fire until he reached the buckle on his pants.

"You sure, Drummer Boy?"

"Yes."

Kellet felt his belt coming undone before his pants were unzipped; the fine wool releasing to give his straining cock some relief. Jamie's hands slipped into the opening before running around to his ass, pushing the pants down his thighs. Kellet whimpered as Jamie removed his hands and stepped away. He opened his eyes to see Jamie undoing his own shirt and slacks, quickly shucking them off.

Kellet's breath hitched at the lean body before him. He greedily ate up the sight of tanned skin stretched over defined muscles. His fingers itched to trace the musical notes dancing around Jamie's rib cage. His gaze dropped to the bulge between Jamie's thighs, barely restrained by the black boxer briefs. He licked his lips, and Jamie's groan scarcely gave him time to react before Jamie was plastered against him and his mouth devouring Kellet's.

"Wanna taste you," Jamie huffed against his ear. Kellet's dick got harder at the words and he nodded, unable to speak.

Jamie pressed one last kiss to Kellet's throat before dropping to his knees. Kellet almost came at the sight. Jamie pushed his pants further down his legs, and Kellet lifted his foot to let him tug the fabric away. Warm hands traveled up Kellet's naked thighs before coming to a stop just before his groin. Jamie's gaze never left Kellet's, again, wordlessly seeking permission to continue. In response, Kellet nudged his hips forward.

Jamie ran his thumbs up each side of the straining shaft, causing Kellet to curse. With a chuckle, Jamie hooked his fingers into the elastic waistband of his boxer briefs and tugged them down. Kellet's dick slapped against his stomach and he heard Jamie moan.

He kept his eyes closed, head resting against the door, knowing that if he looked at Jamie, the show would be over before even beginning. He felt Jamie's thumbs track down his hip bones and his dick twitched, aching to be touched, but nothing happened. Jamie's breath hitched, and he opened his eyes to glance down and saw Jamie staring at the small tattoo that was etched in the skin at the edge of his pubic bone.

Kellet laid a hand on Jamie's head as brown eyes filled with emotion lifted to meet his.

"When? Why?" Jamie whispered.

"A week after you left," Kellet replied, his thumb caressing Jamie's cheek. He didn't need to tell him why he'd gotten the tattoo of a skylark in flight. He knew.

Jamie blinked rapidly before leaning to press a gentle kiss to the spot, his mouth lingering. With a shuddering sigh, he rested against Kellet's stomach, his breath tickling against the swollen head of Kellet's dick.

"JJ?"

Jamie didn't reply, just nodded to show he was okay. He brought his hand up from Kellet's thigh and gently gripped Kellet's aching dick, causing Kellet to hiss. Two firm strokes before Jamie swirled his tongue around the tip, flicking into the leaking slit before taking Kellet into his mouth.

Kellet's hands slammed against the door behind him, and he shuffled his feet slightly wider apart as Jamie slowly bobbed up and down, drawing him in further on each downward stroke. Kellet was assailed with sensation. It had been so long since anyone had gone down on him and the fact it was Jamie sucking him now had him edging closer to his orgasm by the second.

One of Jamie's hands was at the base of his cock, holding it in position as he licked and sucked. His other hand slid between Kellet's thighs and tugged at his heavy balls before stroking against Kellet's taint.

Kellet couldn't stop the cry that echoed around the room any more than he could stop his hips thrusting forward into Jamie's mouth. A grunt from Jamie had him fighting to hold still, not wanting to hurt him.

Jamie pulled off and looked up at Kellet, his face flushed and lips swollen and glistening.

"It's okay, just let go, Drummer Boy. I'll catch you."

Kellet grasped the base of his cock and gave it a squeeze before pointing it at Jamie's mouth. Jamie let him rub the leaking head against his lips before he opened and sucked Kellet back down, humming as he did.

Heat burst through Kellet's veins and his fingers tangled in Jamie's hair as he thrust into the heated cavern of his mouth.

"Oh God, JJ... I'm... ahh... Jaaay..." His voice gave out as his orgasm exploded from him, his toes curling into the carpet as his thigh muscles tensed and body shuddered. His breath came in short pants and he was vaguely aware of Jamie moaning around him before his mouth slid off Kellet and he gave his own shout.

Kellet looked down in time to see him stroking his own cock as he came, spurting up his chest. Jamie fell forward, his head resting on Kellet's thigh as he stroked himself through the last throes of his orgasm.

"Fuck, JJ," Kellet panted out. He got a low chuckle in return.

"I couldn't have said it better," Jamie replied as he got to his feet. He pressed his body against Kellet's before taking his mouth in a slow, languid kiss. Kellet could taste the remnants of himself on Jamie's tongue. Snaking a hand between their bodies, he swiped some of the come from Jamie's stomach and brought it to his mouth. Heat flared in Jamie's eyes as he watched Kellet taste him.

"Fuck, that's hot," Jamie ground out.

"Well, seeing as you deprived me of tasting it fresh from the source, it will have to do... for now."

"I think that can be arranged," Jamie replied with a sexy grin that did all sorts of things to Kellet's insides. "But first, let's clean up and get into bed. As fun as it is to be on my knees for you, they aren't as young as they used to be."

Kellet laughed, joy filling him. He knew that the next few months on tour were going to be tough, but he'd be able to get through them with Jamie at his side. He climbed into the bed, reaching for Jamie, who wrapped his arms around him. With a feeling of utter contentment, he fell to sleep.

Chapter Eighteen

Jamie tapped on the adjoining door that led from his hotel room to Kellet's. After a few seconds, the lock snicked, and he found himself face to face with a grinning Wil.

"This is so cool," Wil enthused as he stepped back to let him in. "I thought our suite in the LA hotel was great, but this one, wow!"

Jamie laughed as Wil gestured to the space. He supposed it was grander than what they'd normally have, but in deference to Wil traveling with Kellet, Jax had organized a small suite with adjoining rooms on each side for their stay in New York City. It meant Wil had his own space but was still close by, and a little bribery from Jamie to Jax had ensured he'd got the room on the other side. The knowing looks from Seth and Liam as they'd exited the elevator meant he knew he was in for some ribbing later.

"Where's your Dad?" he asked, not seeing Kellet in the small sitting area.

"Oh, he's just cleaning up," Wil replied, nodding towards the bedroom and Jamie could hear the faint sound of the shower. A mental vision of Kellet all wet and soapy flashed into Jamie's mind and it took all of his willpower not to go and see if he needed a hand to wash his back, or in fact, any other part of himself. It had been a long five days since their date and Kellet had fallen asleep in his bed.

Wil's chuckle brought him back to reality, and he grinned ruefully at the young man. Jamie made his way over to the couch and dropped down onto it. "Are you all ready for tomorrow?" he asked Wil.

Wil collapsed bonelessly into the recliner opposite, draping himself across the arms as only a teenager can do. "Definitely. Jax has put me in charge of the band's Instagram account, and I'm going to document the day in a mix of live posts and back-stage photos."

"Just don't get up into people's personal spaces," Kellet said as he walked into the room. He was dressed in a pair of dark sweatpants that rode low on his hips and was pulling on an old, faded t-shirt that had the East Bank logo on the front.

"I won't, Dad," Wil replied, his voice exasperated. "I'm not stupid. I know the guys all have their own special routines and rituals they go through before going on stage. I'm just going to get a general feel for everything happening."

Kellet hummed as he dropped next to Jamie on the couch. Not close enough to touch—much to Jamie's disappointment—but close enough for the clean, fresh fragrance of his shower gel to waft over Jamie.

"Are we eating up here or going out?" Wil asked, his gaze bouncing between Jamie and his father.

"Umm..." Kellet looked to Jamie for an answer. Going out had not occurred to him, judging by the relaxed state of his outfit.

A knock at the door had Wil jumping up to let in Seth and Liam.

"Thought we might find you in here when you didn't answer your own door," Seth remarked with a smirk.

"I only just got here," Jamie defended himself. "We were deciding what to do for dinner."

"As long as it involves a good steak, I really don't care where we go," Liam said as he dropped into the empty recliner where Wil had been sitting.

"I... I didn't realize we'd be going out," Kellet said, moving to stand up. "I'll change. Where do you think we'll go?" he asked, a small frown furrowing his brow.

"Why don't we just do room service?" Jamie suggested. He wasn't particularly in the mood to go out either, even if it was only to one of the three in-house restaurants the hotel boasted.

Seth and Liam exchanged glances before Liam sighed and stood up, pulling his wallet from his back pocket. Seth gave a gleeful cackle as he was handed a crisp twenty-dollar bill.

"Perfect idea, young Jamie. Was going to suggest it myself," he crowed as he pocketed the cash.

"Wait, what's with the exchange of money?" Kellet asked, looking at Jamie, who shrugged. "Am I missing something?"

"Seth said you'd want to stay in for dinner and I said we'd go out," Liam explained with another sigh. "I should have known better."

"We can go out if you prefer to," Kellet said, pushing to his feet. "It will only take me a minute to get changed. I don't want to break any traditions."

"Traditions? What traditions?" Seth asked.

"Well, don't you, y'know, have certain things you do before a show? I mean, tomorrow is the first night of the tour. I should have figured you'd go out to celebrate."

"Kel, wait," Jamie said. "You're okay. We often go out for dinner the night before the start of the tour, but not always. Mark was happier to stay in and order from room service, so that's what we'll do tonight."

At the mention of Mark's name, Kellet gave an almost imperceptible wince, but Jamie saw it. He knew that Kellet had been getting more anxious the closer they got to the launch of the tour. He knew he was dreading the inevitable comparisons that would be drawn between him and their former drummer.

"Jamie's right," Liam said. "We can stay in and chill. S'all good."

"No, I'll get changed, and we can go out," Kellet insisted.

"Kel, for fuck's sake, sit your ass down. We're staying in, and that's final," Seth told him. As Kellet hesitated, Seth sighed and leaned forward in his chair. "We can see you're putting on a brave face, but we all know that you're shitting yourself about tomorrow."

Kellet looked as if he were about to deny it, but Jamie jumped in.

"It's okay, Kel. We get it, we really do." He gestured to the others. "These clowns may look like they don't have a care in the world, but I can guarantee you they have nerves too. We wouldn't be human if we didn't."

"Yeah, but..." Kellet began to protest, but Seth shut him down.

"No but's. We're gonna have a great tour, whether we go out for dinner or not."

"You say that at the beginning of every one," Jamie replied.

"I know, but I dunno, I've just got this feeling that this tour is going to be different and we're all going to come out of it better for it," Seth declared, leaning back and crossing his arms.

Jamie quirked an eyebrow at his friend. "Not like you to be so philosophical," he said. "That's more Liam's wheelhouse."

"Seth's right. I feel it too. I know we've had great tours before, but Kel adds something to the mix that Mark never did," Liam said.

"You really think so?" Kellet asked, his tone uncertain.

Liam nodded. "Definitely. Look, Mark and I are best friends, and he's an amazing drummer. I won't deny it; him leaving the band was a huge blow, and I'll admit I wasn't sure if you'd be able to cut it, Kel."

"And do you think I can cut it now?"

"Hell, yes! Like I said, you bring something to the set that I can't put a name to. It's like there's an invisible bond running between us all. We just seem to be more in sync with each other. I'm not the only one who's noticed, either. Miles said the same thing the other day after the dress rehearsal."

Tension dropped from Kellet's shoulders at Liam's words, and he grinned. "Thanks, Lee. That means a lot to me."

"Only saying what's true," Liam responded with a shrug before smiling slyly. "Of course, the bond between you and J isn't quite as invisible."

Kellet's gaze swung to Jamie, who shrugged. He wasn't about to deny anything. He wanted Kel, and he didn't care who knew it.

Kellet turned to glare at his son.

"What?" Wil looked between his father and the rest of the group. "I didn't say anything. Jeez, don't blame me. You two are about as subtle as a lighthouse in fog."

Seth burst out laughing. "He's right. I know you want to keep your thing on the down-low, but seriously, you need to stop looking at each other like you're about to have your last meal, and the other one is the only thing on the menu!"

Kellet winced again, this time noticeably, and Jamie's heart went out to him. He'd obviously thought they'd been more subtle than they had been. It didn't help that they hadn't progressed any further than a couple of make-out sessions since their date. Apart from rushing around finalizing the last-minute details for the tour, Kellet had been spooked by doing anything further after Wil found them kissing in the pool the day after their date. The teenager had just grinned and told them to carry on before disappearing back into the house.

"Kel, seriously, don't worry. Everyone on the crew signs an NDA, and I promise you it will be fine," Jamie said, placing a reassuring hand on his arm and squeezing. A subtle tremor ran through Kellet, and he nodded and settled back into his seat.

"I'm sorry guys," Kellet apologized. "I don't mean to make things weird between us all. This is something I never expected to happen in my life, and well, I just…"

"Seriously, Kel. Stop stressing," Seth commanded. "Wil, grab the room service menu, and we'll order up a feast. Tonight's all about relaxing and enjoying ourselves. Tomorrow is another day."

Jamie snorted. "Thanks, Scarlett O'Hara. Your wisdom knows no bounds."

Seth winked, and Jamie was grateful that he'd eased some of the tension Kellet was feeling.

♫ ♫ ♫

Kellet stared out of the hotel window, the bright lights of New York City spread before him. How was this his life now? Two months ago, his biggest concerns had been making sure Wil was prepared for college in the fall and how he was going to cope as an empty nester. Now he was on the eve of debuting as the drummer for one of the biggest bands on the planet at Madison Square Garden, no less.

The steak he'd had for dinner sat heavy in his stomach. Despite being perfectly cooked, it could have been a piece of stringy rubber for all the notice he'd taken of it. He knew the others had done their best to make the evening as relaxing as possible, but even with all their reassurances that everything was going to be fine, his brain was coming up with every worst-case scenario imaginable.

"You need to sleep, Drummer Boy."

Jamie's soft voice broke through the silence in the room, and he turned from the window to where the other man was standing by the door adjoining their rooms.

"So do you," he retorted.

Jamie grinned as he crossed the suite. Kellet tracked his movements, feeling like prey. Jamie stopped just in front of him.

"I'll sleep better with you next to me," Jamie said, reaching to twine their fingers together.

"Would we actually get that much sleep?" Kellet countered, quirking his eyebrow.

Jamie nodded, stepping closer. Kellet couldn't help but slide his arms around his trim waist as Jamie's hands slid around his neck, his fingers idly playing with the curls at the nape of Kellet's neck.

"Yes, we would." Jamie rested his forehead against Kellet's. "I'm only going to lie awake worrying about you, as you lie awake worrying about tomorrow, so we may as well lay awake together."

Jamie's concern hit Kellet in a spot that had been buried for years. He was used to being the caretaker and the feeling that, for once, he had someone to take care of him was heady. He tugged Jamie closer, the warmth from Jamie's embrace absorbing into his soul.

"We shouldn't," he whispered, a token protest at best.

"We should. No one in our immediate circle cares, Kel."

Kellet was torn. The thought of being wrapped in Jamie's arms for the night appealed, but knowing Wil was in the next room had him balking.

"Come on, Drummer Boy. Wil's a big boy. He understands what's going on." Jamie pressed a soft kiss to Kellet's mouth, pulling away before he could get a proper taste.

"My room or yours?" he asked, his resolve crumbling.

Jamie grinned and tugged his hand. "Mine. That way there's an extra room between Wil and us."

Kellet stumbled at Jamie's words. "I thought you said we were only going to sleep?"

"We will... eventually."

"Jamie," Kellet growled, squeezing the hand in his, trying to get Jamie to stop.

"Kellet," Jamie retorted in the same tone as they passed through the door into Jamie's room. He closed the door on his side and pulled Kellet into his arms.

"I want you, Drummer Boy," Jamie murmured as his mouth tracked along Kellet's jaw.

Kellet all but melted on the spot. "I want you too, JJ, but I can't, not tonight." He felt bad. He did want Jamie—there was rarely a moment he didn't—but he was too wound up to give him the attention he deserved.

"I know. It's okay. Even just this, having you here, in my arms and in my bed, is enough for now. I want to do this right, Kel. I want to take my time with you and not have to rush."

Kellet let himself be led over to the king-size bed. He stripped out of his sweatpants and t-shirt, goosebumps pebbling his skin as Jamie's eyes raked over him. It only took a few seconds for Jamie to strip down to his own underwear before pulling him into the bed.

After settling the comforter over them, Jamie leaned over him and kissed him lazily, taking his time to savor every inch of Kellet's mouth.

With a final press of his lips, Jamie settled back onto his pillow, pulling Kellet into his arms. Kellet rolled, so he was snuggled into Jamie's side.

"Sleep, Drummer Boy. I'll be right here."

Kellet slowly relaxed as the heat of Jamie's body seeped into his. The familiar scents of wood and leather enveloping him as he drifted off to sleep.

Chapter Nineteen

Kellet went through the moves of his warmup routine, starting slowly to warm his muscles up. They were less than an hour away from going on stage and he was doing everything in his power to focus on the familiar pull and stretch rather than the churning of his stomach.

He'd slept fitfully, sneaking away from Jamie's bed just as the sun was rising over the city's skyscrapers. He'd made use of both the hotel's gym and pool, trying to expend some of the nervous energy that was buzzing through him. He hadn't overdone it though, knowing that adrenaline would only get him so far through the performance tonight and he needed to be on his best form. He couldn't—no, wouldn't—let the guys or the fans down.

Jamie hadn't said anything about his early morning departure, just given him an understanding look and a gentle kiss before heading off to the gym. The rest of the day had simultaneously dragged and rushed by. The morning had been spent doing their own thing, and Wil had disappeared early to get to MSG to document the day for the band's official social media outlets.

After a light lunch that Kellet hadn't eaten much at, the four of them had headed over to the venue to run through soundcheck. Being out on the stage had ramped up Kellet's nerves, but there was also excitement bubbling through him. The air at the stadium was humming as it came alive with vendors prepping for the incoming crowds.

He'd soon discovered the time after soundcheck until the show started was some of the longest hours known to man. Jamie had warned him that there was a lot of downtime and had suggested he pack his e-reader, but Kellet had known that he'd be too hyped up to concentrate on even one of his favorite reads.

Liam, Seth, and Jamie had all disappeared into their own small dressing rooms to do whatever it was they did before a show. Not wanting to intrude, but feeling lost, he had taken a slow climb to the very top of the arena where he'd collapsed in a seat and watched as the crew put the final touches on the set. Wil and Cal had provided a distraction as they laughed together posing and taking selfies on the main stage.

A tap at his dressing room door sounded just as he finished the last set of scales. He called out and Cal's blond head poked in.

"Hey, Kellet," the younger man smiled at him.

"Hey, Cal. Everything okay?"

"Yep. This is your ten-minute reminder."

"Ten minutes?" His eyes flew to the large clock on the wall. It was twenty minutes until the scheduled start time.

Cal nodded. "Yeah. Jax said you need to be at the tunnel entrance in ten minutes."

Nausea rose in Kellet's throat, and he swallowed hard. Shit! It was time. "Um… of course. Thanks, Cal," he managed to get the words out.

"Break a leg, Kel," the younger man replied, a huge grin gracing his face, and Kellet could see the excitement vibrating off him, which did nothing to help Kellet's nerves.

Cal closed the door, leaving Kellet alone. It wasn't completely silent in the room; he could hear shouts and a bark of laughter from someone on the crew as they rushed past. The beep of an incoming message had him shaking off his stupor, and he placed his drumsticks on the snare drum before crossing the room to pick up his phone off the small table at the end of the couch.

Andi: Have a great show. So proud of you. Wish we were there to see you rock the roof off. Love A & R xx.

Kellet smiled at the message and thumbed back a brief reply of thanks. He was sad that they weren't there either. She and Ro were currently in Italy, and from all accounts, having an amazing time.

Another quick tap at the door had him looking up, and this time it was the gorgeous brown eyes and dark hair of Jamie that appeared.

"Time to go, Drummer Boy."

Kellet blew out a breath and nodded. He stood and wiped his clammy hands on his thighs. He could do this. He was good enough to be here.

He put his phone in his bag and locked it in the small safe in the room. He'd broken too many screens from his phone falling from his pocket when playing to know not to have it on him. He picked up the drumsticks and crossed to the door where Jamie stood waiting for him. Jamie ran a hand down his arm before pressing a chaste kiss to his lips.

"You've got this, Kel. You're finally where you're meant to be."

Kellet nodded, and with a final glance around the dressing room, he stepped out into the corridor and followed Jamie to where Seth and Liam were waiting.

As they reached the others, Sam appeared and handed Kellet his in-ear monitors. Kellet's hands fumbled as he attached the pack to the back of his jeans and dropped the connecting wire down the back of his shirt, leaving the earpieces resting above his collar. He'd put them in once he was behind his kit.

Sam deftly connected the equipment up and patted him on the shoulder. "All good to go. Have a great show."

"Okay then, everyone ready?" Jax's voice had Kellet looking up from his unseeing perusal of the concrete floor. Where had she come from? He noticed that Cal and Wil were also there, and Wil gave him a huge grin and quickly stepped up to his father to give him a hug.

"I can't believe this is happening!" he said excitedly before stepping back to snap some pictures of them all.

"Let's go. You're on in five minutes," Jax said as she began herding them towards the stage. Kellet noticed a hum that seemed to get louder, and he realized it was the crowd of nearly twenty thousand people cheering and shouting.

His steps faltered as his stomach swooped and his lungs froze. He couldn't do this. God, what had been thinking? He was thirty-seven for crying out loud. Too old to be entertaining thoughts of being a rock star. He should be back in Juniper having dinner with Wil and his parents, not walking to the stage at Madison-fucking-Square Garden.

A shiver went through him. Why was it so cold? His chest felt tight, and he absently ran a hand over it, trying to ease the pressure.

"Dad? Dad?" Wil's voice sounded like it was coming from down a long tunnel. Kellet's feet felt like they were encased in concrete and he couldn't go a step further. He pressed his palm to the wall next to him and closed his eyes. He needed to move, but he couldn't.

He was vaguely aware of his name being called, but it was all he could do to force air into his lungs.

"Kellet! Kel! I'm going to touch your shoulder, okay?" Jamie's voice was low and reassuring in his ear, and he managed a brief nod.

"Kel, it's okay. You're having a panic attack. You're fine, and you're safe." Warm fingers pressed into the nape of his neck as a hand took his and he felt the soft cotton of Jamie's shirt beneath his palm.

"Okay, Kel. I want you to breathe in and out when I do. Can you do that for me?"

Kellet's fingers scrunched into Jamie's shirt. He could feel the steady thump of his heartbeat as Jamie slowly breathed in and then held his breath for a few seconds before exhaling slowly. Kellet squeezed his eyes shut and tried to copy the action. It took a few breaths, but he was soon matching Jamie, and as he did, awareness began trickling in. Jamie's voice was low as he murmured encouragingly.

"That's it, Kel. You're good. Just keep breathing, calmly and deeply. There you go." Jamie's fingers pressed gently at the back of his neck. He dimly heard the crack of a can of soda being opened and the cold press of metal in his hand as Jamie wrapped his free hand around the drink.

"Here, take a couple of sips of this," he said, nudging Kellet's fist. Kellet did as he was told, grimaced as the sickly-sweet taste of cola hit his tongue as it fizzed in his mouth.

"Gah!" he spluttered but took another mouthful when instructed to. He opened his eyes, and the concerned look on Jamie's face eased as he gave a small smile.

"There you are. You okay now?"

Kellet nodded and looked up as Jamie stepped back, giving him space, but keeping a reassuring hand on his shoulder. "Thanks, JJ."

Kellet's gaze flitted to the small group of people surrounding him, concern etching their features. He immediately sought Wil and found him standing with Liam; his face pale and eyes wide as he stared at his father. He saw Liam murmur something to Wil, who nodded and then took a hesitant step forward.

"Dad?" The anxious tone to his son's voice had Kellet reaching automatically for him. In seconds he had his arms full of shaking teenager.

"I'm okay, Wil. Sorry, I scared you," he said, running a reassuring hand up and down his son's spine, just as he had when Wil was ten years younger.

Wil nodded and sniffed before Kellet let him go to

look at his bandmates. "Sorry, guys. Not sure what happened."

"Fuck, don't apologize. If anything, we should be apologizing to you," Seth said, grabbing him into a tight hug.

"What? Why? I'm the one that freaked out."

"We've left you alone all fuckin' afternoon. We should have been with you, not off in our little worlds. We've got so used to doing all this, we forgot that you've never done this before," Seth ground out, agitation and remorse vibrating through him.

"What? No. I'm more than capable of looking after myself," Kellet replied, shocked that Seth would feel like he did. He glanced at Liam and Jamie to see if they felt the same way and froze when he saw the pain and anguish on Jamie's face.

"JJ, don't," he said, stretching out his hand. "Don't go blaming yourself."

Jamie shook his head and stepped out of Kellet's reach.

"JJ," Kellet growled and snagged the sleeve of Jamie's leather jacket.

"Kel, are you able to go on stage?" Miles asked, and he dragged his attention away from Jamie, not realizing their manager had joined them.

Kellet took a few seconds to center himself before replying. "Yeah. I'm good."

Mile's cool gray stare assessed him before he nodded. "Right then. The natives are getting restless, so you'd better get out there."

Kellet smiled at Sam as he passed him his drumsticks and relieved him of the can of soda. He took a couple of deep breaths. Nerves and excitement warred in his stomach, but he pushed them down and fell into step as the group made their way to the stage entrance.

They paused, and Seth grabbed at Kellet's shoulder, pulling him into a group huddle. Liam was opposite him and Jamie on his left. The familiar scent of wood and leather that was uniquely Jamie washed over Kellet, settling him further.

"Okay. Here we go. We give it our all. We're the best damn band on the planet, and we're going to give the folks out there the night of their lives." Seth thrust his right hand into the middle of the circle. Liam and Jamie copied the action and Kellet did the same, creating a four-way fist bump. "Love you guys," Seth said before he broke the circle and reached for the guitar his tech was holding for him.

Kellet watched as Jamie threw him a grin and a wink before disappearing under the stage, Seth on his heels. Liam moved to his position, and Kellet carefully climbed the dimly lit steps up to his drum kit. He settled himself onto the stool and put his monitors into his ears. He glanced over his gear, studiously avoiding looking out to where the audience was. There was a large filmy drop screen curtaining the front of the stage, so he couldn't see anything, but he could hear the growing crescendo of noise as the crowd realized the band was close to starting. Cracking his knuckles, he ran his sticks through his fingers before glancing at Sam and Wil in the wings. They both grinned and gave him a thumbs up. Kellet focused on his breathing as he waited for Larry to give him the cue to start. Here goes nothing.

♫ ♫ ♫

Jamie fixed his in-ears and adjusted the volume as Larry's voice echoed through them, his thoughts all about Kellet. How could he have been so stupid? He'd wanted to give him space to process and get his head together. Given the way he'd snuck out of Jamie's bed that morning. Jamie hadn't wanted to be a distraction and had automatically dropped into his own routine of quiet meditation before the show. All the calm he'd achieved in the last hour had disappeared as soon as he'd seen Kellet's pale face and how he'd frozen. Liam had moved to help Kellet, as he'd always done with Mark, but Jamie had beaten him to it.

"Confirm all in place." Larry's command broke through Jamie's thoughts and brought him back to reality. He gave himself a mental shake and focused on the replies from the various techs.

"Lead in place."

"Guitar Lead, check."

"Bass guitar in place."

"Drums, set."

Jamie risked a glance over his shoulder to where Kellet was perched above the stage. He could see the tension in the other man's face, but it was one more of concentration rather than panic. He watched as Kellet twirled his drumsticks between his fingers, and his dick twitched at the thought of those nimble fingers playing with his body.

"Confirming all in place. Smoke machine, go."

The sound of Larry's voice had all thoughts of Kellet and his amazing digits flying from his brain as Jamie closed his eyes and tapped into his stage persona.

"Lights one, three, and five, set to go. Cue drums. Curtain drop in five, four, three, two…"

He didn't hear Larry say 'one'. The glare from the spotlights struck him as the curtain shimmered to the ground. Less than a heartbeat later, over the roar of the crowd, he heard the clack of Kellet's drumsticks before the opening beat to their first song sounded.

Jamie grinned out at the screaming audience as he began to sing. The familiar rush of adrenaline hit, and he rode the wave, reveling in every second.

Chapter Twenty

Kellet watched with amusement as Jamie worked the crowd, bringing the excitement to a low hum. They were over halfway through the show, and Jamie was doing his 'chat' section.

"Is everyone having a good time tonight?" he yelled out. The cheers and screams rolled over the stage like a wave. It had been happening all night, and Kellet found his nerves had been replaced with a buzz, unlike anything he'd felt before.

"So, as you all know, our friend and drummer Mark left the band a few weeks ago." A few boos met Jamie's statement, and Jamie waved a hand, palm down, as though trying to calm them. "No, it's all good. Mark's health, in fact, the health of every single person involved with Larkspur, from the band to the crew, is always our priority and we're happy to report Mark is feeling a lot better."

Kellet was surprised. He didn't know that Jamie had been in touch with the former drummer.

"Mark sends his love and thanks to everyone for all the messages of support he's gotten." Jamie paused to take a sip from the drink bottle in his hand. "I'd like to introduce you to our new drummer."

Kellet tried not to wince when a spotlight beamed down on him, giving a smile and a wave.

Ever the showman, Jamie grinned and swept an arm towards Kellet. "New York, this is Kellet. Kel, this is New York."

Kellet's heart lurched as the crowd responded and pulling the small mic hanging above his kit towards him, he grinned and replied.

"Hi, New York! It's great to be here and thanks for making me feel so welcome."

"He's doing a pretty okay job, don't you think?" Seth said, mischief and amusement clear on his face.

He pretended to be affronted by the statement, knowing that it was all being captured and shown on the huge video screens that flanked the stage.

"Okay? I'll show you okay!" Kellet retorted and launched into a quick flourish across the drums, ending with a clash of symbols on the hi-hat.

"Oooh, dem's fightin' words, Seth," Liam chirped, flashing a wink at him.

Seth threw his shoulders back and posed dramatically, hip and leg thrust forward as his fingers flew up and down the fretboard, the riff screaming around the arena.

"Show off!" Kellet said, grinning as he glanced over to where Liam and Jamie were leaning against each other laughing.

"Idiots! I'm working with idiots," Jamie declared.

"Ahh, you love us really," Liam said.

Kellet's breath hitched as Jamie looked directly at him as he placed his water at the base of the drum podium. "Yes, I do." With that, Jamie winked and turned back to the audience.

"Right, enough chitchat," Jamie said as he moved to the front of the stage and Kellet couldn't help fix on his denim-clad ass. Had Jamie's ass always looked that good in jeans? Kellet shook himself as Jamie gave the cue for their next song. He counted them in and was soon swept away in the joy of making music and having it appreciated by so many people.

Forty minutes later, they were taking their bows after their second encore, and Kellet was being dragged off stage by his bandmates.

"Dad! That was amazing. You were amazing." Wil launched himself at his father, and Kellet laughed as he caught his son in his arms. He was riding high on adrenaline, all signs of his earlier panic attack gone.

Wil was pulled out of his arms, and he found himself in the middle of a group hug with Seth, Liam, and Jamie.

"Fuck! That was one of the best shows we've ever done," Seth crowed.

"How are you feeling, Kel?" Liam asked, his gaze searching Kellet with concern.

"I'm flying. I feel ten-foot-tall and bulletproof!" Kellet replied with a laugh. The others squeezed in tighter, and he felt a connection that he hadn't realized he'd been missing.

"Kellet!"

Whipping his head around at the sound of his name, he gaped at the sight of his parents. He pulled away from the guys and moved towards them.

"What? How? Why aren't you in Juniper?" he spluttered out as he was enveloped in another group hug.

"Surprise!" his mom said with a huge grin. "We

flew in this morning. We didn't want you to stress about knowing we were here watching. You were fantastic. It looked and sounded like you'd been part of the band for years."

Kellet was humbled by her words and was thrilled that she and his father had made the long trip to see him perform. He accepted a lengthy hug from his dad, who smiled at him.

"Very proud of you, Kellet," he whispered.

"Thanks, Dad."

A smiling Miles interrupted their reunion. "I hate to break this up, but Kellet and the guys need to get changed so they can do the meet and greet we have organized. They'll see you back at the hotel in a couple of hours for dinner."

Kellet said his goodbyes and headed to his changing room. He quickly swapped into a fresh shirt and jeans after a wipe down with a towel and a spray of deodorant. Nerves briefly assailed him again but were swiftly dispelled when Jamie slid around the door.

"Ready to meet your adoring fans?" he asked with a grin.

"I think so," Kellet replied. "I only have to sign a few posters and smile for selfies, don't I?"

Jamie nodded as he wrapped his arms around Kellet's waist, his gaze scanning his face.

"I'm so proud of you," Jamie told him. "Are you okay, really?"

"Yeah, JJ, I'm good. I'm sorry I freaked you out before the show," Kellet murmured, resting his forehead against Jamie's.

"Shh. You're fine. Seth was right; we shouldn't have left you alone. I'm sorry."

Deciding that they were going to end up in a never-ending circle of apologies, Kellet pressed his mouth to Jamie's. Jamie opened for him without hesitation, his tongue meeting Kellet's in a smooth slide.

"Oi, you two. You can fuck later; we've got fans to meet." Seth's yell was accompanied by a loud banging on the door, which had them reluctantly drawing apart.

Kellet stared into Jamie's flushed face, noting the flare of desire that had darkened his eyes to almost black.

"Later, yeah?"

"Always," Jamie replied, before pulling open the door just as Seth was about to bang on it again.

Seth looked them up and down and grinned. "Come on, you two. Let's not keep everyone waiting."

As they fell into step behind Seth and Liam, Kellet was distracted by the thought of being alone with Jamie later rather than on meeting the fans that were expecting them. It was time to stop running and make the most of every minute they had together.

Chapter Twenty-One

Jamie reached idly for his beer bottle as he watched Kellet and Wil interact with Mr. and Mrs. James at the other end of the table. Wil was showing them something on his phone while Kellet looked on, a beaming grin spread across his face. Jamie knew he was riding the high that came from doing a sell-out show. He had his own buzz going on, heightened by the thought of being alone with Kellet later.

Liam dropped into the vacant seat next to him and nudged his shoulder as he tipped his own bottle against Jamie's in a toast.

"Good show tonight, Jay."

"Yeah, it was," Jamie agreed, glancing briefly back down the table towards Kellet.

"I feel bad we let Kel down, though."

"We should have realized that Kel would be nervous." Jamie picked at the label on his bottle, remorse washing through him. He'd let Kellet down badly.

Liam nudged his shoulder again. "Jay, don't feel like that. We're all to blame. Shit, even Miles should have said something. It's like Seth said, he's fitted in so smoothly that we all forgot."

"I know, it's just…"

"Jamie, stop. Look at him. He's on top of the world right now. He played really well. Another couple of shows under his belt and he'll be an old hand."

"But what if he ends up like Mark?" Jamie asked quietly, his voice almost a whisper. "What if the anxiety gets too much, and he decides he can't do it anymore? Then what happens?"

"He's not Mark, Jay." Liam leaned in. "Look, tonight was a one-off. Yes, he may have a few nerves before each show, but hell, we all do. I was closer to Mark than either you or Seth. He struggled all the time with his anxiety, not just before the shows. I think part of the reason we didn't think of Kel today was that Mark always ran on nervous energy, whereas Kel is laid back and chill about most things."

Jamie couldn't help looking down the table again, only this time, shining moss green eyes met his. Kellet grinned and gave him a wink before returning his attention back to his family. Warmth spread through him as he drank a mouthful of beer.

"I think he'll be okay," he finally agreed, and Liam chuckled next to him.

"Just for the record, I'm more than happy to be the go-to guy for calming nerves before a show. However, you're the only one that can sort out the unresolved sexual tension between the two of you."

"Yes, for fuck's sake, can you two screw each other's brains out already," Seth said, slinging an arm around each of their shoulders as he leaned between them.

"Really, Seth?" Jamie said, twisting to look up at his bandmate. "Look, we're going at his pace. I'm not going to lose him again, guys."

"Maybe I should give him a nudge in the right direction then," Seth declared, standing up straight, a look of determination on his face.

"Seth," Jamie growled. "Leave it!"

"Jamie, it's as plain as day that he wants you as much as you want him. I thought you two would have gotten down to it already."

"It's not that simple, Seth, and I don't need you sticking your nose in where it's not needed," he snapped back.

"Okay, both of you just chill," Liam said, ever the peacemaker. "Seth, it's Jamie and Kel's business, and you need to stay out of it."

"Yeah, it's not like we're mentioning anything about you and Cal," Jamie said, smirking when Seth gaped at him.

"Whadda mean? Me and Cal? There's nothing going on. F'r fuck's sake, he's the intern," Seth said the last word on a hiss.

"I've seen the way you look at him. You can pretend that you won't go near him because he's part of the team, and for all your other fucked up morals, you do actually respect the golden rule of not screwing the crew. I'm just sayin', if he wasn't staff, then you'd be all over him like a rash."

Liam chuckled and held out a fist to Jamie, who grinned as they bumped knuckles.

"Don't forget that being Sarge's cousin also adds another layer of 'do not touch' to the whole scenario," Liam commented, winking at Jamie as he finished his beer.

"Assholes. That's what you both are," Seth declared. "I'm leaving now before someone gets offended. I'll see you later."

They managed to hold their laugher until Seth had disappeared from sight.

"Oh brother, I think we've touched a nerve there,"

Jamie said, still chuckling.

"Hmm. We'd better keep an eye on him. You know he'll only go and do something stupid to prove us all wrong."

"Dammit, I hate it when you're right." Jamie heaved a sigh as a sudden wave of fatigue rolled over him. He recognized it as the post-show high wearing off. All he wanted to do now was crawl into bed, preferably a bed that contained a six-foot-tall, brown-haired, green-eyed drummer.

Glancing down the table, he noticed Kellet stifling a yawn and decided it was time to call it a night. Jamie patted Liam on the shoulder. "I'm turning in," he told his bandmate.

Liam smiled and nodded in agreement. "Yeah, good idea. Might as well make the most of sleeping in a decent bed while I can. This time next week it will be the bunks on the bus."

A shudder went through Jamie at the thought. Their tour bus was extravagantly fitted out, and the beds the best they could get, but still, Liam had a point.

"Night, Lee. Thanks for tonight."

"Anytime."

Jamie slipped on his jacket as he stood before making his way down to where Kellet was with his family. Mrs. James spotted him over Kellet's shoulder and gave him a huge smile.

"Oh, Jamie. It's so good to see you again. You were amazing up there on stage. Your parents must be so proud of what you've achieved."

"Thanks, Mrs. J. Mom and Dad love dining out on the fact that their son is in a world-famous band," he replied. "I bet you're just as proud of Kel, though?"

"So very proud," Mrs. James said with a grin. "I've always been proud of him. I'm proud of all of you. You were always good kids, and it looks like you've turned into good men."

Jamie's skin heated at the praise and glanced over to see Kellet looking at him with his own look of pride. Kellet gave him a wink before covering his mouth as he yawned.

"I've just come to say goodnight," Jamie said. "Looks like you're ready to hit the pillows too, Kel."

"Yeah. It's been a long day," Kellet admitted as he pushed out from the table. He crossed around to his mother to give her a hug before doing the same to his father. "I'll see you for breakfast in the morning?"

"Yes, son. No rush, though. Our flight isn't until tomorrow evening. We're going to do some sight-seeing before we head home." Mr. James stood and helped his wife to her feet.

"Dad, I'm going to go with Pops and Mimi to check out Times Square. I'll be back soon," Wil said.

"Okay then. Don't be too late. We've got another busy day tomorrow," Kellet told his son before hugging him.

They made their way to the elevators, and while they waited for one to arrive, Jamie noticed the tired slump of Kellet's shoulders and the faint bags under his eyes. Once inside the elevator, Kel leaned tiredly against the back wall closing his eyes. Jamie stood as close as he could, their arms brushing. He gave a small smile when callused fingers wrapped around his and lightly squeezed.

The elevator came to a smooth halt at their floor, and Jamie tugged Kellet along behind him. When they reached the suite door, Kellet fumbled with his key card before deactivating the lock and letting them into the room.

Before Jamie could get far, Kellet had pulled him into his arms, and soft lips were on his. His tiredness was washed away by the warmth of desire sweeping through him. He met Kellet kiss for kiss, burying his hands in the tousled curls and tangling his tongue with Kellet's insistent one.

They broke apart with a breathless pant and Kellet buried his face in Jamie's neck.

"Want you, JJ," he murmured.

"Want you, too," Jamie breathed back, tightening his hold around Kellet's shoulders.

They stood where they were for a few moments before Jamie realized that despite initiating their kiss and proclaiming his want, Kellet wasn't actually doing anything to further the cause.

"Hey, Drummer Boy, why don't you have a quick shower and then meet me in my room?"

Kellet moaned in protest at the suggestion, pressing his hard length into Jamie's.

"I know, babe, ten minutes, max. You'll feel better for it." Drawing away, he pushed Kellet towards his bathroom. Kellet gave a put-upon sigh before trudging away. Jamie grinned before racing to his own room.

Ten minutes later, Jamie emerged from his shower, rubbing the last vestiges of water from his hair to find Kellet James sprawled face down across his bed clad only in a towel that clung to his fabulously tight ass… and fast asleep.

He gave a rueful chuckle and looked to the heavens. "Really? You couldn't keep him awake for a little longer?" he implored of whatever God was listening.

Throwing his towel back into the bathroom, he crossed to the bed and nudged Kellet's warm shoulder. All he received in return was a soft grunt and Kellet snuggling further into the pillow he was clutching. Jamie managed to get the sheet and comforter from under the sleeping body before climbing in next to him. He tugged the sheets over the two of them and then spooned in behind Kellet. This wasn't quite how he imagined the evening ending, but he'd got part of his wish for his drummer to be in his bed. He'd just wanted him awake as well.

"I love you," he whispered before tucking his nose into Kellet's nape. With a sigh, he let sleep take him. There was always tomorrow night.

Chapter Twenty-Two

Kellet woke slowly, not wanting to leave the dream he'd been having. He tugged the pillow closer, trying to find that perfect sweet spot so he could drift off again. He stretched a foot out from under the covers, wanting to cool down but not escape the warmth that surrounded him.

The sheets rustled softly as a hand ran up his chest and Kellet grasped the long fingers and entwined them with his own. A foot nudged his calf, and he automatically lifted it slightly so it could slip between his legs. A small groan sounded behind him as a hard cock rubbed against his crease, and he sighed and pushed back. There really wasn't any better way to wake up in the morning. Warm and toasty with a hard body against his own.

Wait. Hard body? Kellet gave an experimental nudge of his hips backwards and was rewarded with a gasp and the hand entwined with his tightening. Warm breath feathered across his neck before a soft kiss was pressed to his shoulder.

Memories of the previous night flooded Kellet's brain as he woke up fully. Shit! He'd fallen asleep before Jamie could even join him in bed. He groaned and tried to roll over to face the man currently draped around him like a limpet, but Jamie squeezed him tighter and rubbed himself against Kellet's ass.

"JJ," he gasped out as Jamie's deft fingers let go of his hand and slid down to where Kellet's morning wood was making its interest known.

Jamie didn't reply, just wrapped his fingers around Kellet's hard length and began to leisurely stroke him. Anything else Kellet had been about to say disappeared in a haze of desire, and he reached a hand back to pull Jamie closer.

Warm lips nibbled at his neck before sharp teeth nipped his earlobe. Kellet gasped and rolled onto his back as Jamie rose over him. He got a glimpse of a wicked grin and brown eyes so dark they were almost black before Jamie was kissing him deeply, tongue probing his mouth.

Kellet tugged Jamie on top of him, his thighs opening so Jamie could slot between them. He groaned as their erections brushed together, and grasping Jamie's hips, he pulled him in tight as they began to thrust against each other.

"Fuck, Kel, you feel amazing," Jamie huffed out as he rolled his hips.

"Mmm... don't stop."

They continued to grind against each other, precome easing the slide. Kellet whimpered as Jamie sat up and then groaned as a firm hand wrapped around both of them and he opened his eyes to find Jamie watching him intently as he stroked them hard and fast.

Familiar heat pooled in his groin and his skin tingled as his orgasm approached.

"Jay, I'm close," he muttered. Jamie dropped a hand next to his shoulder and leaned over to capture Kellet's mouth in a bruising kiss while maintaining the rhythm of his strokes.

"Come for me, Kel," Jamie whispered against his lips, and Kellet gave a final thrust before his release was spattering over his stomach.

Jamie cursed as he tensed and came all over Kellet. Jamie eased his grip and stroked them both gently through the last tremors before collapsing onto Kellet's chest. His arms wrapped around Jamie and he buried his nose into Jamie's neck, taking comfort in his scent.

"You okay?" Jamie's question was muffled by the pillow he was face down in. Kellet rolled them onto their sides, sliding a thigh between Jamie's.

He mapped the familiar features that were stamped with concern.

"I'm better than okay," he replied with a small smile. "Sorry for falling asleep on you last night, but really you only have yourself to blame."

Jamie arched a brow at him. "How do you figure that?"

"You made me have a shower. I was literally in there for three minutes, but it was enough to knock me out once I hit your mattress."

"You were asleep on your feet, Kel. Even if you hadn't had a shower, you would have crashed the minute you got anywhere near the bed," Jamie told him as he pushed a wayward curl from Kellet's brow. "And you've made up for it this morning," he continued as he ran his hand over Kellet's ass.

"Do we have any commitments after the show tonight?" Kellet asked, pulling him closer.

"Just the meet and greet. Why?"

"So, we can skip dinner with everyone and come back here. Have an early night?"

"If you want to call midnight an early night, then sure. We can order room service. Why, what did you have in mind?" Amusement glittered in Jamie's eyes. He knew what Kellet was thinking.

Kellet nuzzled the skin under Jamie's ear, grinning when a small gasp escaped. "I was thinking we could do this again. Maybe more, if you're up for it?"

Jamie groaned and pushed his hips against Kellet's. "Oh, I'll definitely be up for anything and everything."

"Good," Kellet whispered before claiming Jamie's mouth.

They were well on their way to round two of the morning when a bang sounded at the door.

"Um, Jamie? Is... um... Dad in there with you?"

Kellet froze and inched away from Jamie, who chuckled at what must be the horrified look on Kellet's face. How could he have forgotten about Wil?

"Yeah, I'm here, Wil," he said, his voice rough.

"Oh... ah... good. That's... ah... good then," Wil's stammered reply made Jamie start to laugh, and Kellet glared at him, which only made Jamie laugh louder.

"Ah, Jamie, are you okay?" Wil called out.

"I'm fine, Wil. Thanks for asking. Is there something you need?"

Kellet flopped onto his back and covered his eyes with his arm. He was never going to be able to look his son in the face again.

"No. Just wanted to remind Dad that we're meeting Mimi and Pops for breakfast and then don't you guys have a meeting or something this morning?"

"Yeah, we do," Jamie called back as Kellet rolled over to look at the clock.

"We'll be down in twenty minutes, son," he said, and his statement was met with a disgusted snort.

"Whatever, Dad. Just don't be too long, alright?" he said with a knowing snicker.

Kellet turned to glare at Jamie, who was still laughing beside him. "Y'know, I'm really regretting bringing him along," he muttered as he rolled out of bed.

"Hey, wait. Where are you going?" Jamie sat up in bed, and Kellet took a moment to drink in the sight of tousled hair and flushed skin.

"Shower and then to breakfast," he retorted as he headed to the bathroom. He stuck his head around the door. "Well. Are you going to join me?"

Jamie jumped out of bed and strode towards him. "You really think we're going to be done in twenty minutes?"

Half an hour later, they entered the private dining area where they were meeting for breakfast.

"Glad you could join us," Seth said with a knowing grin before bursting into laughter at the finger Kellet flashed at him before greeting his parents.

After serving themselves from the large buffet, they sat down at the table.

"I have to leave shortly, so if you two don't mind talking business as you eat, I'll get started," Miles said from where he was sitting at the end of the long table. Jax on one side of him and Larry, their tour manager, on the other.

At Kellet's nod of agreement, Miles tapped on the tablet in front of him.

"Reviews from last night's show are in," he said, pausing as Kellet choked back a cough. "You okay there, Kel?"

"Yeah, sorry. I didn't realize there'd be reviews, but I don't know why. Of course, there'd be reviews. Why wouldn't there be?"

"Dad, you're babbling," Wil said, nudging him in the side.

Kellet realized he was right and heat flushed his skin. He mumbled an apology and took a drink from his coffee to cover his embarrassment.

"That's okay, Kellet. You've had more than enough to think about," Miles reassured him. "And all the reviews are very positive, so there's nothing to worry about."

"He's right," Liam said as he passed Kellet his own tablet. He read the highlighted article.

!MUSIC NEWS NOW!
LARKSPUR WEAVE MAGIC AT MSG

Last night was the opening night of Larkspur's North American tour at the famed Madison Square Garden. It was also the debut of their new drummer, Kellet James, brought in to replace Mark Sullivan, who quit the band two months ago citing personal health reasons.

I'll admit I was not convinced that bringing in an unknown to replace a key member of the group was the best idea. However, I am happy to report that any misgivings I had were dismissed less than ten minutes into the show.
James' nerves were obvious to anyone who has studied band dynamics. However, once into the rhythm (no pun intended), the connection he has with his bandmates was easy to see.

Kellet looked up from the tablet and found Miles smiling at him. He returned the smile, relief settling into his bones. It was better than he'd expected, and he knew that he would only improve with each show they did.

"As I said, reviews are favorable, so Kellet, just keep doing what you're doing," Miles said, pulling their attention back. "Moving along, there didn't seem to be any technical hitches last night, but as always, let Larry know if something isn't working as soon as you notice."

Miles glanced down at his tablet before turning to Jax. "Do you have anything to add?"

Jax's blond ponytail swung across her shoulders as she shook her head. "No, everything is in place for today and tonight. Tomorrow morning we'll leave here by 9am by bus for Boston. Soundcheck is scheduled for 2pm." She looked at them pointedly. "So that means in the lobby, ready to go by 8:50."

"Are all the hotel bookings confirmed?" Larry asked.

"Yes," Jax replied with another nod before glancing down the table. "You'll be pleased to know that you're staying in hotels for the Boston, Philadelphia, Pittsburgh, and DC shows. After that, it's the bus until we get to South Dakota."

There was a round of muted grumblings from Seth, Liam, and Jamie. Wil looked excited at the prospect and Kellet was intrigued. The guys had told him stories of the tour bus, and he knew it wasn't going to be as comfortable as staying in a hotel, but surely it couldn't be that bad.

"Okay then, if there's nothing else, I'll hand you over to Larry's capable hands," Miles said with a nod to his colleague. "Please try to behave while you're out there and I'll see you at the end of the month."

Miles said his farewells before stopping next to Kellet. "Kel, you got a moment?"

"Um, sure, yeah." Kellet stood, wondering what Miles had to say that he couldn't say in front of the others. Falling into step with the other man, they moved to the lobby.

"I just wanted to check in that you are feeling okay with continuing on with the tour?"

"Yes, of course. Why wouldn't I be?" Kellet rushed to reassure him. "Last night was a one-off, I'm sure. I just got a bit overwhelmed with it all and started second guessing myself. I realize now it was unfounded, but you know how sometimes your irrational brain takes over?"

"Good. I'm glad to hear it." Miles paused and rested a hand on Kellet's shoulder. "But, please, let someone know if you're questioning anything. Don't hide away and think you can cope on your own. Jax will be around, so will Larry."

"Thanks, Miles. I'm sure it will all be fine. To be honest, I think the guys are still feeling a little guilty for yesterday. So I know they'll take it to the extreme and be checking on me every two minutes before the show tonight."

Miles barked out a laugh and, not for the first time, Kellet noticed how handsome their manager was.

"You're going to do just fine, Kel. Have a good show tonight. I'll talk to you soon."

Kellet shook the proffered hand and then watched as Miles strode across the hotel lobby, noticing with amusement the appreciative glances the older man got from both the women and men that were milling around.

"Everything okay?" The familiar scent of leather and wood let Kellet know that Jamie had stepped up behind him.

"Yeah. Miles was checking that I was okay after last night."

"And are you?" Jamie asked, concern edging his tone.

"I'm fine, JJ. Like I said to Miles, it was just a blip. I'm sure I'll be nervous before each show for a while, but now I know what to expect, I'll be able to cope with it."

"Good, but you let me know—"

"Kellet, Jamie, we're heading off to catch the Staten Island ferry, so need to say our goodbyes now." The voice of Mrs. James broke into their conversation, and Kellet turned to smile at his parents.

"Thanks for coming, Mom," Kellet said, giving her a hug.

"Oh, Kellet, it was a dream come true to see you up there with Jamie and the boys after all these years. Your dad and I are so very proud of you."

Kellet swallowed down the lump in his throat. "Thanks, Mom."

"Now, Jamie Larke, you look after my boy, y'hear," Mrs. James mock growled at Jamie as she pulled him into a hug.

"I promise, Mrs. J, I'll be with him every step of the way."

After another round of hugs and promises to talk in a few days, Kellet waved his parents off, smiling as his father reached for his wife's hand as he led her out of the hotel lobby.

"They haven't changed a bit," Seth commented as he and Liam joined them. "You're lucky, man, to have parents that care as much as they do."

"I know I am, Seth. I certainly couldn't have done what I have without them backing me every step of the way," Kellet agreed. "Even now, the only reason I could say yes to coming on tour with you guys is that Mom and Dad are helping Andi keep an eye on the bar while I'm away."

"Yeah, like I said, lucky," Seth muttered before stalking off towards the elevators.

"Is he okay?"

"He'll be fine," Liam replied. "Give him a few hours, and he'll be back to his lovable, obnoxious self."

"So, what do we do now?" Kellet asked as they crossed the lobby.

"I'd suggest packing as much as you can, so it's not a rush in the morning," Liam said as he pressed the elevator button. "Only leave out the bare necessities for what you'll need tonight and fresh clothes for tomorrow."

"Are you always this organized?" Kellet asked with amusement at Liam's serious tone.

"Listen to what he says, Kel," Jamie said. "What he says is true. Guaranteed, if you leave your packing until the morning, you'll oversleep. Then you'll have to rush, and inevitably, you'll leave something behind. We've all done it."

"Yep. Oh and set a reminder on your phone to pack your charger cable. You'll lose at least a couple during the tour. Jax always has replacement ones, but she'll charge you double to replace it."

"I'll leave that to my trusty PA, then," Kellet said, grinning at Wil, who rolled his eyes.

Back in his room, Kellet did as Liam had suggested and packed most of his gear. He threw a change of clothes into his duffle bag to take to the stadium and remembered to pack his e-reader. He wasn't going to get caught without it again. As he gathered up his toiletries in the bathroom, he paused when he saw the lube and condoms that were tucked into the bottom corner of his kit bag.

He didn't know why he kept stalling when it came to sleeping with Jamie. Sure, they'd traded blowjobs and hand jobs, and this morning's frotting session had been seriously hot, and he wanted to sleep with Jamie so badly. He knew that Jamie wanted him as well, so he really needed to get past this mental block.

What are you afraid of? Andi's voice echoed in

his head. He gave a rueful snort. Of course, it would be her voice that he heard when he was having a dilemma. But then, she'd been his go-to person for the last twenty years.

What was he afraid of? He sighed and clenched the bottle of lube tightly. He and Jamie had always worked. It wasn't like they hadn't slept together before, but back then, they'd been fumbling teenagers. They'd been each other's first in just about everything. And that was part of the problem. He didn't want to know how many others there had been since they'd gone their separate ways, but he couldn't help but feel jealous that there had been others.

Of course, he'd had other lovers too, but he'd never let them get as close as Jamie had. Jamie was the only person he'd ever trusted in that respect. Did he trust him enough now to let him in again? Not only into his body, but into his heart as well?

Who was he kidding? Of course, he did. He trusted and loved Jamie. He always had and always would. It was time to stop messing around and embrace this second chance they'd been given.

Decision made, he made sure the lube and condoms were sitting near the top of his kit bag before zipping it up. He didn't need Wil seeing that.

He wandered back into the suite to do a final sweep to make sure there wasn't anything left behind and glanced up when Jamie came through the adjoining door. His gaze traveled up and down the familiar body. His own tightened at the thought of being with him in every way possible.

"Hmm, what was that look for?" Jamie asked as he wrapped his arms around Kellet's waist. Kellet brushed his nose along Jamie's before kissing him.

"Just checking out what's mine," he replied and then smirked at the quirked eyebrow he got in return.

"I'm yours, am I?"

"And I'm yours, if you'll have me?" Kellet hoped the insecurity that fluttered through him didn't show.

In reply, Jamie took his mouth in a blistering kiss. Tongues tangled and Kellet pulled Jamie as close as he could.

"Oh, jeez! Is this what I'm gonna have to put up with now?" Wil's voice broke through the lust that fogged Kellet's brain, and he drew away from Jamie.

"You said you didn't have a problem with me and your Dad hooking up."

"Yeah, but I wasn't expecting to keep walking in and finding you both making out like horny teenagers," Wil exclaimed, waving a hand at the two of them. "You've got a bedroom each, can you, I don't know, like, keep it to one of those rooms rather than the public areas. I'm young and impressionable. I don't need to see one of my parents doing… that!"

"I'm sorry, son. We'll try to take your sensibilities into account," Kellet said, trying not to laugh.

"Thank you," Wil said sagely with a nod. "Thank God the Moms are past this honeymoon stage. It's bad enough when they get all kissy face. I don't need it from you two as well."

Jamie's words came back to Kellet, and he frowned at his son. "And when did you tell Jamie that you were okay with us hooking up?" He glanced at Jamie. "And I'd like to think we're doing more than just hooking up."

Jamie brushed their lips together. "We are definitely doing more than hooking up. And Wil gave us his blessing your first night in LA."

Kellet glared at his son, who shrugged. "Whatever, Dad. Now, I've finished my packing, do you need any help with yours?"

"No, thank you. I've done everything I can."

"Great. Then I'm off to the stadium with Cal, and I'll see you later this afternoon." With a cheeky wave and grin, Wil headed to the door. "As you were!"

"He's a good kid, Kel," Jamie said, pulling him back into his arms.

"Yeah, I know. It's hard, though, to see him as an almost adult. He'll always be my kid, y'know. The little tornado with bruised knees and sleepy snuggles. The inquisitive and caring teen who looked out for his friends at school and didn't let anyone give him shit for having two moms and a gay dad."

"Now, back to us," Jamie said, clasping Kellet's chin. "We're not just hooking up, Kel. At least, I'm not. I want you in my life, in every way possible. I'm happy to take it at your pace, but you're it for me, Drummer Boy. You always have been, and always will be."

Kellet grinned at the words he'd thought himself not fifteen minutes before.

"What's that grin for?"

"You just said the same thing I thought to myself earlier when I was trying to figure out why I keep stalling when it comes to us in the bedroom."

"Oh, did you work it out?" Jamie asked quietly, his shoulders tensing up.

"Yeah, I did."

There was a moment of silence until Jamie huffed. "And?"

"You're the only one who's ever had all of me, JJ," Kellet explained huskily.

Jamie frowned, and then his eyes widened. "Wait, you mean there's been no-one since me? But you said back in LA that there'd been other guys."

"Yes, there have been a few other guys, but you are the only one that I've ever trusted to give myself to fully."

Understanding dawned on Jamie's face before a big grin appeared. "Well, that's just another thing we have in common."

"Really?" Kellet asked incredulously. "All the groupies and fans over the years and you've never bottomed for any of them?"

"First, there have not been that many," Jamie told him in an annoyed tone. "I told you, I'm not like Seth. I haven't done the stereotypical rock star thing. There've been a few, but I suppose it's part of the image. It's always been expected that I top and, like you, I've never trusted anyone else."

Relief and excitement coursed through Kellet. "So, who's going first?"

"Why don't we just let it happen naturally," Jamie replied with a grin.

The reminder tone from Kellet's phone stopped him from carrying Jamie into the bedroom then and there.

"I suppose it's time to go and earn our keep?"

"Sure is. But, hey, the quicker we go, the quicker we'll be back," Jamie replied.

With a final, heated kiss that promised so much for later on, they gathered their gear and headed down to the lobby. The excitement and anticipation racing through Kellet wasn't just for the show, but for afterwards as well.

Chapter Twenty-Three

Jamie smiled brightly at the young woman in front of him as she passed the glossy photo towards him for signing.

"Hi, thanks for coming to the show tonight," he said as he scribbled his name across one corner, the marker pen squeaking.

"It was amazing," the fan gushed, her face blushing bright red. "Best concert I've ever been to."

"That's great to hear. You have a safe trip home, okay," Jamie said with a final smile as she took her picture and moved along to where Seth was sitting.

He glanced around the room, relieved to see there were only about a dozen more people to see. Next to him, Kellet smiled and chatted to a young man as he signed a drumstick the kid had brought along with him. He tried not to glance at the clock on the wall, knowing they wouldn't get out of there until they had seen the last person. Normally he loved this part, connecting with the fans who'd paid extra to see them after the show. For a lot of fans it was an expense they couldn't afford and had saved up for, and Jamie never took it for granted. Tonight, though, all he could think about was getting Kel back to the hotel.

Laughter had him looking to his right, and he drank in the sight of Kellet grinning as the fan he was talking to gesticulated with his hands as he shared a story. Jamie gave his own grin at them. Kellet had been nervous before going on stage tonight, but there had been no sign of the panic attack from the night before. He'd been a little pale and tense, but once they'd gotten on stage, he'd soon settled into the show.

As if sensing his eyes on him, Kellet turned and winked at Jamie. With an answering smile, Jamie returned his attention to the next person in line. Not much longer to go.

An hour later, they were back at the hotel, and as they crammed into the elevator, Jamie's hands itched to be on Kellet's skin rather than jammed in his jeans pockets. Next to him, Kellet leaned against the back wall, their shoulders brushing. Both Seth and Liam were busy on their phones, and Jamie pressed a little closer to Kellet. Wil had, thankfully, decided to stay and help Sam with the breakdown of the set and wouldn't be back for a few hours.

The elevator came to a gliding halt, and the door opened soundlessly. Seth looked up from his phone and gave them a grin.

"Right then. I'll see you in the morning."

"Don't be late, Seth," Liam called after him as they headed towards their respective rooms. "You really don't want to piss Larry off this early in the tour."

"I'll be there," Seth singsonged and with a wave, disappeared into his room.

Liam gave a resigned sigh and stopped outside his own room. "Night guys. You two don't be late either."

"Night, Lee," Jamie called out as he all but pushed Kellet into his room.

Jamie closed the door behind him and leaned against it, watching as Kellet dropped his duffle bag on the couch. They stood and stared at each other; the silence only broken by the faint sounds of traffic that came from the street fifteen stories below.

"Why does this feel as awkward as our first night together?" Kellet asked, pushing a hand through his hair, making the curls more riotous than usual.

"I don't think anything could be more awkward than that night," Jamie said with a huff of laughter. He crossed the room until he was standing in front of Kellet. "We know what we're doing this time, even if it has been a while."

"Yeah, I know. I just..." Kellet stopped, and Jamie was surprised to see a faint blush tint his face as he dropped his gaze. Laying a hand on Kellet's chest, he could feel his heart beating wildly.

"Hey, Drummer Boy," Jamie said as he tilted Kellet's chin so they were looking eye-to-eye. "It doesn't have to be tonight. Why don't we both get into bed and relax? We'll order some dinner and put a movie on."

Kellet nodded before pulling Jamie into his arms and kissing him. Jamie melted into the embrace, tangling his fingers in Kellet's wayward curls. After a few moments, the kiss turned from comforting to heated, and Jamie gave a soft moan as Kellet's mouth left his and began nibbling along his jaw.

He ran his hand up Kellet's back, tugging at his dark green t-shirt. Kellet paused long enough to pull the material over his head before his mouth was back on Jamie's. Jamie continued his exploration of Kellet's back, skin warm and smooth beneath his fingers.

Kellet gripped Jamie's hips, pulling him closer. The denim of their jeans did little to hide their need for each other as Kellet began a slow grind against Jamie.

"Naked. Bed. Now." Each word was said with a thrust of hips as Jamie clung to Kellet.

They stumbled apart long enough to strip. Within moments they were sprawled on the large king-sized bed, both desperately trying to touch every inch of each other.

"Where's–"

"Top drawer." Jamie cut Kellet's question off, waving a hand towards the cabinet next to the bed.

Kellet rolled away only long enough to snag the bottle of lube and a couple of condoms. He dropped them on the pillow before covering Jamie's body with his own. He shivered at the contact, and he hooked a leg around Kellet's, drawing him closer, moaning as their heated erections brushed against each other.

Kellet kissed him briefly before peppering kisses down his throat and collarbone. Jamie's eyes fluttered shut as Kellet flicked his tongue over his left nipple. He hissed as it was gently bitten and then licked again. Sensation coursed through him and his dick flexed against Kellet's thigh.

"You always did like that," Kellet murmured against his skin as he tracked across to Jamie's other pec.

Jamie hummed in agreement, his capacity for words evaporating. Kellet chuckled quietly as he moved down Jamie's torso, stopping just before he reached Jamie's straining cock.

He cracked his eyes open to see Kellet kneeling between his thighs. Warm hands rested on Jamie's hips. Kellet's eyes had darkened to deep green pools as he hungrily took in Jamie's reposing body.

"Fuck, you're gorgeous."

"I need you, Kel," Jamie whispered, voice heavy with longing.

"You sure?"

"Only you, Drummer Boy. Only you."

Kellet's hand closed around Jamie's cock, giving it a firm stroke from base to tip. The calluses on his fingers adding a layer of friction that had Jamie groaning and punching his hips up. He was vaguely aware of the snick of the lube bottle being opened, and he gasped when Kellet's hot mouth teased the tip before he was engulfed.

He was so lost in the sensation of Kellet's mouth that it took him a moment to realize there was a finger tracing around his hole, causing shivers to skitter up his spine. He whimpered as Kellet edged into him.

"Okay?"

"God, yes. So good. I need more Kel."

Kellet pulled out and then there was a brief burning sensation as Kellet pressed back in with two fingers. Jamie panted through the discomfort, willing himself to relax.

"I can stop, JJ. I don't want to hurt you," Kellet said.

"You're not," Jamie assured him. He leaned up, and Kellet took the hint and met him halfway in a blistering kiss. He pulled Kellet down on top of him, adjusting his position so Kellet could still stretch him. It didn't take long before he was riding Kellet's fingers, wanting more.

He dropped his hand to Kellet's leaking cock, stroking it firmly, feeling Kellet swell further. Jamie's body clenched at the thought of Kellet inside him, and he pulled his mouth away from Kellet's.

"Now, Kel," he growled, and Kellet gave a small nod as he removed his fingers and reached for the condom.

Jamie grabbed it from him and ripped open the packet. His hands trembled, but he steadied himself and rolled the latex down Kellet's cock. Kellet drizzled some lube over himself and then pushed Jamie onto his back.

"I know this isn't probably the best position, but I need to see you, JJ."

"I need to see you too, Drummer Boy," Jamie replied as Kellet settled between his thighs.

Jamie spread his legs wider as Kellet eased over him. He felt the blunt head of Kellet's cock drag over his balls and down his taint. Kellet's green eyes bore into him as he pushed against Jamie's hole.

"Breathe, JJ," Kellet reminded him, and Jamie took a gasping breath in as the tip of Kellet's cock breached his body. Kellet held himself as still as possible, waiting for Jamie to relax. Jamie gave him a small nod, and Kellet inched forward. Jamie gasped and bit his lip at the burn, his breaths coming in short pants.

"Jamie–"

"No! I'm okay. Just go really slow."

A pained expression crossed Kellet's face, and Jamie pulled him down for a kiss.

"I'm fine, baby. You feel good. Don't stop."

Kellet didn't look convinced, so Jamie twitched his hips enough for Kellet to sink further into him.

"Oh fuck! Dammit, JJ." Kellet buried his face in Jamie's neck, pulling his hips backward and slowly thrusting back again. "Ungh. You feel... ahh... Jay." Kellet seemed to lose all power of speech as Jamie's channel relaxed, letting Kellet slide fully in.

Jamie was overwhelmed with a feeling of fullness, and he clung to Kellet's shoulders like a lifeline. It didn't take long for his body to want more, and rolled his hips, which caused Kellet to groan.

"Kel, please," he whimpered.

Kellet balanced on his elbows and began to thrust in and out of Jamie's body. *Oh, yes. This is what I've been missing all these years.* Jamie wrapped his legs around Kellet's waist, urging him on. The change in angle had Kellet brushing over his prostate and Jamie sped up, meeting Kellet thrust for thrust as heat flooded through him, his nails scraping along Kellet's shoulders as he pulled him closer.

"Right there, Kel," he ground out as he pushed a hand between their bodies so he could jerk his cock. Kellet grunted above him as he slammed into Jamie, and the sounds increased Jamie's desire. He barely had time to register the tingling in the base of his spine before his balls drew up tight, and he was coming, his release splattering over his stomach.

"Oh, shit. Jamie. Jamie. I'm… so good… ugh…" Kellet stammered above him before he tensed. Jamie felt Kellet's cock swell and kick inside him as the other man came. His hips shuddering as he rode the waves of his orgasm before collapsing into Jamie's arms.

Once he'd caught his breath, Kellet slowly pulled out and rolled onto his back with a groan. Jamie stretched his legs out, his hip complaining at the unaccustomed angle it had been subjected to. He winced, and Kellet immediately turned to him in concern.

"Did I hurt you? God, Jamie, please tell me if I hurt you."

The other man's distress was palpable, and Jamie rushed to reassure him.

"No, you didn't hurt me. I promise. I'll feel it tomorrow, but no, you didn't hurt me. I'm just not as flexible as I used to be," he said with a self-deprecating chuckle.

Kellet ran a callused hand along Jamie's ribs, and he arched into the caress.

"That was…"

"Yeah, it was," Jamie agreed as he pulled Kellet in for a slow, sensuous kiss.

They broke apart and smiled at each other.

"Shower?"

"Shower," Jamie agreed. "I'll order some food, too."

Kellet nodded and kissed him again before easing off the bed and heading to the bathroom. Jamie watched him go, noticing a couple of scratches on Kellet's back. The sight of them gave him an odd feeling of possessiveness. *I've marked my man up.* Jamie shook his head at his own silliness as he reached for the phone to order their dinner.

Zoe Piper

Chapter Twenty-Four

Kellet stretched out as much as he could in his bunk, trying to ease the kink in his back that had become semi-permanent over the last few weeks of traveling on the bus. Over the rumble of the engine, he could hear Jamie and Wil trash talking each other as they battled on one of the many video games they had loaded on the bus's gaming system.

"Ha! Sucker! Take that, old man!" Wil crowed.

"How the hell did you pull that move?" Jamie groused, and Kellet could imagine the scowl on his face.

"A master never tells his secrets," Wil intoned solemnly.

"I think I may have to ground you until you do," Jamie retorted.

Kellet tensed as he waited for Wil's reply.

"Bah! As if!" Wil said, snorting. "Even Dad wouldn't ground me for that."

"Has he grounded you often?" Amusement rang in Jamie's tone.

"Oh, he's grounded me a few times. Stopped my allowance once and made me work for no pay when I scratched his car."

"Ouch!"

"Yeah," Wil said ruefully. "Luckily, it wasn't too bad, and a friend of Mom's could fix it cheaply, but I learned how to park more carefully after that."

Kellet silently chuckled in his bunk. It hadn't been funny at the time, but he was enjoying listening to Wil and Jamie bond.

"Did you ever want kids, Jamie?" Wil asked.

Jamie was silent for a moment, and Kellet held his breath as he waited for the answer.

"I've never really thought about it, to be honest," Jamie replied quietly. "I mean, I don't not want children, but we've been so busy touring and everything over the years, the opportunity hasn't presented itself."

"You're not too old though, if you wanted to have kids now. I mean, look at Elton John. He was in his sixties when he and his husband had their kids."

Jamie chuckled. "I'm no Elton John, Wil." He paused again. "I suppose there's always the possibility that I'll want to have a kid one day, but right now, I'm happy with my life."

"Well, I think you'd be a pretty cool dad," Wil told him. "Now, load up, and I'll show you how I did that move."

Kellet swallowed the lump in his throat. He agreed with Wil; Jamie would make a pretty cool dad. In fact, he'd be a great dad, and Kellet felt guilty he'd denied Jamie the chance to be one to Wil.

He rolled onto his side, and through a gap in the privacy curtain, he could see their dark heads close together as they leaned towards the screen, urging their characters on. Wil was going to be devastated if he and Jamie didn't continue things after the tour. Hell, forget Wil; devastation didn't even cover how he would feel if Jamie decided it was all too hard after the tour.

He knew he loved Jamie and that he wanted forever with him, and he was fairly certain that Jamie wanted the same, but he still had his doubts about everything. He jabbed at the thin pillow under his head. Once they were on their mid-tour break, he and Jamie would sit down and hash everything out.

♫ ♫ ♫

Jamie grinned as Kellet appeared from the sleeping quarters on the bus and slid next to him on the dining booth seat.

"Have a good nap?"

"Ngh," Kellet grunted and dropped his head onto Jamie's shoulder with a sigh.

Seth laughed at him from the other end of the seating. "Don't worry, Kel, we're in Vegas tomorrow, and you'll have a large, comfortable bed to spread out in.

"Hmm, that'll be good," Kellet replied, nuzzling Jamie's neck, sending goosebumps down his spine.

"Oi, enough of that," Seth told them, taking the beer that Liam was offering him. "You can't be flaunting your thing in front of us when we aren't getting any."

"You, not getting any? That's a joke," Jamie shot back. Seth just raised a finger at him.

"Have you guys decided how you're going to handle everything when it becomes public knowledge you're a couple?" Liam asked, ignoring the antics of his bandmates.

Jamie shook his head. While Jamie wanted the world to know he and Kellet were together, Kellet was, understandably, a little more reluctant.

"I don't want to do anything to jeopardize the band and if Jamie and I being a couple is going to do that—"

"It's not going to affect the band, Kel," Jamie reassured him. "Look, we've already spoken to Miles, and he's let management know. They don't have an issue with it, and if the fans do, then that's their problem, not ours."

"Yeah, but what if—"

Jamie cut Kellet off again, this time by pressing a kiss to his lips. "Shh, Drummer Boy. We've got this, stop worrying."

"Worrying is Dad's default setting!" Wil yelled from his bunk, causing them to laugh.

"Okay?" Jamie asked quietly when Kellet didn't respond to his son's teasing.

"Yeah, I'm okay," Kellet replied with a smile.

Jamie understood Kellet's fears, and he hoped he could ease them as time went on and they settled into their relationship. He had his own fears, but he hadn't shared them, not wanting to add to the situation. He wasn't worried about the fans; he was worried how he was going to fit into the James family. Kellet, Andi, and Ro were a formidable team, and he felt like he was in high school again trying to fit in with the cool crowd. He and Wil had a good relationship, and he really liked the teenager.

His fingers lazily carded through Kellet's curls, and he felt Kellet relax into him.

"Drummer Boy, I understand you're worried. I get it, I really do. But do you trust me?"

"Of course, I do, JJ. I always have," Kellet sat up and took Jamie's hand in his. "I thought you knew that."

"I do," Jamie replied, squeezing their fingers together. "So, trust me when I say that everything is going to be okay, please? I... we've been doing this a long time. We've got an established fan base, and as long as Seth doesn't do something monumentally stupid, those fans will stick with us through thick and thin."

"Hey! Why I am always the one that gets singled out. Lee could do something to upset everyone," Seth protested.

Everyone stared at him until he sighed in resignation and threw his hands in the air.

"Just for that, I'm going to take all your money," he declared, dropping a pack of cards onto the table.

Jamie kissed Kellet on the cheek and got a grin in return. Hopefully, he'd gotten through to Kellet. Only time would tell.

Chapter Twenty-Five

Kellet jogged down the stage steps and gratefully accepted the towel one of the stagehands was holding out and used it to wipe his face and neck. He was riding the high that came from performing in front of the Las Vegas crowd. It had been their second sold-out concert in the vibrant city and had been as electric as all the others they had performed over the last month.

Kellet was secretly glad they only had one more show in Denver in three day's time and then they had an entire week off. Eight glorious days in one place. Eight days of sleeping in the same bed and sharing that bed with Jamie. They'd managed a few nights together in the occasional hotel they were booked in, but the rest of the time had been spent staring at Jamie across the aisle in the sleeping quarters of the tour bus.

Kellet made his way to his dressing room to gather his things, keen to get back to the hotel. He pulled on a fresh shirt and ran a hand through his hair as he glanced in the mirror to check his appearance. His skin was still flushed from being on stage, but he was tidy enough. Once he was back at the hotel, he planned to have a long, hot shower and, if everything went according to plan, Jamie would share it with him.

With a last glance around the room to check he had everything he needed, he left and knocked on the door just a few feet away.

"Coming!"

Kellet grinned and stuck his head into the dressing room. "Not without me, you're not," he said.

Jamie looked over from where he was pulling on his worn leather jacket and gave him a return grin.

"Hey, sexy."

"You ready to go?"

"Yep, but first..." Jamie gathered him in his arms before covering Kel's mouth with his own.

Kellet sank into the embrace, drawing him closer. Moments like these were all too brief and often interrupted.

Jamie slowed the kiss and eased away. "We need to get back to the hotel."

Tangling their fingers together, Kellet opened the door and led them out into the bustling corridor. They quickly made their way to the rear entry of the arena where Liam and Seth were waiting with Sarge. The ex-Marine gave them a side-eye.

"Glad you could join us."

They just grinned at him before following him out to where their car was waiting.

There were a few screams and shouts from some fans who had stayed after the show hoping to glimpse them. The guys smiled and waved before escaping into the confines of the large SUV.

Kellet sank into the comfortable leather and gave a sigh. He was equal parts wired and tired as the post-show rush slowly dissipated. Jamie sat as close as he could without being in Kellet's lap and the warmth of Jamie's hand on his thigh had him wishing they were alone already, and that talented hand was a little further north.

"I s'pose you two are going to disappear the second we reach the hotel, aren't you?" Seth said from the seat behind them.

"Probably," Jamie agreed, giving Kellet a heated look.

"Ugh! Enough with the eye-fucking, Larke," Seth groused before turning to nudge Liam who was concentrating on his phone. "Lee, tell me you're coming out with me for a drink."

"Huh? What? Oh, yeah, sure."

"Why are you so distracted? Have you found a hookup for the night?" Seth asked as he tried to peer at Liam's phone. The other man tucked it in his pocket while shaking his head in denial.

"Nah, just checking the comments about the show," Liam replied.

"Anything we should be worried about?" Kellet asked. He'd soon realized that Liam was the unofficial business manager of the group. Miles took care of the record label and all the official legal stuff, ably assisted and abetted by Jax, but Liam made a point of monitoring their social media accounts and after each show got the attendance numbers and merchandise sales figures emailed through to him.

Jamie had explained that Liam had always done it, not because he didn't trust Miles to look out for them, but because he'd heard too many horror stories of bands being ripped off. He'd insisted from day one that they needed to take an active role in how they were managed. Jamie had told him that Seth, Mark and himself had been more than happy to let Liam take care of it all.

"No, all good. I'll do a proper analysis once we're home after the Denver show, but we're tracking well and slightly ahead of budget for this stage in the tour."

"I think that calls for a celebratory drink," Seth declared. At the groans from his band members, he glared at them all. "We're in Vegas for fuck's sake. Just come and have one or two drinks and then you can all disappear off to do whatever the fuck you like."

Kellet glanced at Jamie who raised an eyebrow in return. He supposed it wouldn't hurt to have a couple of drinks. They had a late checkout the following day, planning to leave for Denver late in the evening to sleep for most of the twelve-hour journey.

"Alright then, Seth," Kellet said. "Give us half an hour to have a shower, and we'll meet you down in the bar."

Seth grinned and stretched across the seats to fist bump Kellet, before looking expectantly at Liam. Liam rolled his eyes and sighed.

"Okay. Two drinks, max."

"Yuss!" Seth crowed in delight. He pointed a finger at Kellet and Jamie. "And if you two are not in that bar in exactly thirty minutes, then I will come and find you."

♫ ♫ ♫

Jamie followed Kellet as the other man strode across the crowded hotel lobby towards the bar they'd agreed to meet in. In dark jeans and long-sleeved t-shirt, he exuded a confidence that attracted more than a few looks from both men and women alike.

There were a few whispers and stares as they were recognized, but Jamie didn't acknowledge them, not wanting to engage. As much as he loved and appreciated their fans, his only plans tonight were to have the required drinks with Seth and then hightail it back to their hotel room. He was counting down the days until they were on their mid-tour break and he and Kellet could relax at home and enjoy each other's company in private.

Not that they were hiding, just not publicizing their relationship. They'd had long talks with Miles and the management team, and with Seth and Liam, and they'd all agreed not to deny it if asked, but they weren't going to announce anything at this stage.

Have no doubt, Jamie wanted to shout from the rooftops that he and Kellet were together, but he was mindful of Kellet's privacy and desire to keep things between themselves as they rekindled their love for each other.

They paused at the bar entrance, scanning the crowd for any sign of their bandmates. Kellet tugged at Jamie's sleeve, indicating he'd seen them. Unconsciously, Jamie twined their fingers together and let Kellet pull him through the throng of people to the small, semi-private booth that Seth had commandeered.

There was just room enough for them to squeeze in, and Kellet slung an arm across the back of the seat, allowing Jamie to press in close, the warmth of Kellet's thigh pressing against his own. Sarge stood sentry duty a few feet away, making sure they weren't hassled by overeager fans.

"Not bad, guys," Seth said with a playful glance at his wrist, pretending to check the time on the non-existent watch.

"We figured the quicker we got here and did this, the quicker we can escape," Jamie retorted with a grin as he accepted the beer Liam pushed towards him.

"Sure is packed in here tonight," Kellet remarked as he looked around.

Jamie nodded in agreement. "Yeah, apparently there's some tech show on?"

"It's the premier software developers' convention. The who's who of the software development world is here," Liam commented.

"And you know this how?" Jamie drawled, though he really shouldn't be surprised that Liam knew. He had a knack for finding out information.

"Cal mentioned it when we were in Houston."

"Damn, I'd forgotten that," Sarge said as he pulled out his phone.

"Everything okay, Sarge?" Kellet asked their burly bodyguard, who was now scanning the bar.

"What? Oh, yeah, fine," he replied, distracted. "Hey, will you guys be okay for a few minutes? I need to check in with Cal."

"Of course," Jamie reassured him. "What's up with Cal? Is there anything we can do?" Jamie was concerned about their assistant. The man had been a quiet presence so far on the tour, but after the crew versus band laser tag battle in Dallas, they'd all looked at him in a new light. He had a dry sense of humor and he, Wil, and Sam had become as thick as thieves.

"It's not my story to tell, but let's just say that there are some real sharks in the IT world and Cal got caught up in some shit that went down," Sarge said.

"Sarge, go find him. We're not going to be here for much longer. I'm sure we can manage to stay out of trouble," Jamie said.

"I've got hold of Rosco. He'll be here in five minutes," Sarge told them, naming one of the other bodyguards on the team.

"Go, Sarge," Seth said, waving a hand at the bigger man. Jamie could see the concern on Seth's face, which was unusual, as Seth rarely cared about anyone other than himself.

With a nod, he disappeared into the crowds. The waitress came over and took their orders for another round, and they settled back into their seats. Both Seth and Liam seemed distracted, and Jamie leaned into Kellet to whisper in his ear.

"You good to go after this?"

Kellet turned his head, their faces so close it would only take a slight movement for their mouths to meet. "Definitely," he murmured, his breath hitching when Jamie's hand traveled up the in-seam of his jeans.

Jamie reached for the fresh bottle of beer the waitress had just placed on the table and took a couple of deep swallows. Kellet chuckled quietly beside him and did the same.

"There he is," Seth blurted, looking to a far corner of the bar.

"Who?"

"Cal."

Jamie looked over to where Seth was pointing and finally spotted their missing assistant. There were two men talking to him, and even though he didn't know Cal well, Jamie could see that he was uncomfortable.

"I'll message Sarge and let him know we've found him," Liam said, pulling up the messaging app on his phone.

"I think I'll just go over and let him know that Sarge is looking for him," Seth said, standing abruptly before downing the last of his beer.

Before anyone could say anything, he'd left the table and was striding over to where Cal was seated.

"He'd better not cause any trouble," Kellet said.

"Seth? Not cause trouble? Have you met him?" Liam said sarcastically.

Kellet acknowledged the question with a rueful nod. "Did you get hold of Sarge?"

"Yeah, he's coming down from Cal's room."

"In that case, why don't we head out?" Kellet said to Jamie. "There's no point in staying if Seth has abandoned us. Liam, are you going to stay?"

"I'm just going to finish this and make sure Seth is good, then I might go and check out the tables."

Jamie fist-bumped his friend before shuffling out of the booth, Kellet close behind him.

Jamie snagged a finger through Kellet's belt loop as they left the bar. They were halfway across the lobby when a muted squeal came from their right.

Jamie groaned internally, but turned and smiled at the young fan who was approaching them.

"Ohmygod, ohmygod, it's really you!"

"Hi, how are you tonight?" Jamie asked, and he felt Kellet straighten beside him, his own smile at the ready. Kellet had quickly learned how to put on a public face when meeting fans.

"Could we get a selfie, please?" the young girl asked, waving her phone at Jamie.

"Sure. What's your name?"

"Oh, I'm Ashlynne and this is my friend, Bethany."

Jamie smiled at them both and waited while each of them posed between him and Kellet. He gave a sigh of relief as Sarge appeared from the elevators as they were capturing people's attention, and he didn't want them getting caught in a scrum.

Sarge deftly got the girls sorted and with giggles and flushed faces, the two fans waved them off. Jamie was relieved the elevator had just arrived and emptied when he and Kellet got to it. They quickly stepped inside, and as the door closed, Kellet cupped a hand around his neck, drawing him close.

"There'd better not be any more interruptions tonight," he growled, moss green eyes dark with desire.

"Don't tempt fate, Drummer Boy," Jamie replied as they pressed their mouths together. Melting into the kiss, he willed the elevator to go faster.

Chapter Twenty-Six

Kellet wasn't sure what woke him; the incessant ringing of his phone or the banging on the door and Wil calling to him.

Years of fatherhood had him alert instantly, and he leaped out of bed to answer the door as Jamie woke and reached for his own phone that was also ringing. Something major must have happened and worry raced through Kellet's veins like ice.

He flung open the door to find his son, flushed faced and with a panicked look in his eyes.

"Wil, what's wrong? What's happened?" Kellet ran his gaze over him, searching for injury. "Are you okay?"

"Dad, have you checked your phone this morning?" Wil demanded, pushing his way into the room, running a hand through his hair; a nervous gesture Kellet recognized as one of his own.

"What? No, I just woke up? What's happened? Are your moms okay?"

"They're fine. Where's Jamie?" Wil asked, glancing around the small suite.

"I'm here, Wil," Jamie said, walking from the bedroom, phone in his hand. Kellet had a second to take in his sleep rumpled form before his attention was back on Wil.

"Oh, good. There's no easy way to say this," Wil said. Eyes skittering between the two of them, and Kellet didn't notice that Jamie had slid his palm into his until he felt a squeeze of his fingers.

"Just get on with it, son."

"The internet is blowing up with pictures of you two," Wil said, a slight blush staining his cheeks.

"Us two, how?"

"Um… holding hands and kissing when you got into the elevator, before the doors shut."

Kellet sank onto the nearby couch, Jamie falling next to him. "How?"

"Must have been those fans we did selfies with last night," Jamie muttered as he scrolled through his phone. "Miles has messaged to say he's on his way up."

"What? I thought he was in LA?"

"No, he flew in yesterday, something about a meeting with a new act he's heard about. He was going to meet us later before we leave for Denver, but he's shuffled his plans and is coming up now."

Jamie brushed an errant curl away from Kellet's brow, concern marring his features. "Are you okay, Drummer Boy? I know this isn't what we'd planned, but we've been lucky so far. It had to come out eventually."

Kellet grasped Jamie's fingers and pressed a kiss to his knuckles. "Yeah, I'll be fine. I'd hoped to keep things between us until the end of the tour, but I know that was wishful thinking."

"Um, Dad?" Kellet glanced up at his son. "You may want to put some pants on before Miles gets here," he said, amusement glittering in his eyes.

Kellet looked down, suddenly aware he was only clad in his boxers. Jamie chuckled beside him, and Kellet realized that the other man had pulled on a pair of jeans before he'd joined them.

"Not that I mind the view, but I don't want Miles and whoever is with him to catch an eyeful," Jamie said with a smirk.

Kellet gave him a quick kiss before standing and heading to their room to grab his jeans and quickly use the bathroom. When he returned, Miles and Liam were following in a room service trolley, and the scent of fresh coffee wafted into the room. Kellet took an appreciative sniff, much to Wil and Jamie's amusement.

Miles greeted them with a grim smile and helped himself to coffee once the server had left the room. The tension in the air was thick, and Kellet was grateful when Jamie put a reassuring hand on his thigh as he sat down next to him on the couch.

Miles stared at them for a moment, and Kellet tried not to squirm under the steely gaze. He and Jamie hadn't done anything wrong, and he refused to feel guilty for anything that had been reported.

"How bad is it?" he asked, needing to break the tension.

"Someone got pictures of you both last night holding hands outside the arena, again in the bar, and of you kissing in the elevator," Miles recited. He ran a hand over his face tiredly, and Kellet couldn't help but notice how worn out the older man looked. "The usual gossip sites are having a field day, and the slightly more reputable press have contacted us for a comment."

"So, you're going to release the prepared statement?" Jamie asked.

"Yes, Jax is adjusting it now, and she'll email it through shortly. Once you've checked it, we'll issue it, and hopefully, that will keep the sharks at bay for a while." Miles leaned forward in his chair, elbows resting on his thighs. "I've sent a couple of guys up to Juniper to keep an eye on your family, Kel. You'll want to ring and give them all a heads up that there'll be journalists nosing around, asking questions."

Kellet groaned and dropped his head onto the back of the sofa. The last thing he wanted was to drag his parents and Andi and Ro into this mess, but there was no escaping it.

"I've already spoken to Mom," Wil said from his seat in the corner, and Kellet snapped his head up to look at his son. Wil gave him a reassuring smile. "It's okay, Dad. She said to tell you she and Ma have been expecting it and they've got it covered. She's arranged for Mimi and Pops to stay with them, and Ma has drafted a brief statement from the family. She's emailing it to Jax, who'll send it out with the official release."

"Good work, Wil," Miles said approvingly, and Kellet swelled with pride at the way his son glowed at the praise. Despite his misgivings about Wil joining him on tour, it really had been the making of the teen and Kellet was seeing more and more the man his son was turning into.

"What do we do now?" he asked.

"We carry on as planned. The bus leaves for Denver at nine tonight. It's probably best that you lie low for the rest of the day. We'll arrange a car to meet you in the parking lot to try to avoid the paparazzi and fans that will be sure to be hanging around downstairs."

"Once the Denver show is over, you'll head home for the week and all being well, some other story will crop up, and you'll be left alone."

Miles stood, shoving his hands into his suit pants pockets. "I have to admit, Kel, you're taking this better than I thought you would."

"Yeah, a bit surprised at that myself," Kellet said ruefully, running a hand through his hair. "I guess I've always known it would happen. I don't want to hide what Jamie and I have; I just don't want to share it with the world. It's no-one else's business what we do once we're off that stage, but I know that's not a realistic expectation to have." He shrugged. "As long as I have Jamie in my life, I don't care what anyone else thinks."

Jamie gave his hand a tight squeeze at his words, and Kellet looked at the man that meant the world to him, surprised to see a shimmer in the familiar chocolate brown eyes. Kellet gave his own squeeze back. He understood the emotions Jamie was feeling.

"On that note, we'll head off, and I'll see you later." Miles offered his hand, and Kellet gave it a shake. "If you need me for anything, don't hesitate to call or message. Jax is also available if you need her."

"Thanks, Miles. We're just going to hang out, and we'll see you on the bus tonight."

Liam stood and came over to give them both a hug. "I'll see you tonight," he said quietly, and Kellet frowned at his friend.

"You okay, Lee?"

"Yeah, just tired," Liam replied, his eyes flitting to Miles before dropping briefly. "I'm going to catch some zee's, and I'll see you later."

As they left the suite, he turned to Jamie. "What was that all about?"

Jamie shrugged. "Beats me."

"I'm going back to my room. I'll see you later, Dad."

Kellet hugged his son. "Just call if you need anything."

The young man nodded and, with a hug for Jamie, quickly left the room.

"Come on, Drummer Boy. I need more sleep if I'm going to face the vultures later," Jamie said, tugging him towards the bedroom.

"JJ, are you okay with all of this? I know we've talked about it, but this is pretty big. I don't want it to affect you or your reputation. This is your life and your career that could be at stake."

Jamie tugged Kellet into his arms and kissed him softly.

"Kel, I've never hidden my sexuality. None of us have. The fans know that I'm gay, and even though I've never really had a serious relationship, there have been pictures and stories of me out with guys. This is only getting airtime because you're an unknown factor and new to the band." Jamie kissed him again, this time for a little longer. "If we have to weather a couple of news articles and the press hassling us for a week or two, then that's fine. As long as I have you, nothing else really matters."

Emotion swelled through Kellet. "Yeah, you're right."

"Come on. Let's hole up from the world for a few more hours. Once we've cleared the Denver show, we've got a week to hide and just be ourselves. We can get through the next few days," Jamie said as he led them to the bedroom.

♫ ♫ ♫

!MUSIC NEWS NOW!
**** BREAKING NEWS ****

Larkspur Lovers?

It appears there is more than friendship and a working relationship between Larkspur's lead singer, Jamie Larke, and their new drummer, Kellet James
.

The pair were seen and photographed last night after their show in Las Vegas holding hands and then locked in a passionate embrace in the hotel elevator.

James joined the band in May, replacing original drummer, Mark Sullivan. Sources close to the band have said that Larke and James have grown closer as the tour has progressed.

MC Management has confirmed the couple is in a relationship. While they appreciate everyone's interest, the couple asks that their privacy and that of their families be respected.

James has an eighteen-year-old son, who is on tour with him. His former lover and the boy's mother, Mrs. Andi Patton and her wife, respected San Francisco lawyer, Rowena Patton, have issued their own statement. In it, they advise they have known of the relationship from the beginning and are happy for the couple.

Wil chortled as he read the article on his tablet. "'… locked in a passionate embrace…'. Really, Dad, couldn't you wait until you were in the privacy of your hotel room?"

Kellet glared at his son. "It wasn't a passionate embrace. It was a simple kiss!"

"Whatever. The photo's not that great, anyway. You can hardly see anything, but you can tell you are kissing."

"Wil, just shut that thing down, please," Kellet implored. They were sitting on the tour bus, waiting for Seth. Their day had been quiet, and they had snuck out of the hotel a few hours earlier than expected, managing to beat the paparazzi lying in wait for them. A few had gathered at the stadium where the massive tour busses were waiting and apart from a few waves, they hadn't engaged.

The door to the bus hissed as it opened, and Goose, their driver, stuck his head into the cramped seating area.

"Leaving in five minutes," he told them before disappearing again to do his traditional walk around the bus. A former air force pilot, he treated the bus like one of his fighter jets, checking everything before they departed.

"Where the hell is Seth?" Jamie asked, glancing at his phone to see if he'd missed a message. The door hissed again, and Miles and Liam climbed aboard.

From the frown on Miles's face, his day had not improved since he'd seen them that morning. Liam walked past them and threw his duffle bag onto his bunk before slumping on the bench seat next to Wil and closing his eyes.

"Where's Seth?" Jamie repeated.

"Seth will meet us in Denver. He's flying in tomorrow afternoon. He's got some personal stuff to deal with," Miles told them, voice flat.

"Personal stuff? What kind of personal stuff?" Jamie asked, glancing at Liam, who seemed to slump even further into the seat. "Lee, do you know what's going on?"

Liam just shrugged, not opening his eyes. Kellet quirked an eyebrow at Jamie, who was looking as flummoxed as he felt.

"It's not my place to say anything," Miles said with a deep sigh. He pinched the bridge of his nose before looking at Jamie and Kellet. "In the seventeen years I've been managing this band, I've never had a twenty-four hours like this one. There must have been something in the water last night," he muttered.

Kellet was stunned. He'd never seen Miles look anything other than in control, but right then, he looked every one of his forty-two years and like a man who'd fought several battles in a short amount of time.

"Miles, is there anything we can do?" Kellet asked.

"Yeah. Stay out of trouble for the next few days. Do the Denver show, then please, just disappear for a week." He gave them both a tired smile. "Everything will be fine. Don't worry. Jax will be around if you need her." The sharp gray eyes fell on Liam.

"Liam."

The bass guitarist's eyes flew open at the sound of his name.

"I'll see you after the next show. Remember what I said." Miles's tone was commanding, and Liam sat up a little straighter and nodded.

"Yeah, okay. I… I'll see you in Denver."

With a final nod to them all, Miles left the bus. Within moments, Goose was in the driver's seat, and the diesel engine rumbled into life.

"What the fuck is going on, Lee?" Jamie growled. "What shit has Seth gotten up to this time, and what's with all the looks and stuff from Miles?"

"All I know is Seth disappeared this morning and that he'll join us in Denver," Liam answered, standing up. "I'm going to bed. I'll see you tomorrow."

Liam climbed into his bunk, pulling the privacy curtain tight, leaving Jamie, Kellet, and Wil to stare at each other.

"I haven't been able to get hold of Cal all day, either," said Wil. "I hope he's okay."

"I'm sure Jax has got him busy, what with the news this morning and now Seth disappearing," Kellet reassured him. "Why don't you put some popcorn on, and we'll download a movie to watch."

As Wil happily took the distraction his father offered, Kellet pulled Jamie into his arms, seeking solace in the one thing that could distract him from the crazy goings on.

Zoe Piper

Chapter Twenty-Seven

Jamie adjusted the volume in his in-ear monitor as he strutted across the Denver stage towards Seth. The lead guitarist threw him a grin, but it wasn't his usual cocky one. Jamie recognized it as the manufactured smirk he gave when he was portraying the role of rock star, not the fun-loving best friend Jamie had known for nearly twenty years.

Slinging an arm around Seth's shoulders, he leaned against his bandmate as he launched into the detailed riff of Hard Up for Love. Seth didn't miss a note, but Jamie couldn't help but notice the tenseness in Seth's shoulders. Usually, the man was so laid back; he was almost horizontal.

Jamie picked up the vocals again, and with a playful hip check, left Seth and ambled towards the rear of the stage where Kellet was. The screams from the crowd intensified, something Jamie had noticed all night whenever he got near the drummer. As he hit the main chorus, he blew a kiss to Kellet, which, of course, the fans lapped up. There had been an outpouring of support and love for them on social media ever since the news of their relationship had broken.

Kellet, now completely at home on stage, winked back at him, which was picked up on the large video screen. With a laugh, Jamie finished his lap of the stage, ending up next to Liam who just grinned and shook his head at him.

Twenty minutes later, the four of them stood at the front of the stage and took their final bows.

"Thank you everyone, stay safe on the trip home," he called out to the audience. With a last wave, they left the stage and Jamie couldn't help breathe a sigh of relief. It had been one of their harder shows, mainly because Seth had not been on his game.

"Thank fuck that's over," Liam said, surprising them all as he rounded on Seth. "Where were you tonight?"

"Umm... about ten feet to your right," Seth bit back caustically.

"Physically maybe, but mentally, you weren't here. What's going on, Seth?"

"Nothing you need to worry about, Lee."

"Yeah, well, I think I do if it's affecting your performance," Liam said, facing off against his bandmate.

"Oh, I've never had any complaints about my performance, don't you worry," Seth shot back.

Liam stepped up into Seth's personal space. "Listen here, Seth. You can put on a show of bravado and arrogance for the public, but this is us. We know you too well to accept your bullshit posturing," he said, poking a finger into Seth's chest.

Jamie jumped between them, pulling Liam away before Seth could retaliate.

"Hey, now guys, come on. We don't need to do this here," he said, doing his best to break the tension.

"We don't need to do it at all," Seth retorted, pulling away from the hand Kellet had placed on his shoulder. "We all have bad days. Today is my turn, alright?" With that, he turned away and strode off towards the dressing rooms, anger radiating from him like a beacon.

"What was that all about, Lee? You know better than to corner him like that," Jamie said.

"Sorry, I just…" Liam sighed and ran a hand through his sweat-dampened hair. "Seth's right. We all have bad days. He's not the only one."

"Talk to me, Liam. What's going on?" Jamie asked as they fell into step towards the dressing room.

"Nothing. I'm tired. We normally don't schedule the break so late into the tour, and I guess I just need some time out from all of this," he replied, waving a hand at the hustle and bustle of the crew breaking down the set.

Jamie took a good look at his friend, noticing the signs of tiredness and strain around the other man's eyes and mouth. Guilt rushed through him. He'd been so wrapped up in Kel, he hadn't noticed that both of his bandmates were going through whatever shit it was.

"I'm sorry, Lee," he apologized, laying a hand on Liam's shoulder.

"Sorry for what?" Liam replied frowning.

"Not realizing you and Seth needed me. I've been so busy with Kel, I haven't spent as much time as I should have with you two."

Liam shook his head emphatically. "No. Don't think that. You and Kel deserve the time you've spent together. Seth and I have been doing this long enough."

"That doesn't mean that we can't be here for both of you when you need us," Kellet said, joining the conversation. He slipped an arm around Jamie's waist, and Jamie relaxed into the quiet strength.

"It's all good," Liam replied, smiling softly. "A week at home, sleeping in the same bed will do me the world of good."

"True that," Jamie agreed. "We're flying straight to San Francisco and then heading up to Juniper."

"But, if you need us for anything, just call, okay?" offered Kellet. "Hell, you can even come and stay too if you want to."

"Thanks, but I'm good hanging at home." Liam extended his fist, which both Jamie and Kellet bumped before Jamie dragged him into a hug.

With promises to call in a few days' time, they parted ways. Jamie quickly gathered his gear from the dressing room, and soon, he and Kellet were on their way to the hotel. In a few short hours they'd be on a plane home, and he couldn't wait.

Chapter Twenty-Eight

Kellet pushed open the front door of his house, and a sense of peace enveloped him as he stepped over the threshold. Jamie shuffled in behind him, closing the door on the shouts from the journalists that were hanging around on the sidewalk.

"Suppose it was too much to expect they wouldn't be here," he said, throwing his keys onto the small hall table.

"Yeah, but Sarge has arranged some of his team to monitor things. I believe he's even spoken to the local sheriff who's going to do regular drive-by's to make sure things don't get out of control," Jamie replied, pressing himself to Kellet's back and kissing the nape of his neck. "We could have stayed at my place," he reminded Kellet, and he sighed and turned to face him.

"I know, but I needed to come home. I have to catch up with Andi and stuff happening at the bar."

"I know you did, and I have no problem being here with you," Jamie reassured him, sincerity shining in his eyes. "When do you see Andi?"

"Not until tomorrow sometime."

"So, we have the whole day to ourselves?" Jamie quirked an eyebrow at him.

Kellet nodded, before kissing him slowly, taking in the familiar taste of him. Jamie hummed and melted into him.

Kellet deepened the kiss, running his hands over Jamie's butt as he pulled him closer. He could feel his erection through the denim of his jeans and heat flared through him. He briefly considered stripping Jamie where they stood, but immediately dismissed the idea at the thought of making love on his hardwood floor.

He broke away and tugged Jamie towards the stairs and up to his bedroom. Shutting the door behind them, he quickly crossed the room and drew the curtains, throwing it into cool shadows. He didn't want any nosy reporter with a telephoto lens peering through his window, even if it was on the second story.

Turning back to Jamie, he found the other man half naked, shirt abandoned and his jeans halfway down his thighs. Kellet ripped off his own shirt and, after toeing off his boots, made short work of removing his own jeans.

Jamie met him on the bed, their mouths meeting in a heated rush, both groaning as their heavy cocks brushed against each other. Kellet threw his thigh over Jamie's, trying to draw him closer. In return, Jamie's hand trailed down his spine to settle at the top of his crease. Fire raced through Kellet's veins, thickening his already hard cock, a bead of pre-come leaking from the slit. He reached back and shoved Jamie's hand further down onto the swell of his ass.

"Do you want something, Drummer Boy?" Jamie asked huskily, his mouth nibbling along the column of Kellet's throat.

"You, JJ. Always you."

Warm fingers traced Kellet's crease before dipping between the firm muscles, and Kellet twitched at the touch against his sensitive nerves. Jamie didn't linger though, drawing his hand back to stroke Kellet's dick before cupping his balls and tugging on them.

"Tell me there's lube nearby," Jamie said, his voice low in the semi-darkness of the room.

"There should be some in the nightstand," Kellet replied, not wanting to let Jamie go for even the few seconds it would take to reach across the bed. Jamie rolled over the top of Kellet, lingering only to kiss Kellet deeply before stretching to pull out the drawer.

Jamie grinned triumphantly as he found his prize and he sat back on his heels, straddling Kellet. Kellet gazed up at the gorgeous man. Jamie's hair was mussed, his face flushed, and pupils blown dark with desire. Kellet had never seen such a glorious sight, and it was one he never wanted to lose again.

He traced a hand up Jamie's abdomen and ribs, fingers skimming over the tattooed musical notes. Jamie twitched under his touch, goosebumps rising along his flesh. His cock bobbed in response, the mushroom head dark against the paler skin of his stomach.

"I love you," Kellet told him, hoping that Jamie could see he meant it with every fiber of his being.

Jamie leaned down to capture his mouth. "Love you, too."

The kiss was slow and sensual, both of them expressing their feelings in a way that words never could. Jamie drew back, flicking the lid on the lube bottle before generously coating his fingers.

He shuffled down the bed until he was kneeling between Kellet's thighs. Without conscious thought, Kellet brought his knees up and opened himself to Jamie.

Jamie's eyes deepened in desire, and he reached for Kellet's straining cock. Kellet didn't have time to prepare himself for the onslaught of sensation as Jamie took him into his mouth, tongue teasing the sensitive spot just below the crown. He gripped the bed cover as Jamie sucked and licked his way up and down his shaft and slid a finger into him.

A loud moan echoed in the room as Kellet jerked his hips up. He ran his hand up his chest, tweaking at his nipples. A shot of heat raced through him as Jamie moaned as he eased a second finger into Kellet.

"Fuck, Kel, you are so hot right now," Jamie huffed as he pulled off Kellet's cock and raised up on his elbow so he could examine every inch of the man spread out in front of him.

Kellet reached for the discarded lube and smeared some on his fingers before wrapping his hand around Jamie's cock. He stroked from base to tip, causing Jamie to thrust into his fist, his glistening cock swelling further.

"Not going to last if you keep that up," Jamie said, pulling away, his breath coming in pants as he fought to control himself.

In reply, Kellet spread his thighs further and pulled his knees up towards his chest. Jamie got the blatant hint and eased himself down, brushing against Kellet's hole.

With a final check to make sure Kellet was ready

for him, Jamie slowly pushed his way into Kellet's body. Kellet gave a small involuntary grunt as he was breached, and Jamie paused until he felt Kellet relax under him.

Kellet took some slow, deep breaths and focused on Jamie's rich brown eyes. As always, he fell into their depths, seeing right to Jamie's soul. A soul that shone with love and desire for him. Once he was fully seated, Kellet wrapped a leg around his waist, holding the other man as close as he could, wanting to hold on to the feeling of fullness and completeness for as long as he could.

He could see how much restraint Jamie was exercising in not moving, and he needed to feel Jamie pounding inside of him. He dropped his leg back onto the bed and rolled his pelvis. Jamie gasped before his control snapped, and he moved until he almost slid out of Kellet before slamming back into him.

They both groaned and then Jamie began thrusting, his movements strong and fluid. He balanced his weight on elbows, pressing his hips as far into Kellet as he could. Kellet's cock was trapped between them, the friction from Jamie's treasure trail sending sparks through Kellet with every pass.

Jamie pushed onto his knees and hitched Kellet's thighs higher, the angle change causing him to brush against Kellet's prostate.

"There… oh yeah…" Kellet arched his back as he drove himself down onto Jamie. He reached for his own cock, stroking frantically as wave after wave of heat rushed through him.

"You close, baby?" Jamie ground out, his eyes fixed on Kellet.

"Yeesss…" Kellet whimpered as his lower back tingled. "Oh, Jay… fuck! Aargh!"

Kellet's last words were a shout as his orgasm hit him, his cock spurting over his stomach. His inner muscles clamped around Jamie, who was thrusting short and sharply into Kellet. Jamie's rhythm stuttered, and he pushed deeply into Kellet as his own release escaped.

Kellet felt the heat of Jamie's come fill him, and he flexed involuntarily, causing Jamie to gasp and thrust again. They'd done away with condoms shortly after sleeping together the first time. They were both negative and had been tested as part of the pre-tour medical.

Jamie gave him a messy kiss as he pulled out. He went to roll away, but Kellet caught him and gathered him close.

"We should clean up," Jamie muttered as he snuggled into Kellet's side.

"In a minute. There's no rush. We don't have to be anywhere."

"Hmm. That's good, 'cos I don't think I could move, even if I wanted to."

Kellet pressed a kiss to the top of Jamie's head, breathing in the scent of leather and wood and the muskiness of sweat and sex. Nope, he wasn't going anywhere either.

Chapter Twenty-Nine

Kellet parked in his spot behind East Bank and glanced up at the familiar brick building. It felt strange to be here. He'd been working here in one capacity or another for over twenty years, and he'd enjoyed every minute. But now, he felt like an interloper instead of the owner.

As he walked down the short corridor from the rear staff entrance, the recognizable smells of beer and cleaning polish were evident. He could hear muted chatter from the front of the building where the cleaning crew would be clearing up from the night before, and the bar staff would set up for the day.

His body ached, but in all the best ways. He and Jamie had made love again, finally falling asleep just after midnight. They'd slept for a good solid eight hours, with only their grumbling stomachs waking them, rather than an alarm or Wil calling them to get ready to leave.

He'd reluctantly left Jamie on the couch, where the other man had settled in with the tv remote. With a lingering kiss and a promise not to be too long, Kellet had been pleasantly surprised to see no waiting reporters outside of his house. As he'd pulled the Mustang out of the driveway, he spotted a police car sitting a couple of doors up the street. He lifted a hand in thanks and got a nod in return.

Walking into the main bar area, he smiled at the sight of Andi taking stock of the liquor bottles lining the back of the bar. She scribbled something on the clipboard next to her, and as she raised her head, she caught sight of him in the mirror that backed the bar.

She gave an excited squeal and spun to face him. He grinned at her and opened his arms as she raced towards him, catching her in a tight hug. Her light floral perfume enveloped him, and he buried his face in the mess of long, dark hair that she rarely had tamed.

"Oh, Kel," she said, eyes bright as she captured his face between his palms.

He pressed a kiss to her forehead before resting his own against hers. "Hey, Andi."

Emotions raced through him as he hugged his best friend. He hadn't realized how much he'd missed her until that moment. They'd rarely had a day when they hadn't spoken or texted each other, but this summer had been the longest they'd ever gone without seeing each other.

Andi stepped back from his embrace but kept her hands on his shoulders as her gaze ran up and down him. "Oh, Kel," she repeated. "You look amazing!"

"I what?" he asked in amusement. "I've been working the strangest hours known to man, surviving on a few hours sleep that was earned in a bunk bed no bigger than a decent-sized tomb, and you think I look amazing?"

"You do," Andi insisted as she swiped his shoulder in a friendly cuff, before leading him over to the bar. She slipped behind and made them both an espresso from the small barista machine they'd installed a few years ago.

"You look like you've buffed up a bit, and yes, you look tired, but there's a... a glow about you that just shines." She handed him his coffee, a mischievous glint in her eyes. "How's Jamie?"

Kellet couldn't help the sappy grin as he thought of his lover.

"Annd, that grin says it all," Andi crowed. He flicked her the bird, and she burst out laughing. "I'm happy for you, Kel. You deserve this." With her own coffee in hand, she joined him at the bar and rested a hand on his knee, the familiar touch grounding Kellet in a way he hadn't realized he'd needed.

"So, tell me all about it. Tell me everything!" she said, leaning forward, her features alight with happiness.

Kellet filled her in on the last few months, and then she returned the favor, telling him of her and Ro's trip to Europe and how things had been going at the bar.

"So, what happens now?" she asked, "now that the tour is almost finished?"

"I don't really know," he admitted. "To be honest, we've not talked about it. You fall into a routine of just focusing on the next show. Travel, soundcheck, perform, sleep, travel. Rinse and repeat."

"But you've enjoyed it?" Andi asked, tilting her head as she questioned him.

"I have. It's been something I never dreamed I'd get to do, and to do it with Jamie and the guys, well..." Kellet blew out a sigh. He wasn't lying. He had enjoyed the past few months, even though they had been hard work and stressful at times.

"What's going to happen with you and Jamie once the tour is over? Are you going to move down to LA to be with him?" Something in Andi's tone made Kellet sit up and really look at her.

"What's going on, Andi?"

"Nothing, I'm just curious what you are going to do come the fall. The tour will be over, Wil will be at college, Jamie will be in LA. What are you going to do, Kel? Or more to the point, what do you want to do?"

Kellet pondered her words as cold reality hit him. "I… I don't know," he confessed. What did he want to do? He wanted to be with Jamie, but how was that going to work?

"I think you need to talk to Jamie, find out what his plans are for after the tour and for both of you. I can't imagine he wants to be apart from you any more than you want to be apart from him."

"But…,"

"And before you say 'but what about the bar, what about us?', think of yourself first for once, Kel," Andi said, laying a gentle hand on his face. "I want you to go home to that hot man of yours and have a really good talk with him. Ro and I will be over with dinner later on, and we can work out some plans for the future. Okay?"

"Don't let Ro hear you calling Jamie hot," Kellet said with a half grin.

"Heh, she called him hot first, so I'm all good," Andi retorted with a wave of her hand. Kellet burst into laughter and hauled her into his arms.

"God, I've missed you," he said, squeezing her tight.

"We've missed you too." With a last hug, Andi let him go. "Now go on. I've got things covered here. You go and talk to Jamie. And I mean talk. No getting distracted, you hear me?"

"No promises there. As you've already pointed out, I have a hot man waiting for me, it's not my fault I'm easily distracted when he's around," Kellet said with a smirk and a wink.

♫ ♫ ♫

Jamie woke from his light doze at the sound of a key opening the front door. He levered himself onto his elbows just as Kellet walked into the room, who gave him a grin when he saw him.

"You obviously haven't moved since I left you," Kellet stated as he leaned over the back of the couch to brush a soft kiss against Jamie's lips.

"Someone wore me out last night," Jamie retorted, sitting up fully and swinging his legs around onto the floor. He glanced at his phone to check the time. "You're home earlier than I thought you would be. Everything okay with the bar and Andi?"

"Yep, everything's fine," Kellet replied, flopping onto the couch next to him. Something in his tone had Jamie looking at him closely. There was a frown line marring Kellet's forehead and tension in his shoulders.

"Hey," Jamie said softly, turning Kellet to face him, "what's wrong?"

Kellet blew out a sigh and rubbed a hand through his hair. "Nothing's wrong. Andi says the bar has been doing well over the summer and she and Ro had an amazing trip to Europe."

"But…"

"What's gonna happen after the tour, JJ?" Kellet asked in a worried tone.

"What do you want to happen?"

"Don't counter with another question, Jamie. I'm serious, I need to know what's going to happen between us and… and everything."

"Kellet, babe. I want to have everything with you. I thought you knew that?" Jamie was starting to feel nervous. Did Kellet not want the same?

"I do, but what is your definition of 'everything'?" Kellet asked, using air quotes around the last word.

"You in my life, waking up with you, going to sleep next to you, every single day." Jamie searched Kellet's face for a clue how the other man was feeling. "Do you… do you not want the same thing?"

"Of course I do," Kellet replied emphatically. "I don't even want to think about not having you in my life ever again, but JJ, we've got to be realistic. How are we going to make it work? You've got your life in LA, and I've got mine here."

Relief coursed through Jamie. Thank God. They were on the same page. He smiled warmly at Kellet before giving him a quick kiss. "That's just logistics, babe."

"But I can't ask you to leave your home and move here, and I can't commute from LA to Juniper to run the bar."

"Ah, Drummer Boy. You still don't get it do you," he said fondly as he cradled Kellet's face in his hands.

"Get what, JJ? What is there to get?" Kellet's confusion was obvious.

"Do you remember, when I came back here, in May, to ask you to join the band?"

"Of course, I do. I'm not likely to forget something like that. I'm old, not senile."

"Firstly, you are not old. We're the same age, and I consider myself to be in the prime of my life, so you must be too," Jamie told him with a roll of his eyes. "Anyway, as I was saying, do you remember telling me I was a long way from home, and I said that this would always be home?"

Kellet frowned and nodded. "But I'm still not seeing where you're going with this, JJ."

"You, my gorgeous, sexy, love-of-my-life, Drummer Boy, you are my home. Wherever you are, that is my home. I don't care where we live, as long as we're together. If you want to move to, I dunno, South Dakota, then I'll be right there beside you, every step of the way."

"South Dakota, huh?" Kellet said with a smirk, and Jamie was glad to see the tension ease from his shoulders.

Jamie leaned his forehead against Kellet's, his voice a whisper. "Anywhere in the world, Kellet. We've lost too many years already; I'm not losing any more."

"Me neither," Kellet agreed as he took Jamie's mouth in a searing kiss.

Chapter Thirty

Kellet's phone buzzed with a message just as he was pulling on a clean, dark green t-shirt. It was from Andi telling him she and Ro were only five minutes away. He ran his fingers through his hair and checked his reflection. Eh, good enough. His skin was only slightly flushed from the shower, and that would have gone by the time the ladies arrived.

He ventured downstairs and found Jamie on the phone, a frown on his face.

"Yeah, okay, Miles. I guess we'll see you in Seattle then. Yeah, I'll tell him. Thanks. Bye."

"Is everything okay? Why was Miles calling?"

"He called to make sure we weren't being hassled by the press and I told him, apart from the odd one or two hanging around, we'd been good," Jamie replied, slipping his phone into his back pocket.

He slid his arms around Kellet's waist. "I like that shirt on you. The color really brings out your eyes," he told him before kissing him.

Kellet broke the kiss and grinned at him. "As much as I'd like to continue this," he said, waving a finger between them, "Andi and Ro are about to knock on the door."

"Is Wil with them?" Jamie asked, moving to lean against the kitchen counter.

"No. He's out with his friends. Andi said there's some party for him so everyone can see him before he heads out with us again next week. Once the tour's over, he's only got a few days before he leaves for college, so he's making the most of the time he's got this week."

A knock had Kellet grinning, and with a wink, he left Jamie to let their guests in. He opened the door to find Andi and Ro laden down with insulated bags, and he quickly reached to take a couple of them.

"How much food did you bring?" he asked as he kissed each of them on the cheek. "You know Wil is staying with you, right?"

Ro laughed as she headed towards the kitchen. "Mama made your favorite, Kel. I didn't think you'd mind me bringing extra. At least that way, the rest of us may get some."

"Tell your mother I love her," Kellet said as he dumped the bags onto the table. He opened the first bag and inhaled the familiar scent of fried chicken. He closed his eyes in bliss.

"Shit, Drummer Boy. The last time you looked like that, we'd just..." Jamie's comment was quickly shut off by Andi's hand across his mouth.

"Don't finish that sentence, Jamie Larke," she mock-growled at him. "I want to enjoy my meal."

"Thank you, Andi," Kellet said with a glare at his boyfriend, who laughed and tugged Andi into a hug."

Kellet laid out the food that Mama Patton had sent as Jamie, Andi, and Ro greeted each other. They served themselves and settled around the table where they chatted as they ate, catching up on each other's news.

Once they'd had their fill, they relaxed, sipping from the chilled wine Kellet had poured.

"So, did you two talk?" Andi asked Kellet with a raised eyebrow.

"Yeah, we did. Apparently, it's just a logistics issue, but we're going to figure it out," Kellet told her. He reached across the table to link his fingers with Jamie's, who smiled at him lovingly.

"I already knew that you would. What I want to know is are you staying with the band?"

He tensed. They hadn't talked about that. He looked to Jamie to see what his response was and found dark chocolate eyes watching him intently.

"You didn't talk about that, did you?" Ro said with amusement.

"Not really, no," Kellet admitted. "Am I going to stay with the band, JJ? I remember you mentioned something back at the beginning about me staying on if things worked out, but did you mean it?"

"Of course, I meant it. I rarely say anything I don't mean," Jamie assured him. "If you want to stay part of the band, then of course there's a place for you. I mean, this tour has been unlike any other we've played. All due respect to Mark, he's a talented drummer and a good friend, but he's not you, Kel."

"Do Seth and Liam agree? What about the label?"

"The label is happy as long as we're happy and bringing in money for them. We've only got one more album on this current contract, and we'll start that in the new year." Jamie leaned across the table, his gaze intent. "You're a part of Larkspur, Kel. You always have been. I know Seth and Liam feel the same way."

Kellet nodded as he mulled over what Jamie had said. He knew, deep down, that the others wanted him in the band, but it was still good to have Jamie confirm it. Although touring was hard work and not as glamorous as everyone thought; just playing music every day and being part of something like Larkspur had awakened something in Kellet he hadn't realized wasn't there anymore.

He brushed a kiss across Jamie's knuckles and glanced over to find Andi and Ro smiling at them indulgently.

"Well, that makes this easier to say," Andi said before taking a large gulp of wine. With an encouraging nod from her wife, she continued. "Traveling to Europe this summer has made us realize that we want to spend more quality time together. Time that isn't locked into school schedules and work commitments."

"What are you saying, Andi?"

"We didn't get to travel and go adventuring in our early twenties like a lot of our peers did," she explained. "Not that I regret a single moment of being a mother and being a partner in the bar, I don't," she rushed to assure him. "But now Wil is off to college, you've got a new adventure of your own, and well, Ro and I want that too."

Kellet sat back in his chair. He was thrown by Andi's statement. It hadn't occurred to him she may want something different than the life they'd chosen, and a rush of guilt went through him.

"Don't, Kel," Ro scolded. "I know what you're thinking, and it's not true. Andi and I have done exactly what we wanted for the last fourteen years, so don't start feeling guilty for thinking you trapped Andi into something she didn't want."

"Dammit, Ro. I wish you wouldn't use your super-lawyer senses on me," Kellet joked, easing the tension in the room.

"I do what I do best, Kel. You know that," she retorted with a wink.

"So, what's the plan?" Kellet asked Andi. "I know you've got something up your sleeve, so drop the innocent act."

"We've had an offer for the bar," Andi told him, watching closely for his reaction.

"Who?"

"Tomas."

Kellet was surprised. "Tomas. Our Tomas. Our manager?" At Andi's nod, Kellet smirked. "How much have we been paying him if he can afford to buy East Bank?"

"We pay him well, as you know, but he and two friends have pooled their resources and made an offer."

"How much?" Kellet asked. He had a rough idea of what the going price would be, but he was curious to see what Tomas and his friends thought it was worth.

"Not quite market value," Andi admitted. As Kellet opened his mouth to comment, she held up a hand, stopping him. "Wait a minute, there's more. They are offering to buy a sixty percent share, leaving us as silent partners with the balance."

"Huh. That's not a bad deal, Kel," Jamie said, chiming into the conversation for the first time. "You'd still have an income from it, but without all the hassle of having to run it."

"I'd still need to do something for money though," Kellet said.

"Babe, I have enough money for both of us. That is not an issue."

Kellet shook his head vehemently. "No. I'm not sponging off you, JJ. I earn my keep."

Jamie groaned and dropped his head to the table. Andi leaned over and patted him on the shoulder.

"What?" Kellet asked, confused by the actions of his boyfriend and best friend.

"You will earn your keep," Jamie told him in exasperation. "You'll have your share of the earnings from the tour, plus you'll get the royalties from the next album. Miles has the papers already drawn up, making you a permanent band member. He's sending them to Ro to go over so you can sign them this week before we head to Seattle."

"Oh. He mentioned something about papers to sign when we saw him in Vegas, but I thought it was all to do with the drama that happened there."

"I think Miles was a bit distracted with everything going on. What with Seth disappearing and who only knows what the hell is happening between him and Liam, with all the cryptic conversations."

"Sounds like a soap-opera episode," Ro said with a chuckle.

"You have no idea, Ro," Jamie told her. "I swear, it's not normally like this. Yes, Seth will usually do something stupid, and Liam will calm the waters and keep us all in line, but this last week has been out of the ordinary."

"Hopefully, the last few weeks of the tour will be quieter," Ro commented as she sipped from her wine.

"You guys are coming to the final show, aren't you?" Jamie asked.

"Wouldn't miss it for the world. We thought about going to the San Francisco show, but then when you offered us a place to stay in LA, we thought we'd make a few days of it," Andi told, excitement shining in her eyes. "Then we can bring Wil home with us to get ready for college." She gave a mini shudder. "Kel, how the hell are we old enough to have a college-age kid?"

Kellet looked at Andi fondly. She was a beautiful woman and one he was proud to call a friend. He couldn't have asked for anyone better to have a child with. "We got lucky, Andi. I know that Wil wasn't in our plans, and who knows what may have happened later down the track, but having the two of you in my life has made it richer." He toasted her with his wineglass.

"Oh, Kel," Andi sniffed as she clasped his free hand. "You are the best baby-daddy a girl could ask for."

"And that's enough wine for you, wife," Ro chuckled, tucking Andi into her side and kissing her temple. She looked over at Jamie. "These two get terribly maudlin and renew their mutual admiration society membership when they've had a few wines."

"Good to know," Jamie said, grinning. "I think we need to do lunch, Ro, and swap notes."

"You stay away from her, JJ. She's sneaky, and she's a lawyer," Kellet teased. "She'll have you revealing all sorts of secrets before you even know it."

Kellet looked around the table as they all laughed, his gaze lingering on the dark-haired man who held his heart. Life really couldn't get any better than this.

Chapter Thirty-One

The Staples Center was lit up like the night sky in the desert, small lights twinkling like stars in the darkness as the crowd held up their cell phones as they joined Jamie as he sang the final ballad of the show and of the tour.

It would never get old—the touring and performing—it was what he lived for. That and Kel, of course. The music quieted as Jamie hit the song's crescendo; his voice strong as he conveyed all the feelings swirling through him. Gratefulness. Joy. Happiness. Love.

The song ended, and Jamie blew kisses to the crowd as he stalked back up the stage walkway. Seth gave him a grin as the spotlights changed color and Kellet rapped out the opening count of the next song on his drumsticks. After a quick mouthful of water, he was once again front and center.

"Ah, Los Angeles, you look so pretty tonight," Jamie said a few songs later. "As you know, this is the last night of our tour. A tour that started back in January in Sydney, Australia, and that has taken us all over the world." Cheers and whistles echoed back at him.

"We've had some amazing adventures, and there have been some big changes in our lives." Jamie turned and grinned at his bandmates before turning back to the crowd. He waved a hand toward the

VIP area. "I am so happy that Mark is here tonight to help us celebrate a successful tour. We've missed having you around, buddy."

He grinned down into the VIP area where all their families were, along with Mark and his fiancée, Selena. Jamie had been pleasantly surprised when Miles had said that their former drummer was coming to the last show. They hadn't had a chance to catch up yet, but Mark gave him a grin and a thumbs up as Jamie caught his eye.

"A tour like this doesn't just happen. It takes months of planning and organizing. We'd like to thank all our amazing management team for the work they put in. To our crew; we couldn't be out here doing what we love every night if it wasn't for you guys preparing the sets and then breaking them down and getting them to the next city, sometimes even before Seth has had time to wake up and have a coffee."

Seth flicked a finger at him in response, a grin lighting his features.

"To Larry, our tour manager; Jax, PA extraordinaire; able assistants Wil and Cal; head of security, Sarge and all of his minions who do their hardest to keep us where we're supposed to be and out of trouble, we thank you."

Jamie paused as the crowd showed their appreciation. "And to you, our fans. Thank you for your support. Thank you for buying our music. Thank you for coming out to shows like this. We love and appreciate you all."

Jamie stepped to the side of the stage so he could see his bandmates. "And finally, I want to say a personal thank you to these guys. Without you, there wouldn't be a Larkspur, and I am grateful that we get to work together every day. You're my family, and I love you all."

"Especially Kellet!"

Jamie laughed at the shout from the crowd. He wasn't a hundred percent sure, but he was certain that had been Andi's voice. He looked up to his Drummer Boy. Apart from the statement they'd issued after Las Vegas, they hadn't publicly acknowledged their relationship. He quirked an eyebrow and Kellet grinned back at him, giving him the permission he sought.

"Yes, especially Kellet. It's been a long wait to have this man back in my life, and I will be eternally grateful that he feels the same way."

Kellet blew him a kiss that was captured on the screens, and the crowd went wild.

Twenty minutes later, the four of them stood at the front of the stage taking their final bows. They had their arms slung around each, and Jamie's face ached from the smiling. He squeezed Kellet's hip, and he didn't break away when they stood for the last time. Kellet's arm was a welcome weight across his shoulders as they filed off stage.

Seth stopped them as soon as they cleared the wings. "Hey guys. Just wanna say thanks for a great tour. I know we've had some ups and downs these last few weeks, but there's no one I'd rather do this with."

Liam drew them into a huddle. "Ditto. I wasn't sure we could do this without Mark, but Kel, you've done an amazing job, and I'm proud to call you brother."

"Thanks, guys," Kellet said huskily, his emotions riding high. "These last few months have been one of the best times of my life, and I thank you for taking the chance on me. I love you all and am honored to be part of Larkspur."

Jamie pressed a kiss to his sweaty temple. "Love you, Drummer Boy."

With a final hug, they split apart and began removing mic packs. Jamie and Kellet were joined by an excited Andi and Ro and their parents. As they greeted each other and accepted their congratulations, a small shout broke above the hub bub of the backstage crowd.

"Seth!"

They turned to see Cal racing over and flinging himself into the lead guitarist's arms. Seth grinned before kissing the man that was climbing him like a tree.

"What the heck is that all about?" Andi asked in wonder. She swatted Jamie on the arm. "You never told me Seth had hooked up with Cal."

"Well, that certainly explains a few things," Jamie replied. He turned back to Andi. "Seriously, none of us knew. All we know is Seth has been more of a cranky bastard than normal of late."

"Wil said that Cal had not been with you since Vegas. He was quite worried as all he was getting was brief text messages," Andi told them.

Their observations of Seth and Cal were interrupted with the appearance of Mark and Selena. He broke away from their group to give his old friend a hug.

"Damn, we've missed you around here," he said.

"I don't think you've missed me that much," Mark replied with a laugh before offering his hand to Kellet. "Hi Kel. It's great to finally meet you. You did an outstanding job up there."

"Hey, Mark. You left some pretty big boots to fill, I have to say," Kellet replied graciously, but Jamie could see he was thrilled at Mark's words.

"Not really, they were your boots first." He looked around at the organized chaos that swirled around them. "I'll admit that I have missed parts of this. I miss playing the music every day, but I don't miss the long hours on the bus and living out of a bag for weeks on end." He looked Kellet in the eye. "And I don't miss the anxiety attacks and second guessing myself before and after each show."

"I get it, man. It must have been tough for you to decide to quit something you love."

"It was the hardest decision I've ever had to make." He nodded at Jamie. "These guys are my family, you know? Not seeing them or speaking to them every day has been hard." He smiled at Selena. "But this lady has been my rock. She makes it all worth it."

"Mark, I'm sorry I haven't been in touch more," Jamie said contritely. "I… I…"

"It's okay, Jay. I know how busy touring is and add in the fact you've been reconnecting with Kellet here, you don't need to apologize at all."

Jamie chuckled and squeezed Kellet's hand. "Yeah, we've been a bit preoccupied."

They were joined by Larry, who hugged Mark tightly. "Great to see you, Sullivan. Have missed your calming influence on this bunch of renegades."

"Hey!" Kellet protested. "I haven't been around long enough to be called a renegade."

"Two words, Kel," Larry said. "Las. Vegas."

"You can't blame us entirely for that. We didn't deliberately flaunt our relationship in the lobby of the Four Seasons."

"Yeah, whatever," Larry said with a wave of his hand. "Your ride to the hotel leaves in ten minutes, so I suggest you get your gear and continue your conversation there."

Jamie stopped Larry before he could stride away. "Thanks, Larry. You'd better not be too late getting to the party. We need to have a drink before you disappear home."

"Have I ever missed a wrap party, Jamie?"

"Very true. I'll have a cold one waiting for you."

♫ ♫ ♫

The party was in full swing two hours later. Kellet was running on adrenaline and a feeling of relief that it was all over. He'd loved every minute of the last few months, but all he wanted now was to start his life with Jamie.

They were staying at Jamie's for the next couple of days to recharge their batteries before heading up to Juniper to take Wil to college. After that, they were going to split their time between the two until East Bank was signed over to Tomas and his business partners.

His eyes scanned the crowded room. Most of the crew and team were here. He spotted Andi, Ro, and the now green-haired Tam talking animatedly in the corner. Just beyond them, he noticed Mark and

Liam standing very close. Mark had his hand on the back of Liam's neck and appeared to speaking earnestly to the bass guitarist.

Kellet nudged Jamie, who broke off his conversation with Larry. He nodded in Mark and Liam's direction. "What do you think that's all about?"

Jamie followed his glance and shrugged. As they watched, Liam nodded and gave Mark a hug before heading across the room towards Miles. Kellet noticed how their manager's steely gaze tracked Liam every step of the way. As Liam got closer, Miles spoke to him, and Liam nodded in response to whatever Miles had asked. Miles reached out and pulled Liam closer, whispering in his ear. Liam nodded again before quickly leaving the room.

"Should we check on him?" Kellet asked, worried for their friend.

"No. I think Miles has everything under control," Jamie told him in a knowing voice.

"What? What do you know that I don't?" Kellet asked, gently pushing his boyfriend into the wall.

"I don't know anything, exactly," Jamie prevaricated. He kissed Kellet briefly. "Just a feeling I have."

"And do you get these feelings often?" Kellet asked, pressing himself into Jamie's body.

"I know I'm having a certain kind of feeling right now," Jamie groaned back at him. "One that is not suitable for where we currently are."

"When can we leave?"

"Now, Drummer Boy. No one noticed that Seth and Cal disappeared half an hour ago, so I think we're pretty safe to sneak away."

Kellet gave him a satisfied grin before entwining their fingers and dragging him towards the exit. They were almost there when he spotted his son sitting alone in the corner. He glanced apologetically at Jamie before changing direction.

He dropped into the seat next to Wil, who looked up at him sadly.

"What's wrong? Are you not having fun?"

"Yeah, kinda," Wil said. "Sam's just gone to get us more drinks."

"Then why are you sitting here looking so miserable?"

"I'm gonna miss all this, Dad. I'm gonna miss hanging with Sam and Cal—not that Cal has actually been around much lately—but you know what I mean."

Kellet slung his arm around Wil's shoulder, pulling him in close. He could smell the faint trace of the shampoo Wil had used for years, and a pang of nostalgia went through him.

"Have I told you how proud I am of you?" he asked. "I'll admit I was reluctant to bring you along, but you have shone, Wil. You've had experiences not many eighteen-year-olds ever get to have, and this time next week, you'll be settling into your dorm as you prepare for the next chapter in your life."

"I know, Dad," Wil sighed.

Jamie leaned across Kellet to pat Wil on the knee. "You're part of the crew now, Wil. We'll make sure the next tour fits in with your school schedule so you can join us again if you want to."

"Really?" Wil's face lit up. "Thanks, Jamie. That'd be so cool."

"We're heading out, but your Moms are still here, okay?"

"Yeah, I'm good now. I'll see you in a few days."

Kellet pressed a kiss to his son's forehead before Jamie tugged him out of his seat.

"Love you, Dad."

"Love you too, son."

Epilogue

As Kellet lifted the last box out of the Range Rover, Jamie closed the door and locked it. Tugging his baseball cap down further over his face, he followed Kellet up the stairs to Wil's dorm. He was grateful they'd got there before the rush, but the halls were bustling with families settling their teens into their new accommodations.

Jamie had been pleasantly surprised when he'd been told he was joining the expedition to get Wil to college. At first he'd protested, not wanting to intrude on such a special family occasion. He'd promptly been shot down and had humbly accepted the invitation, although he secretly thought part of the invite was because his Range Rover was bigger than Kel's Mustang and Andi's Subaru.

He looked around the modest suite of rooms. There was a small communal kitchen and a compact living area. Off this were four bedrooms with two bathrooms adjoining on each side.

"Do you know who your roommates are?" Jamie asked as Wil took the box from his father.

"I only know their names and that they're all business majors like me."

Jamie had been surprised that Wil was considering a business degree, expecting him to do something more music orientated, but Kellet had explained that while Wil loved his music, it wasn't a passion like it was for him and Jamie. After his adventures over the summer, though, it looked like he was going to minor in entertainment management, having got the bug working for Miles and Jax.

As Andi and Ro flitted about making up Wil's bed and helping him unpack his belongings, Jamie and Kellet set up the tv and gaming console. Before long, everything that could be done had been, and the five of them wandered back down to the cars.

Jamie stood slightly apart from the family group, but after a pointed glare from Kellet, he stepped closer.

Wil gave Ro a big hug. "Bye, Ma. Don't go converting my room, okay?"

Ro swiped a tear from her eye and chuckled. "As if we'd do that. You'll always have a room with us, no matter where we are."

Wil squeezed her again before turning to Jamie. Jamie held out a fist, but to his surprise was enveloped in a tight hug. "Look after Dad for me, Pa."

Jamie's stomach dropped at the name, and he blinked rapidly to prevent the rush of tears that hit him. "Every day, son. Every day."

Wil moved onto his parents, and Jamie surreptitiously sniffed and rubbed his eyes. Ro leaned into him. "That the first time he's called you that?" she asked quietly, and he nodded in response. He was overwhelmed with emotion, but he fought it back to deal with later. Today was Wil's, and he needed to be strong for Kellet. He leaned gratefully into Ro as she wrapped an arm around his waist.

Together they watched as Andi and Kellet said their goodbyes to their son. They were definitely the youngest parents there, and more than a few interested glances were being thrown their way.

With a last hug for his mother, Wil stepped away from their group with a cheerful grin. "Bye Moms, bye Dads. I'll see you at Thanksgiving."

"Don't forget to—" Kellet started but stopped when Wil held up a hand.

"I'll call you every week, and I promise that if I need anything, I will ask." He waved his hands at them. "Now go. It's a long drive back to California." He turned his blue eyes on Jamie. "Pa, make sure he doesn't bury himself in work, okay?"

"I will. Have fun, Wil." Jamie tugged Kellet towards the car. "Come on, you heard the kid. Time to go."

Jamie slowly maneuvered the Range Rover through the throngs of people and cars. Kellet sat quietly beside him. As soon as they were on the open road and he was sure that Ro and Andi were close behind, he laid a hand on Kellet's thigh.

Warm fingers entwined with his and he flicked a quick glance to find Kellet looking at him, eyes full of love.

"You okay, Drummer Boy?"

"Yeah. I will be. It's surreal, but it's good." Kellet was quiet again before angling himself to lean against the door and look at Jamie. "He called you Pa."

"I know."

"Do you mind?" Kellet asked cautiously. "I know we haven't discussed it and I don't want you to feel uncomfortable."

"I'm honored he sees me that way," Jamie replied. "I know how much love he has for Ro, but then she's been part of his life since he was a toddler. I don't care what he calls me, I'm just happy to know him."

"If we'd stayed together, if I hadn't said no to signing the initial contract, you would have been his Pa from the beginning. I'm sorry I took that opportunity away from you." Kellet's voice was full of regret, and Jamie squeezed his hand.

"It was what it was, Drummer Boy. We found our way back to each other, and we've got the rest of our lives to make up for it."

They drove for a few miles in comfortable silence before Jamie spoke again.

"Did you and Andi ever consider giving Wil a sibling?"

Kellet gave a short laugh. "It was discussed, once, after she and Ro got together. We all decided that Wil was more than enough for all three of us, and besides, like you, we were all busy establishing ourselves and getting settled."

"What about now, though?" Jamie was curious how Kellet would answer.

"I don't think so," Kellet said thoughtfully. "I mean, if you want to have kids, then, of course, I'll be onboard, every step of the way. But, I suppose I'm selfish, in that I want you to myself for a while. I've got years to make up for, and I don't want to share you any more than I have to, whether it be with a child or the fans or even Seth and Liam."

Jamie nodded in agreement. "I guess I'm a bit selfish too, then, because I don't want to share you either." He flicked a glance sideways before returning his attention to the road. "I'm happy to carry on as we are and if we decide we want kids later, we'll cross that bridge then."

Kellet brushed a kiss across Jamie's knuckles, sending a familiar bolt of heat through him. "I love you, Jamie. I'm glad you came back into my life."

"Me too, but I'm sorry it took so long for me to do it."

"What? No, don't regret the choices you've made JJ," Kellet squeezed his hand tightly. "I think that if you had come back to Juniper years ago, it wouldn't have worked out as well as it has."

"How do you mean?" Jamie flicked a glance to his right before returning his attention to the road.

"You'd still have been busy with Larkspur, recording and touring. I mean, this year alone, you've been away for most of the year. How would that have worked with me at home? It would have been too hard for Wil to have you flitting in and out of his life."

Jamie pondered Kellet's words and realized what he was saying was true.

"You're right," he conceded. "I still wish—"

"I know, JJ, but we've got lucky. Fate or destiny, or whatever cosmic force you want to believe in, has worked so that we're together now, and yeah, we've lost a few years, but we've been given a second chance, and I'll never take that for granted."

"Me neither, Drummer Boy." He flashed a grin. "So, forever then?"

"Forever, JJ, forever."

About The Author

Zoe Piper English by birth and a Kiwi by choice, and having lived in Auckland, New Zealand for over thirty year, Zoe has had a long and varied career, from qualified farmer to international arms dealer, with lots of administrivia along the way.

She is a bookaholic and devours several books a week. When not escaping into other authors worlds, she can be found staring blankly at her screen, trying to wrangle her own words.

Also by Zoe Piper

The Kiwi Guys Series
Winning Love's Lottery
The Sweetest Song
Igniting the Flame

Standalone Novella
Meet Me at the Altar

Manufactured by Amazon.com.au
Sydney, New South Wales, Australia